THE PETRUS PROPHECY

VATICAN SECRET ARCHIVE THRILLERS
BOOK THREE

GARY MCAVOY

RONALD L. MOORE

Hardcover ISBN: 978-1-954123-13-7
Paperback ISBN: 978-1-954123-12-0
eBook ISBN: 978-1-954123-11-3

Library of Congress Control Number: 2022903866

Published by:
Literati Editions
PO Box 5987
Bremerton WA 98312-5987
Email: info@LiteratiEditions.com
Visit the authors' websites:
www.GaryMcAvoy.com
www.RonaldLMoore.com
R1023

BOOKS BY GARY MCAVOY

FICTION

The Confessions of Pope Joan

The Galileo Gambit

The Jerusalem Scrolls

The Avignon Affair

The Petrus Prophecy

The Opus Dictum

The Vivaldi Cipher

The Magdalene Veil

The Magdalene Reliquary

The Magdalene Deception

NONFICTION

And Every Word Is True

PROLOGUE

FÁTIMA, PORTUGAL – 13 OCTOBER 1917

Cesar Vila fell to his knees and crossed himself, praying to the Blessed Virgin to spare him and his family. The sun appeared to wobble and dance as it zig-zagged through the sky, then careened toward the Earth like a spinning disc, casting multicolored lights across the fields near the Cova da Iria quarter of Fátima before receding to its usual place in the heavens.

Cesar's clothing, drenched from the torrential rain that saturated Fátima just moments before, had become instantaneously dry by the heat of the sun. The freshly muddied ground brought by the rain also had become suddenly and completely dry. If he hadn't witnessed it himself, even he wouldn't have believed it.

But he was not alone. One hundred thousand people had assembled for the prophesied spectacle, and all of them reported the same effects of *Milagre do Sol,* the Miracle of the Sun.

The entire event lasted ten minutes and was reported on by newspapers around the world. The once-impoverished village of Fátima had since become a veritable cottage industry of the faithful, welcoming a pilgrimage of millions of visitors each year.

~

SEVERAL MONTHS before the Miracle of the Sun, in the spring of 1917, three Portuguese shepherd children—eleven-year-old Lúcia Santos and her young cousins, Francisco Marto, eight, and his sister Jacinta, seven—had reported apparitions of an angel, followed shortly after by visions of a luminous lady appearing to them, whom they took to be the Virgin Mary. The Lady, as the children called her, told them that they must pray, do penance, and say the rosary every day in order to save sinners and bring peace to the world. The Lady told them various prophecies, including one declaring an appearance of the Dancing Sun on October 13, as later witnessed by thousands.

Then, in October of the following year, the Blessed Mother had appeared to Jacinta, telling her she and her brother would soon be taken to heaven. They died a few months later, victims of the great Spanish influenza epidemic of 1918. Lúcia, however, would experience several more visions of the Lady for years.

But the Blessed Virgin also gave the shepherd children three prophetic secrets, each to be revealed at various times in the future.

Curiously, Lúcia did not write about her and her cousins' apparitions until 1941, when she wrote her memoirs at the urging of the Bishop of Leiria. Only then did she reveal the three secrets given her by the Lady.

The First Secret proved to be a horrific vision of Hell, filled with terrifying black and translucent animalistic demons plunging through great clouds of smoke caused by a raging conflagration of fire, amid shrieks of pain and despair.

The Second Secret was oddly prescient, stating that World War I would end and another great war would erupt during the reign of Pope Pius XI. In 1917, when the Lady gave the children this prophecy, Benedict XV was pope. Interestingly enough, the next pope would not be chosen until 1922 and he would not pick his regnal name—Pius XI—until his election. So Our Lady of Fátima proved doubly correct with the start of World War II in 1939 after Hitler's long draw-up to the war during Pius XI's final months of life.

The Third Secret, however, today remains a sacred mystery, tucked away in that most secure of papal vaults, the pope's personal hidden safe called the Petri Crypta.

As TOLD to her by the Lady, Lúcia declared that the Third Secret could be revealed to the public after 1960. In that year, Pope John XXIII was reported to have opened the secret—which was handwritten by Lúcia on a single page of paper—and he fainted upon reading it. What he read had terrified him, since, according to eyewitnesses, it specifically stated that the pope who publicly released the Third Secret would be the last pope of all, and that he would betray his flock, turning them over to a terrible slaughter devised by Lucifer himself. In apparent resistance to Our Lady of Fátima's instructions not specifically mentioning a year other than "after 1960," Pope John declined to reveal the secret, stating, "This prophecy does not relate to my time."

Consequently, the Church itself had declared that the Third Secret would most probably remain under absolute seal forever, as it was deemed that mankind was simply not ready for it. It has been speculated, and borne out by the facts, that subsequent popes also read the prophecy and chose not to make it public.

But in 2000, eighty-three years after the first apparition of the Lady to the three children in Portugal, Pope John Paul II ostensibly revealed the secret as being about the modern persecution of Christians that culminated in the failed assassination attempt on his own life on May 13, 1981. But this comparatively banal revelation was scoffed at by many as a contrived attempt to put the matter of the unrevealed prophecy to rest, once and for all.

Before she died in 2005, Sister Lúcia dos Santos, the shepherd girl who became a Carmelite nun, was asked about the Third Secret. She only said that it was in the Gospels and in the Apocalypse—and in the Book of Revelation 8:13, which states, "And I beheld, and heard an angel flying through the midst of heaven, saying with a loud voice, Woe, Woe, Woe, to the inhabiters of the earth…!"

CHAPTER ONE

PRESENT DAY

Father Jonah Barlow—renowned and respected Jesuit scholar, biblical archeologist, author, exorcist, and longtime thorn in the side of the Vatican—was nearing completion of his most provocative book yet: a thorough examination of the miracle orchestrated by Our Lady of Fátima in 1917, including disclosure of the presumed Third Secret of Fátima—one that had a long and strange history to it.

Papa Luciani, as Father Barlow endearingly called his old friend the pope, had expressly forbidden him from revealing the secret while the pope was still alive. Sadly, though, John Paul I sat on St. Peter's throne for just thirty-three days before meeting his Maker—but his death was not without controversy. Even today, many maintain Luciani was murdered before he could enact punishing regulations on the Vatican Bank during its most scandalous affair with Banco Ambrosiano.

Working from his modest, two-story brownstone on Chicago's North Side near Loyola University, Father Barlow stood for relief from the long hours sitting at his typewriter. He was anxious to put the final touches on his manuscript, a project many years in the making, before turning it over to his anxious editor, for they both knew this book would surely be a controversial, albeit bestselling, one. The recent addition of resources from a trusted Vatican insider had given him substantial new insights and enabled him to complete the project. But more importantly for Barlow, the book would finally break the Vatican's silence on the mystery of the Third Secret of Fátima, a revelation each pope in turn had brazenly refused to divulge for his own self-serving preservation.

As he stood at the window stretching, looking out over the Chicago River while waiting for a friend to drop by for a visit, the room took on a deep, sudden chill, and his entire body broke out in goose flesh. Jonah Barlow had had experience with this kind of abrupt change in atmosphere before, and though he was undaunted by the presence of supernatural forces—the worst of which he had faced during his most unsettling exorcisms—he instinctively reached for his pectoral cross and gripped it while uttering the Lord's Prayer. He trusted that his prayers and a thick woolen sweater would stave off the chill.

As he turned to go downstairs to fetch the sweater, he had just reached the top of the landing when a violent force from behind shoved him down the steps. He tumbled head over heels to the turn landing of the staircase, where he lay unconscious until his friend arrived and called for an ambulance.

DIAGNOSED with a cerebral hemorrhage caused by the fall, Barlow lay in the intensive care unit of St. Mary of Nazareth Hospital, drifting in and out of consciousness, mumbling gibberish in a foreign tongue. His visiting friend, a fellow Jesuit priest named Lorenzo Marchetti, sat by his side, hoping Barlow would regain his senses and be able to speak with him before administering last rites, for the prognosis was bleak and certain.

After several hours of such mumblings, without warning, the

dying priest opened his eyes wide with fear, stared at his friend, and spoke with an urgency belying his normally calm manner.

"*Lorenzo...!* The book... you must get the book before *they* do.... The secret is in the book!"

"Jonah," his friend asked gently, "we'll get to the book, but would you like to make your last confession first?"

"*Damn the confession, man!* I was pushed by a cacodemonic force! Lucifer does not want the secret exposed yet! You must return and *get the book*... and... and contact Michael Dominic in Rome."

With that, Barlow's entire body jerked violently, the rattle of death shaking even the hospital staff who rushed in and had never witnessed such a reaction before. Blood spewed from his gaping mouth, and his wild eyes reddened with a fevered look. The entire bed rose up and fell back to the floor repeatedly, as if lifted and shaken by unseen hands. Then, just as suddenly, the bed lay still, and he fell back onto the pillow, his bloodshot eyes wide open, staring at the abyss awaiting him on the other side as death took its final clutch on Jonah Barlow's life.

ACCOMPANIED BY FATHER MARCHETTI, Detective Rebecca Lancaster of the Chicago Police Department drove her squad car from St. Mary's Hospital north up Ashland Avenue, then over to the Rogers Park neighborhood near Loyola, finally arriving at Father Barlow's brownstone a half hour later.

"I still don't know why they assigned a detective to this," Marchetti said. "The poor man just fell."

"Sure, he could have just fallen," Lancaster replied, pulling on an earring with one hand while driving with the other. "But from what the nursing staff told me, they heard him say he was pushed. That opens it up to possible homicide, Father. Just doing my job here."

As they entered the unlocked home, nothing appeared out of

the ordinary. Barlow's black cat, Methuselah, sat placidly on the windowsill, watching a murder of crows perched on the electrical lines outside.

"What time did you say you arrived?" Lancaster asked the priest.

"Actually, I didn't say. But it was sometime around one. We were going to have a late lunch and talk about the book he was finishing—one I'm supposed to find and safeguard."

"Well, nothing leaves this place until it's cleared with me, understood?"

Marchetti sighed and nodded. Moving to Barlow's desk, he searched for his friend's work in progress.

"That's odd," he noted, his bushy white eyebrows scrunched together. "When I was here earlier, the book—some seven hundred pages of it—was sitting right there"—he pointed to an empty spot on the desk—"but now it's gone! Who could have taken it?"

"You said 'earlier.' Was that today, or…?"

"Yes! Just a few hours ago. Someone has obviously been here since and taken the manuscript. Oh, this is just terrible. All of Jonah's hard work, gone!"

"So, now we have a missing book *and* a possible homicide. I'll get a forensics team in here and they'll go over the place. Don't touch anything, Father. But we will need a set of your fingerprints as exemplars to eliminate yours from any others."

As Marchetti scanned other items on Father Barlow's desk, he found a scribbled note on a small pad with Loyola's logo at the top. Beneath it read, "Get Michael Dominic's comments on ms."

Curious, he thought. *Father Dominic has a copy of the manuscript? Pity, I'll have to tell him the sad news.*

"Find anything interesting, Father?" Lancaster asked, noting the priest's attention focused on the desktop.

"Only a note here in Jonah's handwriting, reminding himself to get comments about the manuscript from a priest in Rome. A

Father Michael Dominic, whom I know to be prefect of the Vatican Secret Archives."

"The Vatican has secret archives? Why would the Church need to keep something secret?"

Marchetti smiled amusingly. "It's not the same meaning in Latin, *Archivum Secretum*. Well, yes, literally it means the same, but 'secret' in that sense simply means private or personal, since for centuries the Archives were considered the pope's personal library. These days, of course, qualified scholars have access to most of its contents, and some of it is actually being digitized for access via the internet."

"So we might assume this Father Dominic has a copy of the book?"

"Well, I imagine so, given this note." Marchetti picked it up and handed it to the detective. She glanced at it, then returned it to the desk.

"Do you have any plans to leave town, Father?" Lancaster asked.

"Actually, yes, I'm leaving for Rome in two days' time, for the annual International Theological Symposium, an event that's been planned for months now."

"Well, I'm sure I can reach you by phone if we need to follow up on anything."

"I'll be staying at Villa Stritch, the Vatican residence for American priests. You can always reach me there."

DETECTIVE LANCASTER STOOD at the window of a little room in the coroner's office. On the other side of the glass, the medical examiner and his assistant were performing a postmortem on Father Jonah Barlow in the examination suite. Barlow's body was laid out on a stainless steel autopsy table, his internal organs now resting in a red plastic bag in his open abdominal cavity, having been removed and examined before Lancaster had arrived. The examiner, Dr. Polanski, reached up and toggled on the microphone hanging on a cord over the body, his gloved hand leaving a bloody smudge on the chrome.

"Nice of you to join us, Detective. We saved doing the head until you got here."

"Thanks, Doc, especially since you know this isn't my favorite part of the job. Catch me up on what you've discovered so far," she said.

"Well, I read the attending physician's report from the emergency room. The spewing of blood from his mouth right before he expired was caused by a ruptured esophageal varix—basically, an erosion of the lining of the esophagus—and damage to the portal circulation from cirrhosis of the liver. That, combined with a spike in blood pressure from the seizure, caused a vein in his throat to burst. We often see it in alcoholics and some bulimics. From the looks of his liver, though, I'd say he had a bit of a drinking problem."

"So, it wasn't from 'demonic interference'?" she asked.

"I've been at this for over thirty years, Detective, and I've never seen anything that couldn't be medically explained."

"Well, all that blood sure freaked out the staff at the hospital, not to mention that trembling bed. One nurse with him at the time had to be sent home, she was so upset."

Lancaster watched as Dr. Polanski, having used a scalpel to cut through the scalp along the hairline, now scraped and pulled the flesh away from the skull with a stainless steel chisel.

"Okay, we're seeing bruising on the scalp at the forehead, but none on the back of his head. That would be more consistent with being pushed rather than just falling down the stairs. Most of the time, when someone falls down the stairs, their feet slip out from under them and they fall backwards. We would see bruising on the back of the head and often on the tailbone. I didn't see any in this case. So, I suppose he could have tripped over something, but he definitely went down the stairs head first, not feet first," the doctor concluded.

"Well, that would be consistent with the findings at the scene. His stairs take a 180-degree turn about halfway down. He was found on the landing at the turn. There was a forehead-shaped dent on the wall about a meter above the floor in the stairwell wall."

While they were talking, the assistant medical examiner used an electric bone saw to cut the skull open, using a particular pattern of cuts that would enable them to reassemble the skull properly for the funeral. The doctor examined Father Barlow's brain.

"All right, Detective. See here at the frontal lobe? There is the large hematoma, but there's also a smaller one at the back of his head. We call that a coup–contrecoup injury. His brain hit so hard in the front that it bounced back and hit the back of his skull on the inside. I'd say that means there was more force involved than just stumbling forward or tripping, unless he was running down the stairs—which at his age seems unlikely. No, I'd say this is more consistent with being pushed. Looks like you do have a homicide here."

"Before he died, the victim said something about being pushed by a demonic force," Lancaster sniped with a smirk.

"Well, Detective, like you, apparently, I find that dubious," the doctor said, rolling Barlow's body toward the detective to expose the back. "I don't imagine demons leave bruises on your shoulder blades when they push you." He lowered his head as he peered at her over his spectacles. "But then, I skipped Demonology in medical school."

CHAPTER TWO

Father Michael Dominic glanced up from the wooden desk on the raised dais as the Coimbra University Audience Hall slowly began filling. Invited to Portugal's esteemed university—among the oldest continuously operating universities in the world, established in 1290—the prefect of the Vatican Secret Archives prepared his presentation notes as the audience took their seats.

The building he was in, he learned, had been built in 1537. The relatively small audience hall—with its blue-and-yellow Spanish tile wainscoting on the back and side walls, two large windows on either side of the high-ceilinged room, and seven long rows of wooden bench seats on a dark red tile floor—accommodated around two hundred. He thought back to all the people before him who had held audience at this very stage over the past nearly five centuries, and marveled at the resilience of men and women in their quest for academic enlightenment through the ages.

Sponsored by the World Library and Information Congress, Dominic had been asked to speak on the conservation techniques of the Vatican's mammoth holdings. He had brought with him a laptop and a PowerPoint slide presentation featuring some of the Church's most remarkable artifacts, ones sure to entice the assembled students and faculty.

As he was reviewing his slides, wondering where his assistant Ian Duffy was, a man approached him. He looked to be in his forties, with close-cropped facial scruff and wearing a tweed sports jacket with a crisp white shirt and a turquoise-on-silver bolo tie. Dominic took him to be one of the staff and smiled as the man held out his hand.

"Padre Dominic," he said congenially, "my name is Ernesto Vila. I am the Professor of Natural Sciences here at Coimbra and wanted to personally welcome you to our humble university."

"Very good to meet you, Ernesto," the priest said, shaking the man's hand as he remained seated. "I only hope you enjoy what I've thrown together here. I should have taken more time boning up on my delivery, but as your people say, *'Na cama que farás, nela te deitarás.'"*

"Yes," Vila said, laughing. 'As you make your bed, so you must lie on it.' You speak Portuguese very well."

"Not as well as I'd like to, I'm afraid. I do speak Spanish and a few other languages, but I picked up several Portuguese phrases on the plane so I could at least be courteous."

The man's demeanor turned furtive as he leaned down to whisper in Dominic's ear.

"Padre, when you are finished here, may we have a word together? Privately?"

"Of course, Ernesto. I'm here to answer any questions you might have."

"Actually, what I have to tell you is a matter of some importance. But we shall speak later, yes? Until then, *tenha uma boa apresentação."*

Dominic looked lost. "I'm afraid I—"

"That just means 'have a good presentation,'" Vila said, smiling wisely as he patted Dominic on the shoulder, then turned to take his seat.

Ian Duffy, Father Dominic's assistant in the Vatican Archives, finally joined him on the dais.

"Father Michael, I couldn't find coffee but will bottled water do?"

"Sure, Ian, that'll be fine." Dominic took the bottle, uncapped it, and chugged down several gulps.

"Hana and Marco told me they might be late, so don't hold things up for them."

"As if I could," Dominic mumbled, taking another chug. His close friend Hana Sinclair, a journalist for Paris's *Le Monde* newspaper, and her French bodyguard Marco Picard—who had become something more for Hana over the past year—had offered Dominic her grandfather's private jet to whisk them all here to Portugal, a three-hour flight from Rome.

"Where are they, anyway?" Dominic asked.

Duffy faltered for a moment, then said, "They're exploring the university's famed baroque library, the Biblioteca Joanina. Something I'd like to see myself—when we're done here, of course."

"We'll have some time to kick around after this, Ian, don't worry."

With the auditorium now full and people lining up against the back wall and along the sides of the room, Dominic looked at his watch. *Five more minutes. I do hope Hana can make it.*

A few moments later she and Marco strode into the auditorium. Seeing it was standing room only, they took their places against one of the tall windows and leaned back on the sill. Hana gave Dominic a little wave and a smile, mouthing *Good luck* as he smiled and waved back.

As the bells of the Cabra, the university's revered seventeenth-century clock tower, struck eleven, Dominic stood as he was introduced by the university's president and, after a round of applause, the presentation began.

~

AN HOUR LATER, the event ended with a standing ovation for Father Dominic's compelling review of the Vatican's treasures and how they are cared for in the Archives' specialized conservation labs.

Several people surged forward to meet the handsome young priest and offer their appreciation for his coming all the way from Rome. On one side of the room, Hana, Marco, and Ian Duffy stood watching the spectacle, proud of their friend's deserved accolades, while on the other side of the room Ernesto Vila lingered with his hands patiently folded in front of him, waiting for the crowd to clear.

When Dominic finished chatting with the last person, Hana, Marco and Ian walked up to the desk. As the priest gathered his notes together and closed the laptop, Vila approached him as well.

Looking up and seeing the man, Dominic asked, "Would you guys mind if I spent a little time here with Professor Vila first? We shouldn't be long."

"Of course not; we'll meet you in the Biblioteca," Hana said. "Ian wants to see it as well, and there was too much for us to take in before your presentation. See you there?"

"You bet." Then, turning to Vila, Dominic said, "So, what's this matter of importance you mentioned, Ernesto?"

Now completely alone in the hall so they could not be overheard, the man took a seat on the dais next to the priest and leaned forward, placing his folded arms on the desk. Looking directly into Dominic's expectant eyes, he began his story.

"Padre, I am sure you are familiar with the tale of Our Lady of Fátima, and the three shepherd children's many apparitions of the Blessed Mother?"

"Yes, I imagine most every Catholic knows this story. It is one of the most sacred miracles recorded by the Church."

"That was in 1917, as you know. My great-grandfather, Cesar Vila, was among those who witnessed the *Milagre do Sol,* the Miracle of the Dancing Sun. And as it happened, he personally knew Sister Lúcia dos Santos, who was but a child of eleven at the time. In fact, Cesar was her godfather, having been close friends of her parents for many years.

"Papa Cesar, as we children called him, was quite fond of Lúcia, and she of him. He earned her trust at a time when everyone—her family, villagers, newspaper people, everyone—wanted more from her, most of them not believing her stories, at least until the dancing sun event occurred and was witnessed by thousands of people from all around.

"Lúcia told Cesar everything that had occurred during those many apparitions in the months following the first visit of the Lady, things she had told no one else. But most importantly, she disclosed to him alone the three secret prophecies the Lady gave her, for the Lady gave her permission to share them with her godfather, a most pious man."

"But we already know what the three secrets are, or were," Dominic replied. "Pope John Paul II revealed the third and final secret in the year 2000."

The professor looked at Dominic, a skeptical smile crawling across his face. "And if you believe that, Padre, I have a bridge over the Mondego River I will gladly sell you."

Dominic returned the man's skeptical look but surrendered to hearing the rest of his story. "All right, I take your point. Go on."

"We already know the first two secrets, and they have apparently come to pass as was prophesied. But in truth, the third secret prophecy has yet to be fully revealed.

"Lúcia told Papa Cesar that many popes would refuse to take on the responsibility of revealing the third secret, for to do so would surely cast them as the last pope and the Antichrist, and the end of days would surely follow, just as the Lady prophesied, according to Lúcia. This is why every pope who has read the secret has passed it on to his successor, abrogating his responsibility out of fear of the consequences. And that must certainly be why Pope John Paul II issued an alternate version of the secret, to placate all those demanding its revelation. As you of all people should know, the Church has influence over a billion souls worldwide, and since papal authority is infallible, the faithful have little choice but to believe what their pope has told them. Yet, in the end, he fabricated a more convenient story, plain and simple."

Dominic recalled there had been great controversy surrounding John Paul's "disclosure" of the third secret, but as it dealt in the realm of saints and miracles—an area of little particular interest to Dominic's own ecclesiastical mission—he had given it little thought or attention before now. But what Vila had just told him piqued his curiosity.

"And why tell *me* of this, Ernesto? What is it you think I can do about it?"

"Padre, this must be a difficult request for you to consider, but I assure you, the stakes could not be higher. I *must* meet with His Holiness at the earliest possible moment. And I believe you are in a position to make that happen. Everyone knows you are close to the Holy Father."

Dominic looked closely at the man. Clearly, he was earnest and not some crackpot or opportunist. He was a tenured professor at a prestigious university, and a seemingly pious man.

"I'm afraid I'm going to need more than that to consider such a request, Ernesto. What is it that's so important that it requires a papal audience? Surely there are others who might assist with whatever it is."

Vila's face was etched with the obvious frustration of weighing the consequences of divulging to this priest what he needed to discuss with the pope. But he realized he had to offer something.

"As it happens, Padre, I am a member of the Sovereign Military Order of Malta, or what you might otherwise know as the Knights of Malta. Our Catholic order, founded in Jerusalem in 1099, has some 13,000 member Knights and Dames worldwide, in addition to 80,000 volunteers and 42,000 employees, most of whom are involved in our medical, social, and humanitarian projects in 120 countries. We even have Permanent Observer status at the United Nations.

"I tell you this because the Order of Malta is an honorable, respected entity that does good and charitable work." Vila looked anxiously around the room, continuing in a hushed tone now. "But there has emerged a rogue splinter group, a secret society of sorts, one with a more nefarious mission, and they have infiltrated our order to capitalize on its influential standing in the world community."

Vila studied Dominic closely to determine if he would be amenable to what he was about to say, or if he might simply cast him off as a lunatic. Finding more interest on the priest's face than skepticism, he pushed on.

"This group calls themselves Knights of the Apocalypse, or KOTA. The name alone is repugnant, but it succinctly describes their mission. You see, they profess as their goal to shield the Church from the expected Antichrist. But in practice, we believe they have a far more devious objective."

Having established his bona fides, Vila now had Dominic's rapt attention. The priest was eager to hear the man's next words.

"Yes?" he asked anxiously. "And what would that be?"

"To hasten the coming of the End of Days."

CHAPTER
THREE

Dominic felt like laughing, but for the solemn expression on Ernesto Vila's face.

"You can't be serious," he exclaimed. "Forgive me, but that sounds pretty far-fetched, especially coming from such an intelligent man as yourself."

"I did not expect you to believe me out of hand, Padre. One of our members has secretly infiltrated KOTA and has reported this information back to us. Their apparent objective is to accelerate fevered anticipation of the so-called Apocalypse in conformance with biblical scripture.

"I realize this may not make much sense as I have explained it so far, but I am told that within ten days' time, KOTA will hold a press conference announcing their plan to reveal the Third Secret of Fátima. How they acquired the secret, we do not know, for it is believed to be only in the hands of the pope himself. But they also plan to merge two additional prophecies that, together, make for a compelling scenario. Our fear is that people will start to believe KOTA's propaganda, bringing them closer to realizing their vile and ambitious scheme."

"What other two prophecies do you mean?" Dominic asked.

"Well, to begin with, the twelfth-century prophecies of St.

Malachy, who predicted a long line of popes ending with *Petrus Romanus*—Peter the Roman. And call it coincidence or not, but Malachy's predictions have been so closely associated with each pope in turn over the past eight hundred-plus years that scholars are paying attention, with a skeptical eye, of course. Malachy's specific words were:

> In the final persecution of the Holy Roman Church, there will sit Peter the Roman, who will pasture his sheep in many tribulations, and when these things are finished, the city of seven hills will be destroyed, and the dreadful judge will judge his people. The End.

"And, as it happens, *Petrus Romanus* could very well mean our current pope, Ignatius. Is his surname not Petrini, which is translated as Peter? And not only does his family come from Rome originally, but he is Bishop of Rome, the city of seven hills…."

Dominic had no response, for he was at a loss for words. He had long had a special relationship with Enrico Petrini, who, upon taking on the role of pope, had assumed the regnal name of Ignatius. He was vaguely familiar with the prophecies of Malachy, but had given it little heed. Until now.

"This all feels a little too convenient, Ernesto," Dominic observed, raking back his hair with impatience. "And what of that third prophecy you mentioned?"

"That would be the purported Apocalypse of St. Peter himself, in which Christ reveals a vision of the future depicting epic levels of chaos and global destruction, juxtaposed with heavenly rewards for the righteous and hideous torment for the lost souls of the unrighteous. Suffice to say, if they get their message out into the hearts and minds of believers, no telling what kinds of repercussions could develop."

Dominic was still dubious. "Well, as you probably know, the

Apocalypse of Peter is not accepted as a reliable source of doctrine, like many other New and Old Testament Apocrypha."

"That may well be, but there are many people of faith, especially in Third World countries, who often disregard such rationalizations. And not just people of faith. Think back to the imagined apocalyptic scenarios laid out with the 2012 Mayan Apocalypse, for example, which many misinterpreted as an end to the calendar as we know it, with specters of giant solar flares, a realignment of Earth's axis, and planetary alignments that would supposedly cause massive tidal catastrophes. Sales of survival kits soared as a result of global panic. People are instinctively predisposed to self-preservation, and such doomsday scenarios only serve to stimulate such behavior."

"You do have good points there. But how does KOTA propose informing people of these prophecies and gaining broad traction? And more to the point, to what end?" Dominic asked.

"We'll know more within ten days, I suppose. As to what end, from what I know of them, KOTA would surely not undertake such a massive campaign if they did not anticipate some kind of gain in the proposition. So yes, their ulterior motives are rife with suspicion, and they may have some well-planned reasons for causing havoc. That remains to be seen.

"But as you can understand now, I must speak with His Holiness about these things. There is much more he must be told. When do you return to Rome?"

Considering all that he had heard, Dominic's first instinct was to be utterly dismissive of the whole thing. But Vila's reference to St. Malachy's prophecy involving Enrico Petrini as "*Petrus Romanus*" struck him as too close to home. Other things the professor had said also rang true.

"We're leaving this evening. I'll give this some thought, Ernesto, and let you know more in the next few days. Now, though, I need to meet up with my friends. But I will be in touch with you soon."

Rebecca Lancaster leaned back in the creaking wooden chair of her cramped cubicle at Homicide Division in the North Lawndale section of Chicago, reflecting on the Barlow case. The forensics team had found no probative evidence whatsoever at the scene. No latent fingerprints apart from Barlow's and a few of Father Marchetti's. No trace or biological evidence. Nothing.

Still, she was troubled. It was something Father Marchetti had said, something about that missing manuscript. Why murder someone over a book, one that hadn't even been published? Or maybe that was why: someone didn't *want* it to be published. Her instincts rarely failed her, and she suspected the manuscript might be key to her investigation. If something in that book was significant enough to kill a man for, she wanted to know what it was.

Unfortunately, Jonah Barlow didn't use a computer. He favored an old IBM Selectric, and typewriters didn't have backup files.

But that note Barlow left, the one referring to a Father Michael Dominic: that may bear fruit, she figured. How to get the manuscript from him might be the challenge.

Then she thought back to a conference she had attended in London a couple years ago for the International Homicide Investigator's Association. She had met a delightful Italian detective there. *What was her name… Sabrina something?*

Sitting up and pulling her keyboard closer, she checked her Contacts database. Scanning the names on her screen, she found the person she was looking for.

There she is. Capitano Sabrina Felici with the Carabinieri. She must pull a lot of weight with the rank of captain.

Lancaster thought back to the fun they had together off-duty, when the conferences and workshops had ended each day. Crawling the bars of London at night to see what mischief they could get into, what men they could tease and possibly seduce.

Two alluring brunettes dressed to the nines. Good times, she recalled.

She glanced up at the clock on the wall. *Too late in Rome to call now. I'll just send her an email.*

Briefly explaining the situation, Lancaster asked Felici to give her a call the following day.

Hmm. Maybe I can even finagle a trip to Italy out of this....

CHAPTER FOUR

Capitano Sabrina Felici had arrived at her third-floor office in the Arma dei Carabinieri Headquarters on Viale Romania earlier than usual that morning, around seven o'clock, and was savoring her first cup of freshly roasted cappuccino as she opened her laptop to check overnight email.

Scanning the list of senders to parse out the important ones first, her eyes settled on Rebecca Lancaster's waiting message, and a sly smile crossed her face. Memories of good times in London with her new friend flooded her mind. She opened the message and read it.

> Sabrina,
>
> I can't imagine you've forgotten me, so I'll skip reintroductions. I mean, how could you, after the havoc we caused in the pubs of London?!
>
> Anyway, I'm working on a new homicide case here in Chicago that appears to have links to Rome, at the Vatican in particular, and I'd like to discuss it with you. Who knows, maybe we can reprise our adventures on your turf—if I can swing a trip with my boss...

Please call at your earliest convenience.

Warm regards,

Becca

With a seven-hour difference in time zones, Felici decided to wait until four that afternoon to call Lancaster, when she would likely just be arriving at her office in Chicago. She confirmed so in a reply message, then went on about her day solving homicides on the streets of Rome.

Joe Mancini sat at his crappy, cluttered metal desk in the bullpen, glancing around at the forlorn faces of his fellow detectives working the phones, none of whom were particularly chipper this morning. A twenty-year veteran of the Chicago PD, Mancini's attitude was still as cheerful as when he was a rookie. Yet, working Homicide was tough at times—staying strong under pressure, investigating unimaginable crime scenes, prodding confessions out of killers, and that most emotional ritual, comforting the families of victims—but hey, he thought, it was better than being on the other side of the law. Or still driving long-haul trucks, his former job before entering the police academy in his late twenties.

His partner and lead on the case, Detective Rebecca Lancaster, had asked him to look over the forensic evidence on the Barlow file—what little there was, anyway—and that was his first task of the day.

As he read the report of the crime scene, one curiosity stood out. The forensics team had removed the ribbon from Barlow's IBM Selectric typewriter and was now analyzing it to retrieve whatever information might have been on it. Brilliant. CPD's forensics team was among the best. There wasn't much that escaped their attention. He made a mental note to check back with them on what they found.

He continued reading, noting that Father Lorenzo Marchetti, Barlow's friend, mentioned that the victim's seven-hundred-page manuscript also was missing. *There's got to be a connection. If someone killed for the manuscript,* Mancini mused, *that must have been one important book he was writing. If only we knew what was in it, it might help our case.*

But that was on Lancaster. He knew she was angling for a trip to Rome, to try and coax a copy from this… what was that priest's name? Father Michael Dominic.

If this priest didn't willingly hand it over, which he might, Mancini wouldn't want to be in Dominic's place when Lancaster put the screws to him, that's for sure. She was a formidable force in getting what she wanted. And no doubt that manuscript could well be the key to solving this.

"I'LL ONLY BE in Rome for a few days, Lieutenant. And obviously, I'll fly economy. It's crucial we obtain a copy of that book, and apparently this Father Dominic is the only one who has it. This manuscript apparently is connected to the Vatican, and we all know how Mother Church can sometimes be uncooperative in our investigations. I've got a trusted colleague with the Carabinieri there who can help persuade him, if need be." She had loosened her blouse a bit, exhibiting her countless charms in the ways she knew had worked on men. Especially her boss.

The lieutenant sat behind his desk, grumbling about the budget and overtime as he squirmed in the presence of Rebecca Lancaster's sorcery. He was such a sucker.

But it wasn't as if it were the first time he'd had to send his people out of the country to handle things like this. And since Father Barlow had been a priest, the Chicago Archdiocese had now taken an interest, so political pressure was mounting. With over two million Catholics in the city of Chicago alone, the archbishop was indeed a most powerful figure.

"All right, Lancaster, you've got my okay on this," he said

gruffly. "Just make sure you come back with that book, or don't come back at all. Got it?"

"You bet, Chief," she said, trying to keep the exuberance out of her voice. "See you in a few days."

AN HOUR LATER, Lancaster's cell phone rang, precisely at nine o'clock as Felici had promised. She pressed the green button to answer.

"Hi, Becca, it's Sabrina. So, what have you got going there?"

Lancaster kept her jubilant voice low given the lack of privacy in the open bullpen, and after greeting her friend went on to explain the Barlow case and her need for the manuscript from a Vatican priest.

"Ah, the Vatican. Well, that may be tricky, as we have no jurisdiction in Vatican City. It's an entire little country unto itself, with their own law enforcement agencies. But I do know one of the Gendarmerie Corps there. Perhaps he might be of help. Are you able to come to Roma?"

"I just got the go-ahead from my commander. So, yes, I'll be on the first flight I can catch out of O'Hare. I'll let you know my itinerary when I have it. Meanwhile, I'll email the case file to bring you up to speed."

"That will be helpful, Becca, thanks. And bring your dancing shoes." They both laughed, knowing that—beyond the rigors of working an international murder case—there were good times to be had together in the Eternal City.

CHAPTER FIVE

Six kilometers southwest of Vatican City lies Villa Stritch, an opulent complex of two five-story, red brick buildings housing twenty-six comfortable apartments, a kitchen and large dining room, a rooftop chapel, two common living areas with a fully stocked bar boasting five beers on tap, and a tennis court, all behind the security of a wide, black, wrought iron fenced gate.

Owned by the U.S. Conference of Catholic Bishops, Villa Stritch is home to American priests who work at the Vatican or visit Rome periodically. A staff of three Felician nuns and another three Italian lay people attend to the needs of the villa's residents, and as Father Lorenzo Marchetti settled himself into a cushy, red leather chair in the living room waiting for Father Dominic to arrive, one of the lay staff asked him if he might prefer a beverage. He opted for Italy's premium beer on draft, Birra Moretti.

He glanced at his watch. It was just about five o'clock. He steeled himself for the sad news he was soon to impart to Father Barlow's friend. No one is prepared to hear about someone's passing, though in truth he had no idea how close the two men might have been. Marchetti imagined they must have had some mutual bond, since he knew Jonah would rarely ever let anyone see his work in progress while he was writing.

Looking up toward the entrance of the villa, he saw a good-looking priest come through the door and look around, as if he hadn't been there before. On a hunch, Marchetti waved to the man, motioning him to join him in the open-plan living room.

"Father Marchetti?" Dominic asked as he approached the now standing priest.

"Yes, but it's just Lorenzo. And you must be Father Dominic."

"Please, call me Michael," he said, smiling warmly.

"Thank you for meeting me, Michael," Marchetti said as they both took seats. "Would you care for a beer, or something stronger? They have an excellent bar here."

"Sure, I'll have what you're having."

Marchetti got up to get the beer himself. Standing in front of the cherry wood bar, he reached for a glass mug from the shelf and found his selection on one of the five logo-labeled taps. He angled the glass as the beer flowed gently into the mug. Returning to the living room, he set the glass down in front of Dominic.

"*Salute!*" Marchetti said as he clinked his glass against Dominic's. They both sipped thirstily, the thick foam of the draft coating their upper lips.

"Michael," Marchetti began solemnly, "I'm afraid I have some sad news to convey. I understand you knew Jonah Barlow quite well, is that right?"

"Yes, he was one of my professors when I was working on my master's degree at Loyola. But you said 'knew.' Has something happened?"

"I fear our friend had a tragic fall last week and has joined Our Lord in Heaven. May he rest in eternal peace." Marchetti closed his eyes and made the sign of the cross.

Dominic was stunned, likewise making the same sign even as he exclaimed, "But we just spoke only a week ago! When did this happen? And how?"

"Well, to be honest, we're not quite sure. It appears he fell down the stairs in his home. It was a good thing we had a meeting scheduled for around that time, for I was the one who found him shortly after it happened. I followed the ambulance to the hospital, and after the doctors examined him, they told me the prognosis wasn't good. It was a terrible fall and caused significant damage.

"When I was about to administer last rites, he became quite agitated, telling me he believed a 'cacodemonic force' had pushed him down the stairs. Of course, as he was one of the Church's most respected exorcists, I've no doubt he believed what he told me. He'd certainly seen worse."

"You said 'we' aren't quite sure. Who else is involved?"

"Oh, that would be the Chicago detectives. They believe it may have been a homicide. At least that's how they're investigating it. I believe they intend on contacting you, in fact, so you may want to be prepared."

"*Me*?!" Dominic exclaimed. "Why on earth would they want to speak with me?"

"Jonah left a note on his desk with your name on it, something about your providing commentary on his manuscript."

"Yes, well, that does make sense."

"Another odd thing occurred. As he lay in his bed just before he died, Jonah said, 'Lucifer does not want the secret exposed,' and for me to 'get the book,' and to contact you here in Rome. It's all very strange, I must say. But when I returned to his brownstone with one of the detectives, the book was missing! Someone had been there between the time Jonah fell and I returned to his home. I saw the very manuscript itself—well over a ream, probably some seven hundred pages of it—sitting right there on his desk just hours before, when I called for the ambulance. I don't fault the detectives for thinking foul play might have been involved.

"Then there's the... well, there's no other word for it than *supernatural*—behavior of his hospital bed. Just as Jonah died, the bed lifted off the floor and rattled around as if it were possessed! I must tell you, Michael, it unnerved me as well as everyone standing there. Jonah had told me many stories of such paranormal activity during his exorcisms, but I had never before witnessed anything like that myself."

Dominic decided not to belabor that particular point, something better left to others more suited to speculation in the occult.

"I suppose that means that I have the only copy of his book, then. I have yet to read it. He only just sent me the manuscript last week. And since he didn't use computers, it came printed out in a large box. So typical of Jonah."

"Well, don't be surprised if the Chicago police ask for it. The detective... uh, Lancaster. Yes, Rebecca Lancaster. You might expect a call from her. I believe she thinks whoever killed Jonah —*if* he was pushed, as she believes, though it's possible he simply fell—did so for whatever might be in that book."

"I suppose I should get started reading it, then. I'm certainly not going to give anyone *anything* until I see what Jonah's written. He briefly mentioned it had to do with prophecies and how they may come to pass, material consistent with his canon of work, I imagine. He seemed very enthusiastic about it. But I really wasn't paying much attention at the time and told him I would be happy to review it for him. And, of course, he did ask me to treat it confidentially."

"I expect he would have, yes," Marchetti murmured, taking another swig of beer. "Did Jonah seem all right when you spoke with him last?"

Dominic thought back to his final conversation with his

friend and one-time professor. "As I mentioned, he seemed enthusiastic about the book. Or maybe a better word for it might be enraptured. I think he felt this would be his seminal work. Pity it'll be his last. I suppose I should safeguard it, maybe even have another copy made for his publisher, just in case he hadn't sent one to his editor."

"That does seem prudent, yes. Might I also have a copy of it, Michael?" Marchetti asked, his bushy white eyebrows raised expectantly.

Dominic reached for his beer to take a sip, giving him time to gather a proper response.

"To be candid, Lorenzo, I don't feel right about handing out copies of something I was specifically asked to hold confidential. Jonah must have had his reasons; maybe I'll find them once I've read the manuscript. But until then, I'm afraid I can't. I do hope you understand."

Marchetti sat up straighter, his lips pressed together at Dominic's response. The appearance of being perturbed but unwilling to express it was not lost on Dominic, who now found himself curious about the man sitting opposite him. *Am I missing something here?*

"Well," Marchetti said as he rose, a chilly tone to his voice, "I really must get to the dining room for the six o'clock meal. It was good of you to meet me here, Michael, especially given the circumstances. Goodbye for now."

Dominic rose and shook the man's hand, then headed toward the exit.

"Oh, one more thing," Marchetti said as he turned back toward Dominic. "If the Chicago detectives do contact you, please don't tell them we spoke. I'd prefer not to have further involvement with them."

"No problem, Lorenzo. Mum's the word."

As he left the building to catch the bus back to the Vatican, Dominic wondered what the priest might have failed to tell him.

There was something odd about the man he couldn't put his finger on.

Well, at least I know what I'll be doing for the next day or two. I wonder what's in Jonah's manuscript that's causing all this commotion?

CHAPTER SIX

It was late in the afternoon when Swiss Guards Karl Dengler and Lukas Bischoff had gotten off duty, and both were abuzz with excitement. Entering Domus Santa Marta, where Father Dominic's apartment was located, they headed down the hall to their friend's door.

Dominic was lying on the couch reading Barlow's manuscript when he heard the knocking. He got up to open the door.

"Hey, Michael! We're going to Hopside Bar to watch the big game and want you to join us!"

"Big game?"

"The biggest!" Karl exclaimed, rolling his eyes at Michael's lack of sports awareness. "Roma and Lazio are playing in the *Derby della Capitale,* the fiercest football competition in all of Italy. They hate each other so much it always makes for a ferocious game!"

"Why the hatred?" Dominic asked. "Aren't football teams generally known for good sportsmanship among the teams? Off the pitch, I mean?"

"Not with Lazio. Their hostility against Roma runs deep. The rivalry goes way back to 1927, when Mussolini wanted one major team from Rome to challenge the supremacy of the more renowned teams in northern Italy. So, he consolidated three football clubs from the city to form one club, Roma. But Lazio, a club named after the region in which Rome is situated, refused to participate, wanting to reclaim the city as their own. You don't want to miss this! Please, come with us."

"As appealing as that sounds, I'm afraid I can't, Karl. I've got to finish reading this material soon, for several reasons, and this is the only free time I have just now. I'm sure I'll catch another game with you guys soon. But thanks."

Disappointed but still enthused, the two guards left the Domus, headed to the parking lot, and jumped into Karl's Jeep Wrangler for the short drive across the Tiber River to Hopside Bar, *the* place in all of Rome to watch the sport.

DOMINIC RETURNED TO HIS READING, and what he found both intrigued and disturbed him. It was clear the manuscript was not completed, for Barlow had omitted key elements, including the full prophecies themselves.

But from what Dominic had read so far, it seemed Father Jonah Barlow had laid out a chilling indictment of his own Catholic Church for hiding the true text of the Third Secret of Fátima, as well as for not publicizing the imminent unfolding of the End Time prophecies that were contained in the Bible and in subsequent predictions.

Barlow had capably examined the history of the major prophecies that were not in the Bible—that of St. Malachy, the Apocalypse of St. Peter, and the Third Secret of Fátima—and provided his exposition of how these prophecies were being fulfilled in current times, all pointing toward the imminent Final Judgment Day.

He read that the prophecy of St. Malachy predicted that the last pope would be *Petrus Romanus,* Peter the Roman, and

Barlow pointed out that the new pope was named Petrini—a derivative of Peter—who as pope was also the Bishop of Rome.

Dominic thought back to his conversation about this very topic with Ernesto Vila at Coimbra University. He thought it uncannily coincidental that while Vila wished to speak to the pope about this matter, a book manuscript on the same subject from a respected scholar fell into his own hands. *What the…?!*

He kept reading. Apparently, Barlow *did* have a copy of the Third Secret of Fátima, both the "official" version that had been released in 2000, and another copy that the manuscript referred to as the "real" version. He was predictably critical of the Church for, in his words, creating a false prophecy to satisfy the masses: that the prophecy had been fulfilled and need no longer be contemplated. The Church apparently felt that the real prophecy was too terrible for public consumption. But if he did have the alleged final secret given to the three shepherds by the Lady of Fátima, how he had obtained it was impossible to know now.

The alleged real Third Secret was divided into three parts. In the first part—somewhat bizarrely, Dominic felt—Barlow had written that it would be announced that the rogue planet Nibiru, also known as Wormwood, was now on its approach to Earth, and that the effects of that trajectory would fulfill the Book of Revelation, Chapter 8: the sounding of the first four trumpets. Dominic opened his Bible to the relevant chapter and read the verses:

> Then the seven angels who had the seven trumpets prepared to sound them.
>
> The first angel sounded his trumpet, and there came hail and fire mixed with blood, and it was hurled down on the earth. A third of the earth was burned up, a third of the trees were burned up, and all the green grass was burned up.
>
> The second angel sounded his trumpet, and something like a huge mountain, all ablaze, was thrown into the sea. A third of

> the sea turned into blood, a third of the living creatures in the sea died, and a third of the ships were destroyed.
>
> The third angel sounded his trumpet, and a great star, blazing like a torch, fell from the sky on a third of the rivers and on the springs of water—the name of the star is Wormwood. A third of the waters turned bitter, and many people died from the waters that had become bitter.
>
> The fourth angel sounded his trumpet, and a third of the sun was struck, a third of the moon, and a third of the stars, so that a third of them turned dark. A third of the day was without light, and also a third of the night.
>
> As I watched, I heard an eagle that was flying in midair call out in a loud voice: "Woe! Woe! Woe to the inhabitants of the earth, because of the trumpet blasts about to be sounded by the other three angels!"

Dominic paused and looked out the window, lost in thought.

Barlow went on to say that the second part of the prophecy predicted that the pope would publicly denounce the Third Secret and would be struck down while doing so. But it was the third part which shook Michael to his bones. It was just too chilling to even think about.

The last prophecy Barlow wrote about was the Apocalypse of St. Peter. Supposedly penned by the first pope, the prophecy spoke of the rewards for the righteous and the punishment of the unrighteous at the final judgment, and then went on to make some crazy allegations regarding the actions of his final successor and namesake at the end of days.

Dominic was unsettled by what Barlow had written, yet he remained determinedly skeptical of the whole thing. While not an expert on apocalyptic eschatology, he at least knew that some of the assertions Barlow made had contradicted scripture, or that there were historical events which were already accepted as having fulfilled these passages in biblical times, or some time thereafter.

The actual texts of the other two prophecies were not completely quoted in the manuscript, but Dominic was certain he would find them in the Vatican's Archives, curious as to what the prophecies actually said themselves, rather than as interpreted by Barlow.

But as for the Third Secret of Fátima, he knew that was stored in one place inaccessible to anyone but the pope: in the Petri Crypta, the pope's personal hidden safe in his working office. He doubted Pope Ignatius would allow even Dominic to view that —but it was worth a try.

Meanwhile, he would ask Ian Duffy to round up the Prophecy of St. Malachy and the first Apocalypse of Peter. He wanted to see for himself why Jonah Barlow felt these important enough to challenge the Church on its current position on the matter.

CHAPTER SEVEN

Sabrina Felici's sleek red Ferrari Testarossa, an older model someone on a cop's salary might afford, had been parked at the curb of the loading zone at Rome's Leonardo da Vinci Airport for some fifteen minutes now, waiting for Rebecca Lancaster to emerge from the baggage claim area.

An airport security officer patrolling the zone, his customary submachine gun at the ready, looked at her, tapped his watch, then motioned for her to move along. She reached into her bag and withdrew her Carabinieri badge, flashed it at the officer, and he nodded, signaling his acceptance. She could stay.

As she saw Lancaster coming out the doors, her wheeled luggage trailing behind her, Felici got out of the car and waved to her, smiling. Spotting her friend, Lancaster waved back, then made her way down the row of waiting cars to the Ferrari.

"Well, it's easy to spot you in a crowd!" Lancaster said, embracing Felici as the two reunited. "Sorry I'm late, I had to use the ladies' room after getting off the plane."

"No problem," Felici said, "we're in no hurry. But it *is* cocktail time, and I've got big plans for us."

With the luggage tossed in the trunk, Felici gunned the engine and thrust the car out into the turmoil of airport traffic.

"Big plans?" Lancaster asked as she nervously fastened her seat belt.

"Team Roma plays Lazio tonight, in what we call football, but you refer to as soccer. It's the biggest rivalry of the year, so we're going to the city's hottest sports bar, Hopside. It's not far from here, and they not only have beer and generous cocktails, but gorgeous men."

"That sounds like fun. Fortunately, I slept on the plane so I'm good to go. And wherever did you find this sexy Ferrari?"

"Oh, I've had it for years. But she's still my baby. There's nothing like a Testarossa to make a statement. And I absolutely love driving her. She handles Rome's chaotic traffic like a dominatrix."

"And it begins..." Lancaster said, and the two laughed as the car sped off.

HOPSIDE WAS KNOWN throughout Rome as the premier go-to sports bar, especially for watching the city's most beloved sport. It's interior featured alternating concrete and wood-paneled walls, and an oddly eclectic mix of different tables and chairs arranged haphazardly on a red-tiled floor. Nothing at all matched, as if conformity of any sort had been specifically avoided when designing the space. Large, flat-screen TVs were hung on various walls, and bare LED lights hung from the wood-raftered ceiling.

The place was filling up rapidly as the televisions blared nonstop pregame announcements by two enthusiastic commentators. Karl and Lukas had previously reserved a table close to one of the TVs and, having just arrived, ordered beers.

The opening ceremonies began with each player on opposing teams holding the hand of a young child as they escorted them onto the pitch, a tradition symbolizing the element of bringing innocence to the game, while reminding players that children are looking up to them. The large field flags of both clubs bracketed the formation on the pitch as everyone stood for the cameras and was introduced by the game announcer. Play was about to begin.

The bar was virtually packed when Sabrina Felici and Rebecca Lancaster strode through the door.

"*Merda,* it's busy," Felici said despairingly as she looked around for an empty table. Then she spied two chairs available at a table where two younger men sat near a TV.

"See those two *bello ragazzi* over there?" she asked, pointing to Karl and Lukas. "Let's party with those handsome guys. Who knows, they could get lucky…." With a knowing smile, she winked at Lancaster as they made their way through the crowd to the table.

"*Buona sera,* boys," Felici said flirtatiously. "May we join you? There doesn't seem to be any room for us here, and we really don't want to miss this game."

Lukas looked at Karl, smiled, then shrugged.

"Sure," Karl said, as he and Lukas stood respectfully. "We're not expecting anyone else. Join us. Have a seat."

Felici glanced at Lancaster with a winning smile as each of them took a chair and sat down. Introductions were made around the table.

Karl, ever the gentleman, asked, "So, what are you ladies having?" as he signaled for the waitress.

"A dirty martini for me," Felici ordered, glancing at her companion.

"I'll have the same," Lancaster said, slinging the strap of her bag over the arm of the chair.

The server took their orders and made her way back to the bar through the crowd of rowdy patrons.

"So," Felici asked, "are you boys from Rome? What is it you do here?"

"Well, originally we are both from Switzerland," Karl said proudly, "but now we serve in the Pontifical Swiss Guard at the Vatican."

Rebecca Lancaster's eyes opened wide, astonished at her good luck. *Insiders at the Vatican*?!

Felici, too, was impressed. "That must be a rewarding job," she stated. "Are you on the pope's personal protective detail?"

"Yes, from time to time. We all have many functions, but everyone rotates through all the duties of a Swiss Guard. It is a great honor protecting the Holy Father and Vatican City."

"Yes, I imagine it would be," Felici said. "So, either of you married?"

Both Karl and Lukas laughed. Then, while looking at each other affectionately, Karl placed his arm around Lukas and pulled him in closer, saying, "Well, not officially."

Felici blushed while Lancaster laughed. "Well, there goes our romantic evening!"

"So, you're *gay*?" Felici asked with an awkward smile, slightly embarrassed.

Karl looked up thoughtfully, paused, then quipped, "I prefer to think of us as more 'mildly amused.'"

All four laughed as the bar crowd cheered for the first surprise goal of the game.

"So, are you part of the Vatican's so-called 'Lavender Mafia' we've heard so much about in the States?" Lancaster asked, tugging on her earring.

"Well, it's not like there's a club we joined, no," Karl said, rolling his eyes. "But the Vatican does have its share of gay men and women, although we're extremely closeted for obvious reasons. And what about you two? What is it you do?"

Felici was first to respond. "I am a *Capitano* with the Carabinieri, in the Homicide Division. And Becca here is also a homicide detective from Chicago. She's working on the case of a murdered priest and I'm helping her as best I can. We're actually hoping to interview a Vatican priest who knew the victim. Perhaps you know him… Father Michael Dominic?"

"Know him?!" Karl exclaimed with surprise. "He's one of our closest friends! Father Michael is the coolest priest I've ever met.

He's also prefect of the Secret Archives, a very important position."

"Yes, we're aware of that," Lancaster said, a tinge of hope to her voice, surprised at their good fortune. "By any chance, Karl, would it be possible for you to make an introduction for us?"

He thought for a moment. "Sure, I'd be happy to. Michael is a great guy. I'm sure he'd be pleased to speak with you." Another cheer went up around them as Roma scored a second goal.

"But for now," he added, "let's enjoy this game. We can talk more afterward, maybe have a bite to eat?"

"Sounds lovely," Lancaster said, looking at Felici with optimism. "Now, how is this sport played? I know nothing about soccer."

"Well, first," Lukas corrected her, "it's football, not soccer...."

CHAPTER EIGHT

Father Nick Bannon, personal secretary to Pope Ignatius, was on the telephone when Dominic walked into the pope's reception office. Bannon gestured for him to take a seat, and Dominic waited for him to finish up.

As he sat there, he worried for his old friend Jonah Barlow's legacy. Such a respected fellow Jesuit, a highly regarded scholar, writing what sounded like crazy talk. *And what was he thinking, planning on exposing the Third Secret of Fátima? That duty was specifically entrusted to the pope by the Blessed Mother herself, or so the legend went.*

Whatever it says, it must contain something of extraordinary importance, Dominic suspected, since a succession of popes from 1960 onward had declined to reveal it in their time.

"His Holiness will see you now, Michael," Bannon said, gesturing toward the pontiff's tall, double golden doors.

"Thanks, Nick."

Getting up from his desk, Petrini was already making his way toward Dominic as the young priest entered the spacious office. Smiling, he gave his son a warm embrace. "Have a seat, Michael. What brings you to see me today?"

Dominic got right to the point, relating his time in Portugal and his meeting with Ernesto Vila, as well as the professor's hope to meet the pope in order to discuss the Third Secret of Fátima, the Knights of the Apocalypse, and the pope's role as "*Petrus Romanus*"—the last of the popes, according to St. Malachy. He also discussed his reading of Jonah Barlow's not fully completed manuscript, containing outlandish material involving the planet Nibiru, which apparently meshed with biblical forecasts of Wormwood.

"This last part, Your Holiness, though it sounds far-fetched, may have some astronomical merit to it. I had read before that some astronomers believe there *is* a 'Planet X' out there that may be linked to these Nibiru references. In fact, the California Institute of Technology has found mathematical evidence suggesting just such a heavenly body in our solar system. But as it cannot yet be seen, the prospect is still hypothetical.

"But, that won't stop KOTA from claiming it as yet another sign of the End Times. The only thing they claim to possess, which I find to be practically impossible, is the Third Secret of Fátima, since only the pope has access to that. May I ask, have you seen it yet?"

Pope Ignatius was genuinely surprised, not having given any thought to the Fátima prophecy that supposedly was in his care.

"Well, having just got here myself a few short months ago, Michael, I haven't had time to see everything my duties might require. And just where might this Fátima prophecy be? Do *you* know?"

"Holy Father, there must have been some kind of protocol transferring such knowledge to you when you became pontiff. Has no one told you of the Petri Crypta yet?"

"You are the first person to even *mention* those words to me! What is it?"

"From my understanding, the Petri Crypta, or Vault of Peter, is here in your private office, to which only each pope has access."

"Well, that's a fine kettle of fish," the pope exclaimed

sardonically. "Wouldn't you have thought the camerlengo or someone would have informed me about such an important document under my personal responsibility, not to mention some kind of safe in my own office?" He pressed a button on the intercom. "Nick, could you come in here, please?"

A moment later, Father Bannon opened the door and walked in.

"Are you aware of a vault of some kind in this office?" the pope asked.

"Yes, of course, Holy Father. It is the Petri Crypta, hidden behind Raphael's *Transfiguration* painting over there." He pointed to the Renaissance artwork on a far wall, which had been moved from the Vatican Museum's Pinacoteca Room at the pope's wishes when his office was being prepared. "But only Your Holiness has the special key and biometric fingerprint to open it."

"What key? And I've never been asked for a fingerprint! Why was I never told about this?" the pope asked incredulously.

Bannon was unnerved, as if he himself bore the obligation.

"I… I am very sorry, Holy Father, but this I do not know. I only knew about it when I served your predecessor for a short time. Shall I try to find out how you might access the vault?"

"Yes, Nick, that seems appropriate, don't you think?"

"Of course. I shall attend to it at once." He backed out of the room and closed the door.

"Something is just not right about this, Michael. It's as if I were deliberately left in the dark about this so-called Petri Crypta. But Nick will work it out. Until then, what was it Professor Vila asked of you? He wishes an audience, you say?"

"Yes, and my feeling is that you should meet with him. He came across as a studious, impassioned academic, not someone who just wants to meet the pope for some frivolous purpose. He's also a member of the Knights of Malta, a very pro-Catholic order of chivalry. And for whatever reasons he might have, he insisted he could not convey his information through anyone else."

"All right then, please have Nick set it up. Let's see what this Professor Vila can tell us about these prophecies. I must say I'm dubious about being 'the last pope,' though. But he does have my interest."

~

RETURNING TO HIS OFFICE, Dominic sought out Ian Duffy and found him in the digitizing lab working on his software database for indexing the Archives.

"Hey Ian, I need you to round up a couple things, but I'm not really sure where they are."

"Well, if they're not in my database, I can use the old system to find them, assuming they're cataloged. I have yet to consolidate both databases, a more challenging task at the moment."

"However you do it, I need the prophecies of St. Malachy and the Apocalypse of St. Peter. They should be easy to find, even on the internet. I also need the Third Secret of Fátima, but you won't find that anywhere; the pope is the only one with access to it and that seems to be more of a problem than we'd anticipated."

"Okay, I should have those other two to you shortly, Michael."

~

STILL RECOVERING from last night's indulgences while watching the game at Hopside with their new friends, Karl Dengler was grateful he had the late shift today. He felt sorry for Lukas, who had early duty at St. Anne's Gate this morning, but as he always drank more moderately, he was probably in better form.

What was it I had promised to do? And for whom? Some responsibility was gnawing at him as he groggily made his way to the shower. *Oh, right. Introduce those detectives to Michael. Okay, one thing at a time….*

Feeling better after he had shaved and dressed, he headed out of the Swiss Guard barracks just inside St. Anne's Gate and on to Father Dominic's office, taking the Belvedere Courtyard route between the Vatican Museum buildings. Once home to the papal menagerie—where Pope Leo X let his prized elephant roam free—the courtyard had long ago been converted from a series of stepped garden terraces into a spacious asphalt parking lot for Vatican employees.

Weaving between the cars, Karl entered the Apostolic Library building and continued into the Secret Archives, where Dominic was sitting in his office reading.

"Good morning, Father Michael," he said cheerfully. "Have you got a minute?"

"Sure, Karl, come on in." He set the Barlow manuscript aside.

"Last night, Lukas and I were at Hopside watching Roma beat Lazio when we met these two attractive detectives—of the female persuasion, I should mention. One of them is a *capitano* with the Carabinieri named Sabrina Felici; the other is Rebecca Lancaster, an American from Chicago. Both are working on a murder case involving a friend of yours, I think, Father Jonah Barlow? Anyway, they would like to meet with you about Father Barlow's death. I told them I'd ask you."

Michael said nothing but raised an eyebrow. It wasn't being contacted by a detective that surprised him. He anticipated this after his discussion with Father Lorenzo Marchetti. What did surprise him was how quickly these events were running together. Karl, misinterpreting Michael's reaction went on to say, "They're very nice, I think you'd like them. We had great fun watching the game together."

"Okay, how do I reach them?"

Karl handed Sabrina Felici's business card to Dominic. "I expect you could set the time and place, though I'm not sure how long Signorina Lancaster will be in Rome."

"All right, thanks, Karl."

The Swiss Guard left the office, and the priest went back to reading Barlow's book.

This book apparently holds much interest for various factions, Dominic figured. *How does it fit with the odd request from Vila and Father Barlow's death?*

CHAPTER NINE

The Archbishop of Washington, D.C., Cardinal Damien Challis, was a rock star of the Catholic Church. As head of one of the largest cathedrals in the United States, he oversaw a diocese that included the center of political power of the richest and mightiest country on earth, giving him a bully pulpit like no other.

Yet it was still something of a surprise that the U.S. Conference of Catholic Bishops had assigned so young and fiery a preacher to a post typically held by a much more reserved pastor. Cardinal Challis had turned a majestic cathedral into the Catholic version of the modern Protestant mega-church. Masses were packed to overflowing to hear his dynamic sermons, upbeat music and multimedia presentations in several languages.

And that wasn't the only thing Challis borrowed from the large Protestant congregations, especially the evangelicals. He was also a fervent believer that he was living in the End Times, just prior to the long-predicted Second Coming of Christ. He beat the apocalyptic drum at every turn, tying modern occurrences into biblical prophecy, especially as related to events in the Middle East and the State of Israel.

But Damien Challis played another more furtive role apart from his priestly duties. He served as Knight Commander for a secret organization bent on preparing for the End Times: The Knights of the Apocalypse, an ancient order of chivalry with roots in the late seventeenth century. Their purpose? To defend the Catholic Church against the emergence of the Antichrist.

Challis sat at his desk facing the webcam mounted atop his computer screen. A meeting of the group's leaders, the Council of Seven, was about to begin.

His monitor display was divided into six secure videoconference windows, one for each of his fellow members of the Council and all of their images masked to prevent their identities from being known to one another. Their appointed spiritual advisor, a shadowy figure code-named Magnus, a man everyone knew but who remained silent during the meeting, was also attending the conference by telephone and could hear all the participants.

The organization believed it was privy to secret knowledge about the end of the world—knowledge acquired by the studious devotion and divine inspiration of certain modern members and advisors of the order—as well as privileged access to copies of all biblical and apocryphal texts of eschatological prophecy collected over the centuries of the order's existence. Since possession of that information by various governments of the world could prove severely adverse to their mission, it had been closely guarded for over three hundred years.

"Gentlemen," the cardinal Knight Commander began, "recent events have forced me to call you together at this time. As you are aware, *Petrus Romanus*, Peter the Roman, has been elected pope in the person of Enrico Petrini. Thus, we know our time is short, less than the number of years left to the man now serving as pope. But let me turn this over to Nimbus, the Knight of Swords, who has a report on the most recent events."

Nimbus spoke up. "Thank you, Commander. Our operation in Chicago had several unanticipated challenges but ultimately was successful. We have recovered the prophecies that were given to the scholar, Father Jonah Barlow, in the form of a manuscript he was working on. But I'm afraid Barlow himself had to be eliminated in the process, though our agent made it appear to be an accident. Suffice to say he resisted all efforts we made to encourage him not to publish his interpretations until we were better prepared, and instead insisted that the world be made aware of all his findings at once. It was apparent from notes at the scene that at least one copy of the manuscript was sent out to be reviewed by someone at the Vatican, a priest named Father Dominic. There may have been other copies sent out as well, but we have yet to determine that."

A slight but clearly irritated huff came from Magnus at the mention of Dominic's name.

"So, as you can see," resumed the Knight Commander, taking back control, "our hand is being forced, and our timing must be accelerated. This was not totally unexpected, for as it is told in Matthew 24:22, 'If those days had not been cut short, no one would survive, but for the sake of the Elect those days will be shortened.'

"We are the Elect, my brothers. Hence, our time has been shortened. We will make the first announcement very soon now, in a matter of days.

"Incidentally, Magnus tells me this Father Dominic can be quite troublesome; he has had many disagreeable interactions with the priest himself. I have thus dispatched agents to monitor Dominic's movements and make sure he does not interfere with our preparations. Fortunately, Barlow's manuscript does not mention any of us by name.

"I also understand we are now in the process of securing a location for the End Times Last Mass and will have the final approvals and financing in place within days. Clearly, we have been granted divine favor in order to carry out our appointed role in preparation for the return of our Lord. We will meet again before the second announcement. With that, this meeting is adjourned."

Just as Cardinal Challis was shutting down his conference connection, a knock sounded at the door.

"Yes? Enter…."

"Your Eminence," said his production assistant, "Mass will start in ten minutes."

Showtime, Challis thought, as he donned his vestments and checked his makeup.

CHAPTER
TEN

Lukas Bischoff was on guard duty at St. Anne's Gate when the fiery red Ferrari pulled up to the stop sign, its powerful engine thrumming as it idled.

Lukas smiled when he saw Sabrina Felici behind the wheel and her friend, Rebecca Lancaster, sitting beside her. He approached the driver's side door to greet them.

"*Buon giorno,* Sabrina. It's good to see you and Rebecca again."

"Hi, Lukas," they both said at once. "You're looking quite dashing in that uniform." Lukas blushed and stood a bit taller.

"We're here to see Father Dominic, of course. And thanks again to you and Karl for arranging this meeting. We really appreciate it."

"No problem, it was our pleasure. Here are your Vatican passes. Always keep one with you and put the other on your dashboard. See that building over there?" He pointed to the central post office. "Park anywhere in that vicinity where there's a free space. I'll meet you there and escort you to Father Dominic's office myself." He signaled to the gateman to raise the boom barrier, and the Testarossa slowly made its way to the parking area while Lukas followed it on foot.

• • •

"Father Dominic, I would like to introduce Capitano Sabrina Felici with the Carabinieri, and her friend Rebecca Lancaster, who's with the Chicago Police Department. Ladies, I leave you in good hands." Lukas gave a smart but casual salute and turned to head back to his post.

Dominic shook hands with the detectives as introductions were exchanged. "Please, call me Michael." He invited them to have a seat.

Lancaster couldn't take her eyes off Dominic, clearly taken with him. *Such a handsome man!* she thought. *What a pity he's wasted on the priesthood….*

"So, how is it I can be of help? Karl told me it has something to do with Father Barlow's death?"

"Yes, Father," Lancaster said, taking the lead, "we have reason to believe his death was not an accident. We are fairly certain Jonah Barlow was murdered. And we also believe it has something to do with a book manuscript he was working on.

"We also understand he gave you a copy of that manuscript. Is that correct?"

Dominic studied her as he considered his response. He decided to let it play out for the moment.

"Yes, that's correct," he replied simply.

Lancaster glanced at Felici, then turned back to Dominic. Her usual steely resolve as a hardened detective was being tested as she tried not to think about his body. *Snap out of it! You've got a job to do. He's a priest, forgodsake.*

"Father, it might be of significant help to us if I could have a copy of the manuscript. There might be something in it that could have a material impact on our investigation." She swallowed hard and unconsciously reached up to pull on an earring.

"I'm very sorry, but for now I'm afraid that won't be possible," Dominic said politely. "Jonah gave that to me in confidence, and I owe him at least that. I have read most of it, and there's nothing yet that stood out to me as having relevance to someone being murdered."

Not one to take "no" for an answer, Lancaster tried the charm offensive.

"Michael..." She paused for effect as she held his eyes, then purred, "while I respect the honorable position you've taken, couldn't you make just one small exception in this case?"

"Well, if I did, then it wouldn't be so honorable, would it? I truly am sorry, Detective, but you'll have to find leads elsewhere. I seriously doubt the book would be of much help. Perhaps you could try his publisher if you're so inclined."

Slightly perturbed, Lancaster tried yet another tack.

"May I ask what the book is about, Michael?"

Dominic paused to consider how much he should reveal.

"Well, basically, it's about apocalyptic eschatology... prophecies leading up to the End Times. Jonah is—or was, rather —a dedicated scholar respected for his work in that narrowly specialized area, among other things. In the book, he describes several renowned prophecies which he felt were soon coming to pass. Now, I am not one who particularly believes in that line of thinking, but Jonah was certainly an advocate, and apparently had what he considered to be proof of his esoteric findings.

"I can tell you this: the Church itself wouldn't side with Jonah's work, despite his unblemished reputation—" Then, realizing what he had just said, he leapt to clarify himself.

"That's not to say the Church would actually murder him for it, though... That should be absolutely clear."

Lancaster found a thread she could pull on.

"But that's just what we're looking for, Michael. While I might agree that the Church would be hard pressed to sanction an assassination, there may be others who took it upon themselves to ensure that information wouldn't get out. Do you see the dilemma we have here?"

Not missing the inclusive "we" part, Dominic clearly understood the dilemma, one he had just helped to create. He sighed and leaned back in his chair.

"To put it bluntly, Detective, there are parts of that book that only the pope should be privy to. And yet somehow Jonah claimed he'd gained access to the Third Secret of Fátima, a prophecy given only to three Portuguese children in 1917. That prophecy has been handed down from pope to pope for decades, and its revelation can only be disclosed by the pope. For whatever reasons of their own, however, all popes since 1960—the year the Blessed Mother dictated that the secret should be revealed to the world—has each evaded his responsibility, passing the duty on to their successors."

Accustomed to ferreting out clues from evidence or data they came across, both Lancaster and Felici quickly glanced at each other.

"Michael," Felici prompted gently, "do you not see how this might look from our perspective? What you have just told us can certainly be viewed as motive for someone inclined to obtain and reveal this so-called Third Secret of Fátima, or even to prevent its disclosure, depending on their ambitions."

Dominic realized he had dug a deeper grave by disclosing what he already had. But there was no taking back what he had said. Perhaps part of him subconsciously wanted the detectives' help in better understanding Jonah's work—and death—himself.

"Well, yes, I suppose I do see that now," he admitted, averting his gaze from the women and staring out the window to the Vatican gardens. Several nuns, their blousy black sleeves rolled up, were working in the vegetable patch, chattering amongst themselves as they tended the plants, blissfully unaware of the grave matters being discussed a mere six meters away in Dominic's office.

Turning back to the detectives, he offered a feigned proposal in order to buy time.

"Let me discuss this matter with the Holy Father. As he can be a hard man to get time with, it may take several days.

"In the meantime, I'd be happy to give you a tour of the Secret Archives, if you wish...."

CHAPTER ELEVEN

Before Giovanni Greco had been promoted to cardinal and then to Vatican Secretary of State—replacing Enrico Petrini when he became pope—he briefly served as personal secretary to Pope Xavier II, who had resigned due to poor health during his reign. But Greco was always on a fast-track in the Vatican hierarchy, and some day he himself hoped to lead the Church.

In the meantime, he was quite content with his current job as the second-most powerful person in the Vatican, overseeing the city-state in all matters except ecclesiastical, which fell under the pope's domain.

When his own secretary informed him that the pope's personal secretary was on the phone, Greco was only too happy to oblige him, as Nick Bannon could well be considered the third-most important person, being the gatekeeper to His Holiness. Few people could meet with the pope without Bannon's personal concurrence.

"Ciao, Nick. What is it I can be of help with today?"

"Your Eminence, we seem to have a problem with the Holy Father's safe, the Petri Crypta. In his transition it seems he was not given formal access to the vault, the key and biometric fingerprint. Without those, he is unable to gain access, of course. Have you any idea where the key might be, and how we go about this biometric process?"

Cardinal Greco thought back for a moment to his own time with the previous pope.

"Nick, I must admit this is all news to me. To my knowledge, Pope Xavier never went through that process. We didn't even know there *was* a vault! But I served as his secretary only for a short time, replacing Cardinal Dante when he went to prison—what, about two years ago now? You don't suppose…."

The line was silent for a few moments as both men considered the unimaginable.

"Eminence," Bannon asked, "do you think former Cardinal Dante is somehow involved in this? That would be *my* first guess."

"I just had the same suspicion, Nick. I'd bet my sapphire ring Dante never turned over the access protocols to Pope Xavier, and now Pope Ignatius suffers the same dilemma. Where is that bastard Dante these days, anyway?"

"Last I heard, he and Bishop Silva had boarded an airplane, destination unknown, as they fled prosecution for their roles in that P2/Opus Deus scandal. Where he is now is anyone's guess.

"Nick, if you'll hold on for a moment, let me check the Secretariat's Protocol Manual for this."

"Of course, I'll stand by."

Greco set the phone down and reached behind him for the binder containing nearly every custom and procedure for such arcane Vatican protocols. Paging through to the proper section, he found details on the Petri Crypta. He picked up the phone.

"Here it is, Nick. Let me read you the notations:

> "The Petri Crypta is no ordinary lock safe. The lock is both mechanical and biometric. His Holiness must place his thumb on the fingerprint reader on the key handle, and then put the

special Crypta key in the lock. Once inserted, the key transmits its code to the lock, then the key is turned, and the lock opens. The key codes and the lock were synced when the lock was first initialized.

If any attempt to open the lock is made in any other manner, the keyway closes for twenty-four hours. If three attempts are made using anything other than the correct keys, the safe fills with a highly penetrating solvent that dissolves all inks, making the documents inside unreadable. The biometric key can be associated to a new thumbprint, but for the fingerprint to be changed, two physical keys are required simultaneously, together with an encoder the Vatican locksmith maintains that will allow each new pope to change the mechanism to accept his biometric thumbprint.

One key stays with the pope, and the spare is held by the Secretary of State. When a pope dies, the camerlengo gives the former pope's key to the Secretary of State, who arranges to have it recoded to the new pope, using his key to authenticate it when the Vatican locksmith is summoned once a new pope is elected.

There are two additional spare keys, to replace the pope's and Secretary of State's key, if necessary. They are stored off-site with an individual known as the *Clavis Domini*, the Key Master, who resides in the Benedictines' Abbey of the Dormition monastery in Jerusalem."

When Greco had finished reading, both he and Bannon were speechless, each considering the extraordinary logistics required. Greco broke the silence.

"Great pains have been taken to ensure the Petri Crypta remains secure, Nick, so obviously there are exceedingly special contents meant only for the pope's eyes. And we both know that, historically, the Third Secret of Fátima is kept there as well."

"Yes," Bannon agreed. "And as it happens, that's what started this whole matter. His Holiness is dealing with that very issue as we speak. So he must gain access to the vault as soon as possible.

"Let me take this up with Papa Petrini," Bannon continued, "and I'll let you know if we need your further assistance. Thank you for your help, Eminence."

CHAPTER TWELVE

Once Father Dominic had confirmed that Pope Ignatius would take the meeting, Ernesto Vila had driven up the Portuguese coast from Coimbra to Porto. Only in Porto could a man find the exclusive men's atelier begun by Ayres Carneiro da Silva over seventy years ago, which still thrived, hand-stitching the finest bespoke suits in all of Portugal.

Pleased with his sartorial investment, the professor sat proudly in the vast marble foyer outside the pope's private office, trying hard not to wrinkle the dark blue Mongolian cashmere as he waited to be summoned by His Holiness.

But he was also deeply apprehensive. He knew he was taking a great risk by challenging the pope with his urgent plea. It would be tragic if the Holy Father spurned his request, for dire consequences far greater than even he might be able to foresee, much less explain, would certainly follow. He prayed to God the pope would understand and comply with his appeal.

MONSIGNOR DIEGO FERRETTI, the Vatican's official heraldist, was ensconced in the sitting area of the pope's personal office, with the Holy Father seated next to him and Father Dominic sitting across from them. Spread out on the table before them all were various cutout charges, stars, helms, and crests with which to prepare Pope Ignatius's personal coat of arms, the custom for every new pope.

"We will begin, of course, with the papal tiara and the Keys of Saint Peter, features unique to and consistent with the papacy. Then comes the Petrini family shield, an honored escutcheon that goes back to the year 1280," Ferretti explained, as he moved the historic shield to the center of his workspace. "As you will note, Your Holiness, the tincture is divided into three horizontal partitions across the field: the top partition features the lion, depicting the tribe of Judah, fighting the dragon, which represents evil.

"Three stars feature on the second partition. The first is the seven-pointed star standing for both the seven days of creation and the seven trumpets of the End Times. And in accordance with Revelation 17:9, it also stands for Rome, the city that sits on seven hills over which you are the bishop. Next to that, the six-pointed star, representing both the sun and the nation of Israel. Finally, we have the five-pointed star, the symbol for the Virgin Mary.

"In the final partition we have placed the Maltese cross, associating the eight points with the Eight Beatitudes of Jesus. And beneath that is the personal motto I have suggested, and one I truly hope you'll adopt as befitting your papacy: *Fidelis ad Ultimum*—Faithful to the Last.

"I am very pleased with your design, Diego, thank you for your fine artistry," the pope said as he admired the heraldic imagery. "It is with great pride that I embrace this as my papal coat of arms. But I would prefer the motto be *Fides, Spes, Amor:* Faith, Hope and Love. What do you think, Michael?"

Dominic was silent for a moment as he stared with warm sentiment at Ferretti's beautiful work, for he knew that he too shared the Petrini family's history although in a most unconventional and surreptitious way.

"It is without equal, Holy Father," he said, holding the pope's gaze in mutual understanding. The moment was not lost on either man, as both their eyes clouded with emotion given the close bond they shared, a rare moment of love between father and son.

"Thank you, Diego. Can you leave this here awhile so I can

appreciate it a bit longer? I am grateful for your time and effort. This suits me perfectly."

"It was my honor, Holy Father," Ferretti said as he gathered up his tools and other materials, reaching for his walking cane. He smiled inwardly as he prepared to leave, pleased at having manipulated the pope into accepting the most meaningful heraldic representations of importance to his masters in the Knights of the Apocalypse. "Unless there is anything else, I shall be on my way."

"MICHAEL, these detectives… Do they honestly believe Jonah was murdered for a *book*?" The pope sat in the white, high-backed chair behind his desk after Ferretti left as Dominic paced the grand office, having explained about his meeting with Lancaster and Felici and their desire to get a copy of Barlow's manuscript.

"I've known the man for many years," Petrini continued, "and, yes, he has put himself at odds with the Vatican on numerous occasions. But, truth be told, he hasn't been wrong most of the time. The Church does have her share of dark secrets, not to mention the infernal workings of the Curia. But just maybe he'd gone too far this time, and it cost him his life. What's your advice on the matter? *Should* the detectives be allowed access to Jonah's work?"

"I need to give this more thought, Holiness. Let's go ahead and bring in Professor Vila, who may shed more light on the subject, since they are related." Dominic picked up the phone on a side table and punched the intercom button. Father Bannon, the pope's secretary, answered promptly.

"Nick, could you send in Signor Vila?"

A few moments later, the two golden doors swung open, and Father Bannon escorted the professor in. Dominic made introductions and Vila, who was clearly overcome with emotion, respectfully knelt and kissed the pope's ring.

"Please, Ernesto, do have a seat," Dominic offered, gesturing to a cozy sitting area by the fireplace. All three men sat down as Father Bannon put another log on the fire, then left the office, closing the tall doors quietly behind him.

Dominic took the liberty of explaining to the pope the topic of his earlier meeting with Vila in Coimbra, setting the stage for Vila to take over the discussion.

"Most Holy Father, first I wish to thank you for the great privilege of your time, which I know must be very tightly scheduled. You honor me by accepting my request to meet, but now I have another request of you, a most urgent one: You *must* release the Third Secret of Fátima publicly, and at the earliest possible opportunity. Let me explain.

"As I told Father Dominic, my great-grandfather, Cesar Vila, witnessed the Miracle of the Sun as prophesied by the Blessed Lady in 1917. Cesar also knew Sister Lúcia, one of the shepherd children, quite well. He was her godfather, in fact, having been friends of the family for many years.

"A longtime friend of mine, Father Lorenzo Marchetti, introduced me to Father Jonah Barlow while the latter was working on his book dealing with three specific prophecies leading up to the End Times. As you likely know, Father Barlow was a renowned expert on apocalyptic eschatology, that part of theology dealing with death, judgment, and the final destiny of the soul and humankind.

"As it happens, he was using me as a source for stories from my great-grandfather to support the theories he put forward in his book. In our discussions, the one thing he was absolutely certain about—and please forgive me here, Holy Father—was the fact that Pope John Paul II told the world something substantially different about the Third Secret than what it actually contained. Cesar told me the real secret, and it's not the one the pope revealed in 2000, which is more aligned with what a group who calls themselves the Knights of the Apocalypse wanted the public to hear. Their intentions are evil and self-serving, but somehow they were able to get the pope to falsify the Third Secret."

The pope leaned forward and clasped his hands together as if in prayer. "Then what do you believe *is* the true Third Secret, Professor?"

"Holy Father, it is not a question of what I believe. It is a matter of the truth."

In hushed tones, Ernesto Vila related to Dominic and the pope what he was told about the Third Secret of Fátima.

The shock on the faces of both Dominic and the pope were evident, which surprised Vila.

"But, Your Holiness, you of all people should already know what the Third Secret is! Is that not the case?"

Petrini looked at Dominic as the two flushed with embarrassment. Dominic spoke on their behalf.

"Ernesto, forgive us, but we are not yet prepared to reveal what is known at this stage. There are... certain complications...."

Vila was taken aback. "It is not for me to forgive the pope, nor you, Father Michael! No doubt you have things well in hand. Regardless, Your Holiness *must* release the true Third Secret before Father Barlow's manuscript is published, or the Vatican is sure to suffer unwarranted complications and harsh public criticism, much like when Pope John Paul gave the world his false testimony about the prophecy. Please do not misunderstand me. I do not wish to castigate nor offend John Paul's memory, for surely he was manipulated by KOTA operatives, since that was the message they wanted released at the time.

"But now, they have long-planned vile objectives, and from what I am to understand, you and the Church will look very bad if they come to pass. Please, do *not* let that happen!"

Dominic and Petrini looked at each other, now understanding the urgency.

"Thank you, Ernesto," Dominic said. "It does look as if we have work to do on the matter sooner than later. I appreciate your coming all this way to meet with the Holy Father and me. May we contact you again if need be?"

"Of course, Father, I will make myself available at your convenience."

With that, Nick Bannon was called to escort Ernesto Vila out of the pope's office and back to St. Anne's Gate for his return to Coimbra.

When Bannon returned, he rejoined Dominic and the pope.

"Your Holiness, after some effort I now have information on how to access the Petri Crypta—but it's not going to be as easy as one might expect.

"Someone needs to go to Jerusalem to get the keys from a monk who goes by the name *Clavis Domini*."

CHAPTER THIRTEEN

"Clavis Domini?" the pope inquired. "Who in God's name is the Clavis Domini?"

Bannon answered, "Apparently, Your Holiness, it has been a long-standing tradition that, given the secure nature of the Petri Crypta, the Benedictines' Abbey of the Dormition monastery in Jerusalem has been selected by the Curia to act as custodian for the backup keys to your vault, in the event of such a quandary as we find ourselves in now.

"The current Clavis Domini, or Key Master, is a monk named Brother Moshe Hadani. I have contacted him already and he is expecting the arrival of your designee to acquire the keys, but he wishes to speak with whomever it is soon. He seemed somewhat urgent about that too. Do you have any suggestions as to who that might be?"

The pope turned to Dominic. "I do have one person in mind...."

Dominic's face lit up. "I'd love a visit to Jerusalem! Thank you, Holy Father. And it would be an honor to meet Brother Moshe."

"You must leave as soon as possible, Father," Bannon urged, "for Hadani leaves on sabbatical in two days, and he is the only one who can transfer the keys. He also asked after Simon Ginzberg. Apparently, they are old friends. He wishes you to call him at your earliest opportunity on this private number. I must say he seemed quite distressed." Bannon handed Dominic a piece of notepaper with an Israeli phone number on it.

"I think I can manage that," Dominic said, thinking, hoping, that Hana might be available for a quick trip to the Holy Land. "I'll give him a call now."

"Excellent," Pope Ignatius said, "and Nick, please get me Simon Ginzberg on the phone."

Now back in his office in the Archives building, Dominic picked up the phone and dialed the number.

"Is this Brother Moshe Hadani?" Dominic asked.

"Yes, this is Moshe speaking," said an anxious voice with a thick Hebrew accent.

"Good afternoon, Brother. I'm Father Michael Dominic from the Vatican. We seem to have an access issue here with the Petri Crypta, and His Holiness has given me the task of acquiring the keys from you as Clavis Domini. May I ask what your availability might be?"

"Father Dominic," the monk said, clearly agitated, "you must come at once! My life has already been threatened over these keys and I fear for my safety."

"Threatened?! By whom?"

"I cannot say. Two brutish thugs, both wearing seven-pointed stars pinned to their lapels, visited me here at the abbey demanding I turn over the keys to them. *How* they discovered I am the Clavis Domini is beyond me, and rather shocking in itself! No one but the pope, the Secretary of State, and I know of this secret arrangement with the Vatican. It is highly classified. Mysterious forces are at work here in Jerusalem, Father, poised to take the keys from me for whatever nefarious reasons. I feel as if I am being followed wherever I go, and I cannot even sleep peacefully in fear for my life."

"That makes my immediate visit now more critical," Dominic replied tersely. "Hopefully I can be there tomorrow morning, if I can make the arrangements. Where shall we meet?"

"Here, at the abbey. I will be waiting for you. In the meantime, as an extra measure of caution given the threats, I have sent the keys away to separate hiding places by trusted couriers. Certain friends have been holding special safes to put a key into should it be required. They will protect the key until the correct designee comes to retrieve it. When you arrive, I will tell you exactly where the keys are. But since this line may not be safe, if anyone gets to me before then, I will give you specific clues as to where to find the keys which only you will understand. Now, pay close attention...."

Hadani gave Dominic clear but coded instructions for the locations of each key, in Latin—a language Dominic would understand—and using metaphors he should be able to figure out.

"Is all that clear to you, Father Dominic?"

"Yes, I think I understand it, Moshe. You're a very good cryptologist, I must say. And the Latin was a nice touch."

"Now, one more thing. You must be sure to—*Hey! Wait! What are you doing here?! Stop! No, please don't... please, I...!"* Dominic heard a struggle, then a thump. Then silence.

"*Moshe?!* What's happening?!" he asked frantically.

Then he heard something else. Heavy breathing on the line.

"Who is this?" a deep voice asked in an unknown accent. "What did the monk say to you? Tell me!"

Dominic looked at the phone, then hung up, his hands slightly trembling.

He searched online for a phone number for the abbey but found nothing. *Of course. They're Benedictine monks; they probably don't even allow technology in the monastery....*

He didn't even know the man, yet he felt sorrow for such a

trusted colleague of the Vatican. *Hopefully he isn't dead. But who do I call in Jerusalem? I don't know anyone in the city… I've got to get there, quickly!*

He picked up the phone and dialed a number in Paris.

"Hana? How does a quick trip to Jerusalem sound to you? Just trust me, I'll explain everything later."

"Anything you need, Michael. When?"

"Great, thanks. We need to leave first thing in the morning. Just pack for a few days."

AT THE VATICAN SWITCHBOARD, Sister Mary Oliphant, a nun of the Pious Disciples of the Divine Master that handled all calls in and out of the Vatican, noticed Father Dominic's office line light up. On her display she recognized the country and area codes as being those of Jerusalem. Tapping a button on her console, she listened in on the call but muted her microphone.

Having listened intently to that call, she also eavesdropped on the next call Dominic made immediately afterward. When he ended the last call, she opened a secure texting app on her personal cell phone and sent just five letters to a private undesignated number in her contacts: "**MD2CD**."

MAGNUS FELT the burner phone vibrate in his pocket. Withdrawing the phone, he read the message. *So, Michael Dominic is going to the Clavis Domini. Interesting….*

Then, using the same burner, he made his own call to Jerusalem.

CHAPTER FOURTEEN

Detective Rebecca Lancaster was rattled. Here she was in the Eternal City, her investigation going pretty much nowhere, and having to rely on a disturbingly attractive Vatican priest to hand over the keys to her kingdom. Or their shared kingdom, really.

Meanwhile, she had done all the retail therapy she dared at the Prada, Armani, and Bottega Veneta outlet shops in Rome, and had a nice new wardrobe to return to Chicago with—once her work was done.

It's been two days already, and I have yet to hear back from the good Father Dominic. Let's give Sabrina a call....

Pulling out her cell phone, she looked at the time. *Four o'clock. Surely, she's still in her office.* She called Felici's number.

"Hi, Sabrina, it's Becca. Say, we need to get things moving, and I haven't heard back from Father Dominic yet. What do you suggest we do now?"

"I was just about to call you, Becca," Felici replied. "Earlier today, I met with the Vatican Gendarmerie on another matter and told them I was working with you on your investigation. Since it involves the death of an American priest, and I was already up to speed on the case, they temporarily deputized me to represent the Holy See in your investigation, as long as I report back to them on our activities. So we now have official standing with the Vatican and can act in its name!"

"That's fantastic!" Lancaster cheered. "Will this open the door wider for Father Dominic?"

"You bet it will. To some degree, anyway. It is still his decision as to whether or not he will share Jonah Barlow's manuscript. But at least he can feel more amenable to helping us. Shall I give him a call?"

"No, let me do that. I'll call him right now, in fact. I'll let you know how things go."

Ending the call, Lancaster was now more enthused. She tapped in the number she had written on the back of a business card, Dominic's direct line. The priest answered after two rings.

"Hello, Father Dominic. This is Detective Lancaster. I'm just calling to see if you've had time to discuss our matter with His Holiness, and if we might now have a look at Father Barlow's book."

"Hi, Rebecca. Good to hear from you."

We're on a first name basis now?! she thought. *Good. That makes things easier.*

Feeling bad about his ruse of using the pope to buy time, Dominic continued anyway. "Actually, no, I'm afraid the Holy Father and I have yet to discuss this."

"Well, in that case, I should mention that Capitano Felici has just been deputized by the Vatican Gendarmerie to assist in my investigation, since it does involve the suspected murder of a priest. Does that help matters? Can we have a look at Barlow's manuscript now?"

Dominic considered this new angle. And given Brother Moshe's predicament—whatever that might be—the assistance of two detectives, especially with the blessing of the Vatican, might well be useful in Jerusalem.

"Interesting," he said. "Given that new development, I might have another proposition for you. I'm leaving for Jerusalem in the morning to deal with an important matter, but I fear my contact there—a monk at the Abbey of the Dormition monastery —may have met with foul play. Your and Capitano Felici's investigative skills may come in useful there. Would you like to join us? To sweeten the offer, I'll bring portions of the manuscript with us which you can read on the plane, but I cannot give you a full copy of it, and there are certain parts I'm not going to reveal, at least not yet, since they won't be relevant to your case anyway. Oh, and we'll be traveling by private jet. Sound interesting?"

Lancaster was over the moon but held back her enthusiasm.

"Of course, we'd be happy to assist you in any way we can. And even just reading the manuscript on the plane would be a huge help, Michael, thank you for suggesting it." She pumped her fist repeatedly in the air of her hotel room.

"Good. We'll pick you both up at seven o'clock tomorrow morning at your hotel. See you then."

CHAPTER FIFTEEN

While Hana's grandfather, Baron Armand de Saint-Clair, was vacationing on his yacht docked at the Portomaso Marina in St. Julian's, Malta, Hana as usual had free use of his private jet. The Dassault Falcon 900LX had just taken off from Fiumicino Airport in Rome, bound for Ben Gurion Airport in Tel Aviv, when Hana's guests—Michael Dominic, Marco Picard, Rebecca Lancaster and Sabrina Felici—settled in for the three-and-a-half-hour flight.

"What is it your grandfather does to merit this kind of luxury, Hana?" Lancaster asked as she took in the plush surroundings of the spacious main cabin.

"He's in the banking business, Rebecca. Our family has owned Banque Suisse de Saint-Clair in Geneva for generations, and despite his age—he just turned ninety-two—he still travels quite a bit. He's now on holiday in Malta for a month or so, where he has many friends and banking colleagues. Grand-père always seems to mix business with pleasure when he can, and he's also a member of the Knights of Malta, so he has other responsibilities there as well."

"I never knew that!" Dominic exclaimed, explaining to the others, "The Knights of Malta are a chivalric order of Catholic lay people. They have a rich history, although these days they mainly focus on providing international medical humanitarian assistance where it's needed. I'm impressed the baron is a knight, though I'm not surprised. Members are elected for life in a secret conclave and must be approved by the pope, and the baron has been on the popes' Consulta for years."

"What's that, Michael? The Consulta, I mean," Lancaster asked, sidling up next to him on a loveseat set against the hull.

"The Consulta is an intimate group of the pope's closest personal counselors, people who advise him on administrative and political matters. All popes going back hundreds of years have had one."

"Are you a member?" she pursued, crossing her legs and fondling an earring.

"No." He laughed. "I give His Holiness enough day-to-day advice without making it so formal. He and I have known each other since I was a child."

"Now *that's* fascinating," Lancaster gushed, moving a bit closer to Dominic—as if there were any more space on a loveseat on a jet. "Tell me more about that...."

Sitting in a single seat across from them, Hana watched Lancaster make her moves, heard her purring voice, and grit her teeth at the seductress's subtle lean forward. Like a dog glaring at a threat, Hana's hackles rose. She saw Michael swallow hard, his eyes avoiding the cleavage before him, but she knew that, being polite, he wouldn't reveal his discomfort.

"Michael, there's something I need to speak with you about. Can you join me in the forward cabin?"

"You bet," he said, clearly relieved of the burden his charms had often caused in the past. Then he pulled out Barlow's manuscript from his bag. "Rebecca, here's Jonah's book to keep you busy during the flight."

Disheartened that Hana had spoiled her game, but happy to get her hands on the book, she acquiesced. "Thanks, Michael. Yes, this *will* keep me busy."

Now past the cabin divider and having closed the door, Dominic looked at Hana awkwardly, then spoke quietly. "Thanks for rescuing me. I was getting a little hot under the collar." He feigned pulling on his white clerical collar and grimaced.

She chuckled at his response. "I've had to rescue you more times than I can count from damsels in no distress whatsoever. You need to stop working out, maybe let yourself gain a few pounds and go bald."

"Not a chance! With my sedentary work I need all the exercise I can get. And I like my hair." He reached up to rake it back, then shook his head to let it settle.

"So, tell me, what *are* we going to Jerusalem for? Though I'm always happy to oblige your engaging exploits, you've been circumspect about our mission there." She grinned as they both took seats.

"I'm glad you take it as 'our mission,' and I'm really grateful Marco is here, too, since we may run into trouble. But it wouldn't be the first time, right?"

"'Trouble?!' What kind of trouble?"

"Well, I'm not really sure myself yet, but..." Since Hana was his closest confidant and she *was* accommodating him with transportation, Dominic went on to give her the background on everything in play: Brother Moshe Hadani and their strange phone call, and the need to acquire the pope's keys for the Petri Crypta; Father Jonah Barlow's death and the detectives' involvement; Ernesto Vila's contacting him to meet with the pope and their discussion about the prophecies of Fátima; and meeting Father Lorenzo Marchetti at Villa Stritch.

"It's a good thing I have nothing pressing going on at the moment," she confessed, "because this sounds way more fun than writing about European immigration policies, about which I spent the last two months researching." Hana's job as an investigative journalist for *Le Monde* kept her busy, and despite her family wealth, she had always strived to make her own mark in life. And having just finished up a major assignment, she was grateful for another adventure with her priestly friend.

"Just watch out for that woman," Hana cautioned, a tinge of jealousy in her tone. "She's obviously using her wily charms to get you defrocked." They both laughed quietly, then hysterically, until tears rolled down their cheeks. Then, settling down and composing themselves, they returned to the main cabin.

ONCE THE JET had landed on Runway 12 at Ben Gurion Airport, it taxied to the Fattal VIP Terminal, where passengers were met by a shiny black Mercedes Sprinter van to take them southeast to the Abbey of the Dormition in Jerusalem, less than an hour away.

Passing through numerous checkpoints where their passports were validated, the group finally arrived at the monastery, an imposing tan-brown structure resembling a small basilica. Located on the revered Mount Zion, the abbey had been constructed in 1910, but its original foundations went back to the fifth century.

As everyone exited the van, they admired the ancient historic buildings and surrounding scenery just outside the Old City of Jerusalem.

"Why is it called 'Dormition,' Michael?" Sabrina Felici asked. "In Italian, *dormire* means 'to sleep.'"

"That's exactly why they named it so, in fact," he replied, "and it's the same translation in Latin. Legend has it that Mary, mother of Jesus, died on this spot, or in the actual language of scripture, 'fell asleep' here. Mount Zion was also the location of the Last Supper. This is very holy land we're standing on, sacred to billions of people around the world.

"Let's find the abbot and see if we can learn more about Brother Moshe."

Dominic led the group to the entrance of the abbey, where,

after passing through the vestibule, they entered a gorgeous round, brilliantly lit chapel chamber with surrounding arched alcoves painted with ancient murals, and a high domed tiled ceiling over a vast, intricate floor mosaic.

"I don't know what it is," Hana remarked, "but even for an agnostic like myself, churches always have a profound impact on me. This really is stunning, Michael."

"It is breathtaking, isn't it?" he replied, infatuated with the exquisite tile work of the mosaic floor.

As they were admiring the room, a monk approached them. He was tall and thin with white hair and wore a loose black robe with a hood resting behind his shoulders and black leather shoes, clerical garb somewhat unique to Benedictine monks.

"Good afternoon," he said in German to his visitors. "I am Brother David Kunnas, abbot of this monastery. Are you just visiting or is there anything in particular I might help you with?"

Responding in German, the official language of the Teutonic monastery, Dominic replied, "Good to meet you, Brother David. I'm Father Michael Dominic, Prefect of the Vatican Apostolic Archives." Dominic introduced everyone else, requested they switch to English out of respect for the others, then got to the point of their visit.

"Yesterday I spoke with Brother Moshe Hadani about a certain matter of mutual interest. While we were talking, it seemed as if he was being attacked, and then the line went dead. First, is he all right, and if so, may I see him?"

Kunnas's face took on a serious look of concern. "I'm afraid Brother Moshe passed away yesterday peacefully in his cell, apparently from a heart attack. I am very sorry to deliver such sad news. It is a great loss for all of us here." At this point, the abbot cocked his head. "But, Father Dominic, you say you *spoke* with him? How?"

"By phone. I called a specific number given to me for him."

"That is most unusual, as we have no telephones here. Technology of any sort is forbidden for abbey residents." Kunnas looked mystified, even disturbed. "Perhaps he had a hidden mobile phone… but for what reason?"

"Brother David, may we have a look at his cell?" Dominic inquired. "As it happens, we have two homicide detectives with us, and I must say, Moshe sounded as if he were in some peril when we were speaking. He was clearly fending off others whose presence had surprised him. Maybe closer inspection of the scene might be advised."

At the mention of homicide, Kunnas appeared startled, then exasperated. "Well, yes, I can see your point now," he said, seeming surprised. "Perhaps it wasn't a heart attack, then. Please, follow me."

Kunnas led them all outside and down a long breezeway to the residential wing adjacent to the main chapel. Entering the building, the abbot opened Hadani's cell door, which Dominic noted did not have a lock on it.

With second nature guiding them, Detectives Felici and Lancaster wasted no time inspecting every nook and cranny of the room. Eventually, Lancaster looked under the bed, discovered something of interest, and stood up. She reached in her purse for a pair of latex gloves, then bent down again and pulled out a long plastic tube of sorts, sealed at one end.

"What's that?" Hana asked, looking at it closely.

"It's the needle cap of a syringe. Unless Brother Moshe was a drug addict or insulin user, I would consider this to be rather unusual."

"Yes, as would I," Felici concurred. Then, directing her attention to Kunnas, she asked, "Did Brother Moshe have diabetes?"

"Well, no, he didn't. I would certainly know if he were diabetic. In fact, he was in excellent health. We were quite surprised when the medical examiner ruled his death as being from natural causes."

Marco leaned closer to look at the cap in Lancaster's hand. "In that case, one might assume he had been injected with a quick-acting drug. And if he died from a heart attack, any number of substances might have induced it: KCI—potassium chloride—or possibly aconite, also known as monkshood, which would seem ironic, wouldn't it?" A trace of a smile crossed his face until Hana glared at him.

"Is his body still available to view?" Felici asked.

"I'm afraid not," Kunnas replied with a relieved look and sad smile. "Our custom is to cremate the body within twenty-four hours. That duty was performed last night."

"Pity," Hana said. "Well, given what you've told me, Michael, this does seem suspicious."

"Yes, I agree. Brother David, is there a room my friends and I might use to speak privately? We have much to discuss."

Kunnas met Dominic's eyes with curiosity. "Of course. You can use our meeting room; it's just down the hall." He led them to a small spare room with a conference table and several chairs, and a window looking out over the gardens.

"Take as long as you like. I will be in my office at the other end of the hall if you need me."

After he left the room, shutting the door behind him, Kunnas rushed down the hall to his office. Closing and locking the door, he went to his desk, opened a drawer, and pulled out a set of headphones. Placing them over his ears, he flipped a switch on a recorder in the drawer and listened to every word his guests were saying.

"For the record," Lancaster submitted, "I don't trust that abbot. There's something fishy about him."

"I get the same feeling," said Hana, "but Michael, isn't it time to share with the others why we're here?"

"I'd wondered that myself," Marco said, "but I always trust you have proper motivations, Michael, so I didn't ask before now. Is there something else going on we might help with?"

Dominic had been overly discreet long enough, he realized.

Standing up, he went to the window, not looking at anything in particular, just formulating his thoughts. He was grateful to have everyone here, each of whom might offer helpful advice.

Turning around, he gave them all the same story he had told Hana on the plane, omitting only certain parts.

CHAPTER SIXTEEN

"Brother Moshe, who was the Clavis Domini, told me the keys to the pope's Petri Crypta are hidden in keystones, one at the chapel of the Grail Chasers in Scotland, and the other in another place I'll reveal later, after we figure out this first clue and get the key."

"Grail Chasers?" Hana exclaimed. "You mean as in the legends of the Knights Templar? That could only mean Rosslyn Chapel in Roslin. There have been rumors for centuries that the Templars found the Holy Grail and hid it in the historic chapel there. I only know this because Rosslyn Chapel has been owned by the Saint-Clair family for centuries—since 1446, actually. A cousin of mine oversees its operations now."

"Seriously?!" Dominic beamed. "That's exactly it! I had no idea your family had connections there, but of course it makes sense. Now that I recall, the Saint-Clairs have had a long association with Rosslyn. How could I have missed that?"

"You can't know everything, Michael," Hana teased.

Dominic briefly looked at her askance, then continued. "Each of the two keys is closely guarded by a sentry. Once we've established our bona fides, the sentries will disclose the location of their respective keystones, and we can then retrieve each key.

As to the purpose of all this? Those keys are essential to opening the pope's personal vault and retrieving, among other things, the true Third Secret of Fátima. And we can't just use an ordinary locksmith, since extreme anti-coercion measures are built into the safe's mechanisms. Forcing entry would thoroughly destroy its contents."

"That's quite an effort Moshe made, to hide both keys," Hana noted.

"I expect he had legitimate fears that he might be compromised by the Knights of the Apocalypse, which it now appears he had good reason to be. That's why Moshe had trusted couriers to carry the keys to safe places within his control. He gave me special codes to access them, codes the sentries are authorized to respond to.

"Moshe also gave me instructions that I should 'meditate on the Stations of the Cross.' This was just before he was attacked, so he had no time to clarify it, though maybe that was meant for our face-to-face meeting, which sadly won't happen now. Perhaps we'll find more when we get there—and we just need to get there safely." He looked at Marco, who just smiled confidently.

"I wish now that I'd invited Karl and Lukas to join us," Dominic added.

"No worries, Michael. I have a *confrère* I can call on if we need additional muscle," the French commando obliged. "As we say, '*Une fois soldat, toujours soldat.*' Once a soldier, always a soldier."

MAGNUS LISTENED INTENTLY as Brother David Kunnas related everything he had heard while eavesdropping on Dominic's conversation.

"The priest and his people must be stopped at all costs," Kunnas demanded. "They cannot get possession of those keys!

But there is nothing more I can do here, having already dealt with Moshe Hadani."

"You have done well, Brother," Magnus said, his cultured, deep-toned voice as imperious as ever. "We will stop them at Rosslyn Chapel. I will have our people there alerted to their arrival."

WITH CAREFULLY CONTROLLED TIMING, the first press release from the Knights of the Apocalypse was issued electronically at exactly midnight Vatican time. Well-placed KOTA members in all major media channels ensured it found its way to the public.

> The end of the world is upon us. Prophecies entrusted to us are being fulfilled.
>
> This is the First Warning.
>
> Prepare for the tribulations to come. Store up food and water and fuel. And in accordance with Luke 22:36, *"Whoever has a purse or a bag must take it; and whoever does not have a sword must sell his coat and buy one."*
>
> The prophet, St. Malachy, was given a vision, that:
>
> *"In the final persecution of the Holy Roman Church, there will sit as bishop, Peter the Roman, who will pasture his sheep in many tribulations, and when these things are finished, the city of seven hills will be destroyed, and the dreadful judge will judge his people."*
>
> Behold, who sits on the chair of Saint Peter but *Petrus Romanus*, Peter the Roman, foretold to be the last pope.
>
> The End is near. The time is at hand. *Petrus Romanus* is here.
>
> Only the Elect will be saved.
>
> This is the First Warning.
>
> Another prophetic fulfillment is expected.
>
> Be watchful.

CHAPTER SEVENTEEN

Later that evening, the Dassault Falcon 900 was en route from Tel Aviv to Edinburgh Airport, an eight-hour flight.

Dominic and Hana were talking quietly in Hana's aft sleeping cabin while Marco and the others were playing cards in the main cabin.

"It's been a while since I've been in Scotland, Michael. I'm really looking forward to visiting the chapel again. I haven't seen my cousin Angus in years, though we've stayed in touch by email from time to time."

"Is he the keeper of Rosslyn Chapel?" Dominic asked, eager to learn more.

"Yes, Angus Brodie. He comes from a good Scots family that goes way back to the Middle Ages, and somewhere along the line the Saint-Clairs joined up with the Brodies. I'm sure he also has some Viking in him. He's my great-uncle's grandson, a bear of a man with a bushy red beard, though it may be graying by now."

"Well, I better catch some sleep while I can. Is this other bunk taken?" He looked at the twin beds in the cabin, then glanced up at Hana, who started blushing.

"Why, Father Dominic, whatever would the neighbors

think?" They both muffled their laughs. "Of course, it's yours, take it. Marco can sleep in one of the seats; he can sleep anywhere, actually. Me, I need to relax a bit first, so I'll read some news, see what's happening out there."

Dominic lay down on the bed and closed his eyes. As Hana paged through the latest news from *Le Monde* on her laptop, a video segment by one of her colleagues caught her interest, with the sardonic headline, ***"Are the End Times Near? Again?"***

"Michael...look at this!"

Dominic sat up and shuffled over to her bunk, looking over her shoulder as she pressed the Play button on the video news alert window. Her friend and colleague in Paris, Jacques Devereaux, was reporting:

> "A fringe Catholic group calling itself the 'Knights of the Apocalypse' has just issued a press release claiming the imminent end of the world. Citing the prophecy of an obscure twelfth-century Catholic mystic, St. Malachy, the group claims that the prophecy predicts a long line of popes, which ends with the final pope who is named *Petrus Romanus,* or Peter the Roman.
>
> They point to the election of Enrico Petrini—Petrini being a derivative of Peter, an old Roman family name—as fulfilling that prophecy. There has been no comment yet from the Vatican. The group went on to say they expect fulfillment of further End Times prophecies in the immediate future, with more announcements to come."

"Well, it's bizarre, that's for sure, but not surprising given what we know now," Dominic said. "Let's share this with the others."

"That's easy." Using AirPlay on her MacBook, Hana streamed the video to the large, flat-screen in the main cabin, turning it on remotely. The TV came to life, causing the others to look up. Putting down their cards, they watched the replay.

Michael and Hana entered the cabin as Devereaux was continuing his announcement. When the video ended, Dominic looked around at the others.

"As it happens," he began, somewhat irritably, "the Holy Father and I did have some advance warning this might be coming. While KOTA certainly believes the End Times are near, that doesn't make it true, of course. How many times has the world been put on edge by such nonsense? All these so-called prophets preaching end-of-the-world scenarios truly believed scripture was being fulfilled, when in fact nothing has ever come of it.

"But I do find the timing interesting, especially in light of Jonah's death and his missing manuscript, which deals with this very topic, not to mention our search for the keys to the Third Prophecy."

"Michael," Lancaster asked, "do you know if Jonah Barlow or Brother Moshe had any connections to KOTA?"

Dominic looked up, thinking about it. "As far as I know, Moshe had no connections. But Jonah may have contacted one or more of the group's members for his research, since his book—which you'll find as you continue reading—deals with the subject of their obsessions."

As it was getting late, Hana yawned and said, "We have a few more hours before we land in Scotland. I think it's time we get a little sleep while we can. The pilots will give us a heads up about thirty minutes before we get there. I've already called my cousin Angus, and he's expecting us later in the morning, though I didn't give him specifics yet. But I got the feeling he was expecting us....

"Marco, did you confirm our arrival with your friend?"

"I did, indeed," said the commando, glancing at his watch. "Duncan will meet us at the FBO at 0600 Greenwich. He'll also arrange for some kind of vehicle that will accommodate all of us. We're good to go."

CHAPTER EIGHTEEN

The jet touched down at Edinburgh Airport just before six o'clock the next morning. Taxiing to the Signature Fixed Base Operator terminal for private aircraft and swift executive customs handling, the plane was met by a black Range Rover Sport SUV, prearranged by Marco's friend Duncan MacKenzie to accommodate all five of them for the trip to Rosslyn Chapel, some thirty minutes away.

"It's too early for us to do much of anything until Angus opens the chapel at nine," Hana said as they began to deplane. "Why don't we have some breakfast first, then see some of the sights on our way there?"

"That sounds great," said Marco. "I'm famished. Hey, there's Duncan now!"

A fit, tough-looking man who looked to be in his early forties with a red beard approached them as they all headed toward the Range Rover. Seeing Marco, the man's face lit up with a huge smile.

"Awright, ye wee bawbag, it's about time we kicked shite oot ane anither again!" MacKenzie gave Marco a great bear hug, squeezing him tightly, lifting him up off his feet before releasing him.

"Duncan, you old bastard, it is *très bon* to see you as well! *Mes amies,* I'd like you to meet my old comrade-in-arms, Duncan MacKenzie. He works here at the FBO, doing the odd special job from time to time."

"Aye, and by the look of it, ye got a wheen o' bonnie lassies here with ye, too, laddie. Will ye introduce me to yer birds?"

As the two detectives' eyes flew open, Marco was quick to point out, "Uh…just so you know, '*birds*' is a form of endearment here, not a sexist remark." He then made proper introductions to everyone as each shook MacKenzie's hand. Ever the Scottish gentleman, he tipped his tartan Balmoral bonnet to each of them in turn.

Rebecca Lancaster eyed MacKenzie carefully, then smiled, saying, "Shouldn't you be wearing a kilt there, Duncan?"

He held her gaze intently with a crafty smile. "Well, lass, I just might put one on for ye a bit later, then we can—"

"Alright, calm down there, boyo," Marco chided. "Let's get that breakfast now, shall we? Duncan, we'll be in touch. Stick around, we may need you."

AFTER A LEISURELY MEAL at the Laird & Dog Inn, a village country pub MacKenzie had wryly told them was "world famous in Edinburgh" for their traditional Scottish breakfasts of square Lorne sausage, fried eggs, streaky bacon, baked beans, haggis and toast, the group got back into the Range Rover for the half-hour drive to Rosslyn Chapel.

The gently rolling hills and green pastures of the Scottish Lowlands quickly came into view after they passed the outskirts of the city, with Marco at the wheel, viewing stop signs merely as suggestions to guide his undisciplined—and characteristically French—driving. When he often found himself turning into the right lane, approaching vehicles kept reminding him that cars drive on the left in Scotland.

Fortunately traffic was light on the A701 heading southeast toward Roslin. They arrived ten minutes earlier than expected, and every passenger in the SUV was relieved when the vehicle came to rest in the parking lot of Rosslyn Chapel.

"I'm driving back," Hana jokingly threatened when she got out, slamming the door.

"We will see about that, my little 'bird,'" Marco replied with a droll smile.

As the group approached the main entrance to Rosslyn Chapel, they took in the extraordinary Gothic beauty of the nearly six-hundred-year-old edifice. Adorned with flying buttresses and pointed arches in an aged medley of colored brick and stone, Rosslyn Chapel exhibited a mysterious and captivating aura.

"Hana, this is simply breathtaking," Dominic marveled as he beheld the ancient building. "How long did you say the chapel has been in the Saint-Clair family?"

"Since the fifteenth century," she reiterated, "but…oh, there's Angus now!"

A hefty man who looked to be in his fifties approached them with a wide smile peeking out from the mass of a peppery red beard.

"Ah, ma Hana, yer looking fair braw, ma lass!" The two embraced each other warmly.

"Everyone, this is my great-cousin Angus Brodie, caretaker of Rosslyn." She made introductions to the others, at which point

Brodie invited them to his rooms in the back of the chapel grounds. As they all took seats near a blazing fireplace, Brodie and Hana stepped aside for a private conversation.

"Angus, it's so good to see you again. But we're here on an important mission. Father Dominic and I—"

"I know why yer here, lass," he muttered solemnly. "The Clavis Domini, God rest his soul, told me before he died that Father Dominic would be the likely claimant of the keystone."

"Keystone?" Hana asked.

"Aye, there's much work ahead. But Ah'm afraid only you and the good Father are permitted for the process. Let's put the others on a tour of the grounds. I'll have one of the docents guide them while we go aboot our business."

Brodie picked up a nearby phone and pressed a button, then requested that one of the tour guides come to his quarters. Then he turned to the group. "Ladies and gents, if I might have yer attention. I've got some business to attend to with Father Michael and my dear Hana here. It won't take but a short while, and in the meantime I've arranged for ye to have a private tour of our fine old property here."

Just then a docent entered the room, a fair young girl of about twenty, wearing a tartan plaid skirt and a white blouse. "This here is Gracie. She knows everything there is to know aboot Rosslyn Chapel and will show ye a good time. Gracie, I leave these fine folk to ye then, lass."

The others stood up and after introducing themselves, Gracie led them outside for a tour of the grounds and the outer buildings. Marco glanced at Hana as he followed the others out, and from the look on his face it was clear that he preferred to be with her and Michael, where the action was, rather than be part of a dull tour. She returned his gaze, shrugging her shoulders as if it were out of her hands. He sighed and gave her a petulant wave, suggesting he would go but he wouldn't have a good time.

. . .

"At the request of Brother Moshe," Brodie began, with Dominic and Hana listening intently, "a courier sent by the Knights of Malta arrived last week with a sealed package. I was instructed to place it in the special keystone that's been here for centuries, used for secret transfers of private papers and such through the ages. When not used, the keystone remains empty and unlocked, specifically in the event the keys to the Petri Crypta had to be concealed for security purposes.

"The combination is unknown to me, having been set by the Clavis Domini himself, which Moshe did on his last visit here. When the package arrived, I did as I was told: I placed it inside the keystone and sealed it shut. Even I do not know the combination to unlock it; that is for ye to do, Father Dominic. My only part in this process is to ask three questions which only ye can answer. Moshe made sure of this, in cooperation with an old freend of yers, a man named Simon Ginzberg."

"*Simon* is involved in this too?!" Dominic sputtered, astonished at the lengths to which Moshe Hadani had gone. "I have to say, so far I'm finding this all inconceivable!"

"As a Knight of Malta myself, Father, it has come to our notice that there are many who desperately want the keys to the papal vault, so ye'll understand the enhanced security measures we've taken. We have our suspicions who actually took the keys which should have been in the hands of the pope and the Vatican's Secretary of State, but that is not for me to say. And despite yer bein' with Hana, who I know, this process is intended only for the claimant, so Ah'm required to ask them anyway. Now, movin' on…."

Brodie reached inside his breast pocket and withdrew a small notepad. Opening it, he flipped through to a specific page.

"To begin, there are three questions I must ask ye, all of which are unique to yer experience. If ye do not have the correct answers, access to the keystone will remain inaccessible."

"Nothing like a pop quiz to put the pressure on," Dominic moaned. "Go ahead."

Brodie stood a bit taller, proud to be fulfilling his duties as sentry of the keystone.

"Question 1: Who inspired this passage relating to the End Times?

The Albigensian truth is summoned,
As the final shepherd of Rome flees:
Mother sacred breathes her last,
The flock wanders in the gloaming.

Dominic instantly recalled the parchment in late medieval French cursive he had once held. "Nostradamus," he answered confidently. "That was one of his lost quatrains that I discovered a couple years ago in the Vatican Riserva."

"That is correct," Brodie confirmed. "Now, on to Question 2. Who was the abbé of Rennes-le-Château?"

"That's not something I'm likely to forget, since I read his Last Will and Testament, among other papers. Saunière. Bérenger Saunière."

"Also correct." Brodie smiled as if he were the host of a game show. "And now to the last question. As ye should recall, the Nazis relied a great deal on apocalyptic prophecies in their search for the Holy Grail. Who was the archeologist sent by Heinrich Himmler on the mission to find it?"

Dominic thought back to their dreadful experiences with the Novi Ustasha and all the havoc of that particular adventure. *What was that guy's name…?*

"Ah, Otto Rahn," he replied. "Yes, Rahn was key to finding the Veil of Veronica which was given to Mary Magdalene. What a mess that was. Remember, Hana?"

"Michael, I don't ever want to think about that evil Dr. Kurtz again." She grimaced.

"Father, you have correctly answered all three questions. Now, I must show ye the location of the keystone, but the rest is up to ye. My part of this is complete."

Brodie escorted them inside Rosslyn and over to a side chapel, then looked up. Over the inside doorway was a Masonic keystone, central to the bricks forming the archway over the entry, with the traditional Masonic emblem in its center. Surrounding that were eight trapezoidal stones, each with an alphabetic character on it.

Pointing to it, Brodie affirmed, "Aye, that keystone is where ye'll find what yer lookin' for. Ah'm afraid I cannae help ye further. I'll get a stepladder for ye, but only ye have been given the combination."

As Brodie stepped away to find the ladder, Dominic looked blankly at Hana. "Combination?! What combination?" he asked.

CHAPTER NINETEEN

Standing on the top step of the ladder while Dominic held it steady, Hana inspected the keystone carefully.

"There appears to be a ring of eight letters on trapezoidal blocks around the central square and compass symbol. Angus said there was a combination, right? It must have something to do with the letters. Wouldn't you agree?"

"Yes, that seems logical. Can they be removed, or do they push in or anything?"

Running her hand across the face of it, she realized that each of the eight lettered trapezoidal blocks was not firmly fixed.

They were slightly loose, and—as she discovered when pressing on one—receded slightly deeper back into their apportioned space, about half a centimeter.

"Ah-ha! So that's how it's done," she exclaimed. "Apparently, we just need to press each block in its corresponding order to open the keystone's vault. Those clever Templars…." She pressed the octagonal center stone and it, too, receded slightly. As she did so, she heard a soft metallic click and the first block she pressed popped back out. "I imagine this center block resets the start of the process if we get one or more wrong. This may take some time, Michael."

"Well, logically, it seems like this might be an eight-character combination lock. Now we just need to figure out the correct order in which to press the letters," Dominic said.

Hana had a thought. "Well," she said pensively, "given there are eight symbols, and we need to put them in the proper order, by my rough count there are over forty thousand possible permutations. How do we know which order they fall in?"

"Let's see what we've got here before jumping to grim conclusions," Dominic replied optimistically.

He thought back to his conversation with Moshe Hadani. Something about the Stations of the Cross….

"I remember now. Brother Moshe said, 'When you get to the chapel, meditate on the Stations of the Cross.' I thought it was some kind of spiritual advice. But now I think it may have been a clue to the combination."

Turning back toward the main chapel, he observed the fourteen stations properly spaced against each of the long walls, seven to a side. Hana came down off the ladder and followed him as he moved to the first station and gazed at it.

"As you may recall, the objective of the Stations of the Cross is to help the faithful experience a spiritual pilgrimage through contemplation of the Passion of Christ. It's a special ceremony commonly celebrated on the Fridays of Lent, especially on Good Friday, just before Easter Sunday.

"But look here," he said, pointing to four stations on one side of the chapel and four on the other. "Above just eight of the stations there's a Maltese cross, something not traditionally associated with the design or purpose of the ritual, but which definitely has Masonic connections. Of course, that cross is also used by the Knights of Malta, which, as you know, is a Catholic order. Angus did say he was a member of the Knights, and that one of his brother members brought him the key. And Rosslyn Chapel has long been associated with the Knights Templar and various Masonic orders.

"The keys, then, must be connected to the specific symbols on these Maltese crosses. Notice only eight of the fourteen stations have such a cross. That's got to be it, Hana! Eight letters, eight crosses." Dominic looked closely at the cross over the first station. "Interesting," he murmured.

He moved from station to station, noting that the crosses at the relevant eight stations had been subtly marked, emphasizing certain lines, extending others, with an added dot on some of the symbols.

"Maybe the correct order of the letters is connected to the symbols on these Maltese crosses. Look at them, Hana. The symbols on each cross are slightly different. My guess is they're cryptograms from some archaic Templar or Maltese cipher. That's what Moshe meant by contemplating the Stations of the Cross! Have you got a notepad or something we can write on?"

Hana reached into her bag and retrieved a small Moleskine notebook.

"Okay, as we walk by each station, make a note of the symbol in each of the crosses." Hana complied as they passed each station. Ever the puzzle fan, she was relishing the process.

When they had finished all eight of the Maltese crosses, they stared at the retrieved symbols:

"This is clearly a substitution cipher. Now we just need to decode them. I left my phone in my backpack in the car. Can we use yours to do a Web image search for the key? It should just be a simple matter of substituting the symbols for alphabetic characters."

"Sure," she said eagerly. Opening the browser on her phone, she searched for *Templar Cipher*. The key was revealed in one of the first results:

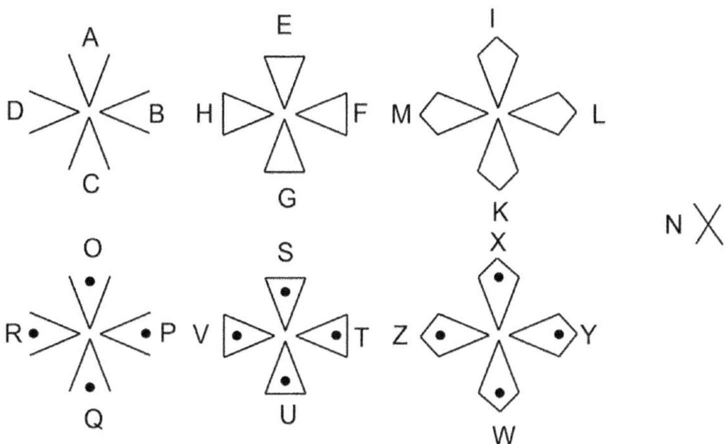

Using the key, Hana quickly transcribed each of the symbols to its corresponding letter, resulting in S-S-W-T-H-T-S-K.

"What order are they in now?" Dominic asked.

"H-T-W-S-S-T-K-S, Hana replied, "assuming you start from the top."

"This is vaguely familiar to me," Dominic mused. "I recall it as being part of a Masonic legend. Now let's search on the combined letters in that order, as an acronym."

Hana obliged, and instantly the translation appeared on a Web page she found: *Hiram, Tyrian, Widow's Son, Sent To King Solomon.*

"Ah, yes, now I remember," Dominic said enthusiastically. "All Third Degree Masons study the story of a man named Hiram, the son of a widow. According to legend, Hiram was the architect for the Temple of King Solomon. Apparently, he was in possession of secret Masonic passwords that a group of heathens, for whatever reason, wanted access to. He valiantly refused to turn over the codes and was killed in retribution. In Masonic teaching, the story of Hiram is perceived as an example of loyalty. That must be the letters surrounding the joined square and compass, another Masonic symbol."

"Interesting," Hana mused absently. They both gazed at her notebook. "So now we try the order from the crosses on the keystone?" she asked.

"Yes, let's try that!" Dominic agreed.

Hana was energized. "I haven't had this much fun since our time in Venice, decoding that cipher we found from Antonio Vivaldi!"

Climbing back up the ladder Angus had provided, Hana inspected the keystone.

As Dominic read off the letters, Hana pushed each one in the order shown on the notebook: S-S-W-T-H-T-S-K. When she was finished there was a slightly louder click than before and the center section popped open about half a centimeter.

She looked down at Dominic, exhilarated. "I believe you Americans would say '*Booyah*' about now, right?"

Turning back, she pulled the center stone out to reveal a secret compartment, inside of which was a brown cardboard tube about ten centimeters long and two and a half centimeters in diameter, with a groove around the middle—just big enough to hold a large key. She handed it down to Michael.

Dominic excitedly twisted the tube at the groove and it slid open, revealing one of the biometric keys to the pope's safe.

"*Booyah,* indeed! So, one down, one to go," Dominic quipped, dropping the key in his pocket. "Let's go save Marco from the hens!"

CHAPTER TWENTY

Gracie led Marco, Sabrina and Rebecca through the gardens and the grounds, coming up on the back side of the chapel near where Dominic and Hana were at work inside. Where the back stone wall met the side wrought iron fence, a large overgrown tree completely hid the corner.

Marco sensed, more than saw, that something wasn't right. He asked the ladies to sit on the wooden bench against the iron fence so he could take a photo of them, looking at them in a way that hinted he had something planned. They didn't question him.

He took out his iPhone and, putting his back to the tree, feigned taking a photo of the two. He flipped the camera view around to face himself and pointed the lens over his shoulder as he began walking backward toward the tree, pretending to be composing the picture in front of him.

As he got closer to the tree, it seemed as if part of the tree just came to life and started running for the stone wall. His intuition validated, Marco turned and tried to dive after a man wearing a ghillie suit—blending perfectly into the tree and bushes—who had dropped a parabolic microphone into the brush as he vaulted over the wall. Marco made it to the wall right behind him, but the mysterious figure had disappeared into the hedges. A ghillie suit, used as sniper camouflage, was so effective a person could be standing right next to its wearer and not see him. Apparently, he had been using the parabolic mic to listen to what was happening inside the chapel.

Marco returned to the detectives, who were glaring at him.

"We could have helped if you'd given us a clue," Sabrina admonished him.

"Well, yes, but I wasn't sure he was even there until he moved. No sense in making a fool of myself if there was nothing there."

"Marco, at some point that bravado is going to make a dead fool of you."

The Frenchman just smiled. "We had better get back and let the others know. Obviously, we were being followed, which means others are aware of our presence here."

UNDERSTANDING his guests had special work to do—work which he could not be privy to—Angus Brodie strolled the courtyard garden while smoking his well-aged Brave Heart pipe, packed with MacBaren's golden brown Burleys and toasted Cavendish blend, as he waited for Hana and Father Michael to finish up.

As the two emerged from the arched doorway of the chapel, both were smiling as they approached him.

"I assume then ye had a good visit here, ma freends?" he asked, assuming by their cheerfulness that the mission was successful.

"Everything is well in hand now, Angus, thank you so much," Hana said, hugging her cousin. She breathed in the fragrant smoke lingering on his woolen argyle jacket and instantly felt a sense of homely comfort in his arms.

"We do have to be leaving now, though," Dominic said. "I wish we could have stayed longer, Angus, but, duty calls."

"Aye, no rest for the, eh… wicked." The Scotsman laughed as

he stroked his beard. "Ye have a blessed trip to yer next port o' call." With that, he shook hands with Dominic as the others rapidly rejoined them from beside the Chapel

"Looks like someone was listening to your activities inside. We chased a guy in a ghillie suit out of the tree in the corner. He got over the wall before I could get to him. He might have called for reinforcements, though, so we better get moving. Did you get what you came for?" Marco asked Hana.

"Indeed, we did," Hana said eagerly. "We found the first key using a most remarkable archaic Templar cipher. Suffice to say, our job is half done."

"Let's get back to the airport quickly, Marco," Dominic said.

"You got it, boss."

EVERYONE GOT into the Range Rover SUV as the Frenchman jumped in the driver's seat and started the engine. It roared to life, and as his foot clamped on the gas pedal, everyone anxiously hastened to fasten their seatbelts.

As he steered the vehicle down the long drive out of the chapel grounds, Marco noticed a black BMW sedan in the distance moving quickly up the road toward them. The road ran between two small hills with shoulders that sloped up on both sides. As the sedan neared the SUV, its driver suddenly swerved, blocking the center of the road, then stopped.

Marco instinctively whipped the steering wheel to the left, aiming for the shoulder but just as he reached it, he immediately spun the wheel to the right, crossing the road in front of the BMW and riding up the berm on the right shoulder. In the confusion, the driver of the BMW first reacted by trying to block Marco from the left side but didn't anticipate the sudden switch to the right. The Range Rover missed hitting the BMW by mere centimeters, but once he was off the berm, Marco raced past it and sped back on the road, the high-performance Hankook tires efficiently gripping the pavement.

Looking back, Marco saw the BMW make a U-turn. "Obviously, that was no accident. They're coming after us now. Does anyone else have a weapon?"

"'Anyone *else*?!'" Lancaster sputtered. "You're *armed*? In the UK?"

"It pays to have friends in low places," Marco jibed, his adrenaline ramped up as they sped toward the village of Roslin. He shouted, "Hang on, everyone!" as if he had to remind any of them, as they were all clenching their seatbelts tightly while turning to see if the BMW was still following.

They were fast approaching an intersection as they entered the town. Seeing the BMW fifty meters behind them and closing, Marco pulled over onto the dirt shoulder and slammed on the brakes, intentionally skidding on the loose dirt. A huge cloud of dust billowed up behind the SUV, obscuring it from view. He then slammed his foot on the gas pedal and the Range Rover leapt forward. Making a hard left turn at the intersection, the SUV disappeared between the buildings on both sides of the narrow street.

Behind them, the driver of the BMW shot through the dust cloud and on past the intersection before realizing he had been duped and lost the Range Rover. He and his passenger cursed loudly as he braked hard and spun the car around back toward the intersection.

Meanwhile, Marco had taken a couple of turns in town to stay out of sight and eventually made it back to the main road.

The BMW driver sat at the intersection, engine thrumming, as he waited for any clue as to where their quarry was. Glancing up at his rearview mirror, he saw the SUV pull out from a side street, now several hundred meters away, and race in the opposite direction, toward the airport. Turning the BMW around, the driver floored it, trying to catch up to the powerful Range Rover.

"Hana," Marco asked rhetorically, "do you know where your grand-père gets his pilots? Both of them flew fighter jets in the

Swiss Air Force. Call them now, *s'il vous plaît*. Tell them we need a hot exfil in fifteen mikes. They'll understand."

Hana whipped out her phone and made the call. Marco reached in his pocket and pulled out his own cell phone.

"Michael, look in my Contacts for Duncan MacKenzie's number. He should be on the gate at the FBO. Tell him we've run into a little trouble and need that gate open and ready when we get there—then to close it immediately when we've gone through. Remind him we're in the black Range Rover, with a bastard BMW on our tail."

As Dominic made the call, rapidly conveying the details to MacKenzie, Marco turned to see the BMW gaining on them in the final stretch to the airport. Then he saw another car on the four-lane road ahead of them, a red Mazda in the fast lane. Marco was fast approaching it from behind.

"Hold onto your seats, everyone. Now!" he commanded.

Marco came up behind the Mazda and just as he reached the rear of it, turned into the left lane. Positioning the SUV's brush guard up against the left rear bumper of the car, with a quick jerk to the right he pushed the Mazda into a spin, then dashed around it to the right as the out-of-control car spun to the left. The Mazda did a full 360-degree turn in the middle of the road as its occupants screamed frantically. Finally coming to a full stop, it blocked a good part of the road, and with no place else to go traveling at speed, the BMW slammed on its brakes to avoid ramming into it.

Marco laughed wildly as he raced on to the airport. "That was fun, wasn't it?! Something the Yanks invented for stopping police pursuits. They call it a Pursuit Intervention Technique or PIT maneuver. We learned it in Special Forces Driving School. Never had to use it until now."

The others didn't seem to need that information at the moment, frenzied from the sudden actions Marco had taken.

As instructed, MacKenzie had the FBO gate open and waiting for them and closed it quickly as they came through. Having finally gotten around the Mazda, the black BMW came to a stop some distance away, its two male passengers now standing outside the vehicle, watching with anger as the Range Rover pulled up to the private jet.

Even from that distance, they could see Marco get out of the vehicle, raise his arm in victory and give them the one-finger salute, a gratified smile on his face.

CHAPTER TWENTY-ONE

As the FBO aircraft fuel handler pulled his jet refueler truck up next to the Dassault Falcon, the pilot anxiously descended the boarding stairs. He informed the fueler they had need of an immediate departure, and urged him to quicken his pace.

"Ah can only go as fast as the hose allows me to, laddie," the man said hopelessly. "We'll have ye departin' here in a few more minutes."

After glancing at his watch, the pilot returned to the cockpit to begin the pre-flight checklist, having already done a quick walk-around inspection of the aircraft.

The jet fuel now topped off, the fueler retracted the hose, disconnected the grounding wire that kept static electricity from igniting the flammable liquid, then went to close the fuel hatch.

Glancing around as he did so, however, he reached into the nearby wheel well and attached a small, magnetic GPS transmitter he had furtively withdrawn from his pocket.

Ah dinnae ken where yer goin', lads, but somebody will, he mused as he drove the truck back to the pump station. *Aye, wouldn't matter anyway. World will be endin' soon. Best o' luck to all o' ye.*

The jet's engines whined loudly as it idled on the apron

outside the FBO terminal of Edinburgh Airport. The copilot flipped on the passenger address system. "Good afternoon, ladies and gentlemen. We have a departure slot coming up in five minutes. If I can ask everyone to please fasten your seatbelts for takeoff, we'll be taxiing to the runway momentarily."

As everyone was settling in, Rebecca took a seat across from Marco, gazing at him lustfully. "I have to say, that was some pretty hot driving back there," she purred, her eyes conveying more than she had said.

"I agree," Dominic echoed from across the aisle, looking at Marco with new respect for the man's superb handling of the Range Rover during their grueling trip back to the airport. "That was some brilliant maneuvering, Marco. Is there really such a thing as Special Forces Driving School?" he asked the Frenchman.

"*Oui,* there is, Michael, but it's called Tactical Mobility Training. We learned to handle everything from a dirt bike to a big rig. Pursuit, evasion, how to wreck a vehicle so it can't be used by the enemy, how to use vehicles as weapons, and in all kinds of conditions—mud, snow, rain, sand, ice—you name it. We were there for more than a month."

As they continued chatting, the jet had taxied to the end of Runway 24, and moments later its three powerful Honeywell turbofan engines roared to life as the plane quickly sped up the runway, then rose west into the clear blue skies over Scotland.

A moment later, the cabin intercom phone from the cockpit buzzed. Hana picked it up. "Okay, Miss Sinclair, we managed to get out of there quickly as you requested, but the tower is giving me all kinds of grief for not having filed a flight plan. Can you tell me what our destination is?"

She turned to Michael, passing on the pilot's urgent request.

"Tell him to set a course for Malta," the priest said.

CHAPTER TWENTY-TWO

From his lavish office in the administrative wing of the Cathedral of St. Matthew the Apostle, patron saint of civil servants in Washington, D.C., Cardinal Damien Challis once again sat in front of his ultra-wide computer display featuring six secure videoconference windows, one for each of his fellow members of the KOTA Council, each blurred to mask that person's identity. And once again, their spiritual advisor, Magnus, listened in by telephone.

"My brothers, the reaction to our first announcement has been even greater than I anticipated. The fulfillment of the Prophecy of St. Malachy has caused panic buying, hoarding, looting. Apparently, many people have been anticipating the end, and certain social media segments are responding intently. Economic markets are reacting as expected. And still, there has been no word from the Vatican.

"I am now prepared to move forward with the next phase of our plan. We have obtained the use of a small chapel just outside the District of Columbia. We have installed a glass case and several Web cameras in a secure room inside the chapel. Tomorrow morning, we will release the Web addresses of the video feeds to the media, along with a recorded message from me—with my identity obscured, of course—which will explain that the remaining prophecies we expect to be fulfilled before The End have been written down and sealed in envelopes inside the secured case. When one of the prophecies is fulfilled, I will go to the chapel, open the case, and reveal that prophecy on the live Web stream. We will, of course, alert the media that a revelation of the sealed prophecy is forthcoming. And given the wide public response to our first announcement, mainstream media will now pay attention.

"As events are moving swiftly, we may have need of you or the other members under your command, likely with very short notice. Be sure you have your secure cell phones with you at all times."

Magnus broke into the conversation. "And know this: Lucifer is watching the signs. At the sealing of the prophecies, I expect a response within days, perhaps sooner.

"Be prepared, my brothers. The End is near."

AFTER THE KNIGHT COMMANDER, Damien Challis, had shut down the videoconference connection, Magnus stayed on the phone for a brief follow-up conversation.

"I must tell you, brother, that I have discovered a way out of what is to come, a special—let's call it a dispensation—exclusively reserved for the Elect among us. I happened across it in scripture and in the Apocalypse of St. Peter. As this will be the crowning achievement of your ministry, *you* will be the one to bring this before the people.

"You shall stand before Christ as a prophet, and hundreds, if not thousands of the faithful will accompany you, all wearing the sacred white robes in which to wash away their sins in the blood of the lamb. And by doing so, you will deal a savage blow to the Antichrist, that accursed Pope Ignatius.

"Here is what you shall do...."

In the private production studio arranged for the Knight Commander's prerecorded announcement to the world, Cardinal Challis—dressed in a jet-black hooded robe with a gold, seven-pointed star on his breast—faced the camera wearing a white mask to hide his features, the hood of the robe pulled over his head. Only his eyes could be seen through the two eerie holes.

A glass display case was positioned behind him, containing the remaining prophecies in envelopes, live webcams pointed at the case to ensure each was never opened until it was time. At the touch of a button, he started the recording.

"For now, these things are hidden, as I myself am hidden from you. But I tell you truly that in due time, a very short time now, all hidden things will be revealed to you. There are live webcams focused on this case that can be watched on the internet at all times, to demonstrate that nobody can alter the prophecies before they are revealed. We have already proven to you the fulfillment of the Prophecy of St. Malachy. The remaining prophecies come from the actual Third Secret of Fátima and the Apocalypse of St. Peter. As portions of the prophecies are fulfilled, that specific prophecy will be revealed. This is to prove to the people that the End Times are here, that the final prophecies are being fulfilled. Our only salvation is for the Church to stand together against the Antichrist. You will not have to wait long for these prophecies to come true.

"Watch, and be ready."

CHAPTER TWENTY-THREE

Soaring at forty-one thousand feet above Belgium, and just crossing over into French airspace, the Dassault Falcon enjoyed smooth weather on its four-hour flight to Malta International Airport.

Carlos, the flight attendant, was making the rounds offering crab salad finger sandwiches and drinks to everyone while they talked about their past few hours at Rosslyn Chapel.

Hana looked up at Carlos with recognition. "Huh. I'd never noticed this before, but doesn't Carlos, here, look a lot like Michael?"

Everyone looked at the fit, good-looking flight attendant, who seemed pleasantly embarrassed as he retreated to the galley.

"He does, actually," Dominic said. "Quite a handsome young man, if I say so myself…." The others agreed as they chuckled.

"If you ever get into movies," Rebecca said, "there's your stuntman."

"Hah! If only…." Glancing at his watch, he figured now was a good time to reveal the day's activity he had planned.

"All right, while we're all enjoying lunch, let's talk about what's ahead. Our goal now, of course, is to obtain the second key. But given the uninvited guests we just encountered, it's clear others are on to our mission now, for whatever purposes. Either they don't want us to get the keys, or they want the keys for themselves. If anyone else can think of other motives, I'm all ears." He waited.

Everyone was quiet, looking around at each other, until Marco spoke up. "At this point, we have no idea who was behind that attack, but it's safe to say the Knights of the Apocalypse would be our prime suspects, given their press release about the prophecies. Whoever it is, they likely have reinforcements, though since the pilots filed a late flight plan, and it's a fairly quick trip there, hopefully they won't be able to gather their forces on Malta until we have finished our business.

"Regardless, keep your eyes open, or as we say in the *Bérets verts*, keep your head on a swivel."

Dominic chuckled at the visual image, then continued. "The one problem we face—and it's a rather significant one—is that I don't know exactly where we're supposed to go on the island. The Clavis Domini's instructions were more than a little vague, and I've never been to Malta."

"I have," Sabrina Felici said brightly. "My father was a Knight and my mother was a Dame of Malta, and before they died we made many trips to the island when I was younger. They often had business there, at *Forti Sant'Anġlu*, or Fort St. Angelo, where the order's Maltese headquarters is located. But I do remember the island fairly well, if that helps."

"Yes, it might," Dominic added hopefully. "In fact, maybe you can help me figure something out. The Key Master gave me what sounds like a riddle. He said, '*Step into the secret fire and quench your thirst. Make sure you ask the sentry for the highest keystone. No other will satisfy your quest.*' I don't have a clue what that means. Anyone else?" He glanced around the cabin. "Hana, you're the puzzle master, any thoughts?"

She squinted as she conjured up an idea. "Maybe we might

try juxtaposing the words for similar ones, like 'Go into the hidden flame to get a drink,' or something."

"Okay," Dominic said, "let's all get our phones out and see what each of us comes up with. Do we have internet access in-flight?"

Yes," Hana replied. "Grand-père had ground-to-air capabilities installed when he outfitted the plane."

"Okay, then. Search for places on Malta that have anything like an eternal flame, or some kind of fire, like candles or bonfires, anything that isn't readily visible. I know it's a long shot, but we've got to try everything."

Ten quiet minutes had passed before anyone spoke, engrossed as they were on searching the Web for likely destinations. Dominic looked over at Felici, who was staring out a cabin window with a curious look on her face, as if she were deep in thought.

"Sabrina? A penny for your thoughts...."

"I was just thinking... what if we approached this from a different, more logical angle? Where would you go just to quench your thirst? A bar, obviously, or maybe a restaurant. But one with a prominent archway, one that has a keystone over it."

"In any old city on Malta that's likely to be every building in town," Hana said. "But 'keystone' *is* the, well, key, isn't it?"

Rebecca Lancaster suddenly looked up, a trace of a smile on her face. "No. It couldn't be that easy...."

"What?" asked Hana.

"It's a crazy thought, but it just occurred to me that in the U.S., a brewing company named Coors makes a light beer called Keystone. I've had it; it's not bad, kind of bready, but very smooth. Think they'd have Keystone beer on Malta? I seriously doubt it."

"Odd," Dominic said, "I've never heard of Keystone beer. After our lacrosse games we'd all go out and have different beers to try them all, kind of a post-game ritual. Personally, I preferred

Stella Artois, and in Italy I drink Birra Moretti. But Keystone? Never heard of it.

"Anyway, where would one go in Malta to get an American beer in a place that has secret fires or hidden flames? Even saying it sounds crazy."

"Well," Felici added, "I don't know much about beers, but I do know that if you want to quench your thirst in Malta, you have to try a Kinnie." Assuming she was introducing something new, she smiled with satisfaction.

"And a 'Kinnie' is…?" Marco asked.

"It's a soda brewed from bitter oranges and extracts of wormwood. Really tasty. My dad would get them with a couple shots of vodka at the pub near our hotel. It's the most popular drink mixer on Malta."

"Sounds awful," Dominic said as he tried to get all this clear. "Okay, so it's a hidden pub with a fire that serves American beers and bitter orange Kinnies made from wormwood?" He laughed at the absurdity of it. "But there's that word '*Wormwood*' again. Another clue, maybe?"

"I may have something here," Felici said, peering at her phone. "There's a hotel just outside the walled city of Valletta called the Phoenicia, with a restaurant named the Phoenix. You know, the mythological bird that rose from the ashes? One of the reviewers here notes they have a fire pit which is used to ignite flaming shots of liquor and—wait for it—a flaming Greek cheese appetizer called *saganaki!* Apparently, those specialties aren't advertised as such, probably an insider kind of thing and certainly good dining theater, but that could easily be a candidate for your Key Master's riddle, '*Step into the secret fire and quench your thirst.*'"

"Great find!" Dominic said. "And here's another possibility. It's a place near the University of Malta called Flames, a Turkish-Asian fusion restaurant. It's on Triq L-Imhallef. Apparently '*Triq*' means street in Maltese."

"I found something too," Hana added. "A place called Fuego

in Paceville—and *'fuego'* means fire in Spanish and Portuguese! Looks like it's kind of a night spot, with a salsa bar and dancing. We'll have to hit that one last just to have some fun, especially if the key isn't at any of the other places. You like to dance, Michael?"

"Okay, well, that gives us several spots to try," Dominic said, ignoring the question. "If it's not at any of those places, we'll regroup and see if we can come at the clues from another angle. Let's wrap it up for now. I'd rather start fresh in the morning, especially if we're liable to run into trouble again. Who knows what's waiting for us in Malta?"

"This is interesting," Rebecca said, still staring at her phone. "Apparently people are starting to panic over some announcement made by KOTA. Market shelves are clearing out of water, batteries, and, of all things, toilet paper. Emergency supplies." She looked at the others with concern.

"What on earth is happening out there?" Hana asked no one in particular.

CHAPTER TWENTY-FOUR

Lucifer paced back and forth, sweating under the hot Arizona sun, making a mental list of the tasks he needed to accomplish in the next thirty minutes before the press arrived. It was easily 110 degrees in the shade, and he just wasn't used to these temperatures. His usual environs were much cooler and at a much higher elevation.

He paced in front of the headquarters of the Mount Graham International Observatory, which was oddly some sixty-four kilometers of twisty mountain roads by car away from the observatory's actual telescopes.

The headquarters wasn't much to boast about. Just a few small, white-painted, cinder block buildings with red trim and a blue stripe, bringing to mind the school colors of the University of Arizona, one of the primary sponsors of the observatory. It sat on the desert plain near the base of the mountains that housed the telescopes, and directly across Highway 366 from the Safford Federal Correctional Institution. Lucifer mused about the irony of putting a federal prison in a place so reminiscent of Hell, for surely many of its inhabitants were destined to end up there.

Of course, Lucifer wasn't his real name. It was the fitting code name he had been assigned by KOTA, since he worked at a telescope that was nicknamed as the LUCIFER—an abbreviation for Large Binocular Telescope Near-Infrared Spectroscopic Utility with Camera and Integral Field Unit for Extragalactic Research—telescope. It happened to be situated on Mount Graham near the Vatican's own Advanced Technology Telescope.

In reality, his name was Boris Ponomarenko. Ukrainian by birth, Catholic by religion, and prone to conspiracy theories by nature and upbringing under the shadow of Soviet Russia. While his primary assignment had to do with calculating the orbital periods of near-Earth asteroids, he used his expertise to make calculations regarding the hypothetical Planet X, supposed to be lurking somewhere in the outer solar system based on gravitational perturbations on the orbits of the outer planets.

Ponomarenko had made his own adjustments to those calculations, based on his additional observed effects of near-Earth asteroids and comets, and had come to the conclusion that Planet X, also known as Nibiru, was on a near-collision course with Earth, and likely carrying a train of Kuiper Belt objects in its gravity well. Kuiper belt objects were large chunks of rock originating out past Pluto from a planet that had failed to coalesce during the formation of our solar system. Nibiru was almost certainly dragging a cluster of them directly into Earth's path, and should they ever arrive—or, in his mind, *when* they arrived—the cluster would certainly rain chaos down on our unsuspecting planet.

Ponomarenko had come down the mountain early on a Sunday morning, when the headquarters would be deserted, in order to hold his press conference. He set up a podium and portable PA system in front of the main operations building, as well as a twenty-five centimeter Celestron Edge telescope on an Advanced VX mount next to the podium as a prop, its black optical tube glinting under the hot sun. The scope was used for star parties at HQ, but was nothing like the telescopes the observatory had up on the mountain.

• • •

WHEN THE MEDIA had arrived—two TV crews from local Arizona affiliates and a reporter for the *Arizona Daily Sun*—Lucifer stepped up to the podium and began his presentation.

"Good morning. My name is Dr. Boris Ponomarenko. I am an astronomer here at the Mount Graham Observatory. I have asked you here to share with you some shocking findings that are verified by NASA, but are being suppressed by not only the American government, but by other major countries worldwide.

"As many of you may know, two CalTech researchers published their findings in the *Astronomical Journal* in 2016, indicating evidence of an enormous object ten times the size of Earth that is orbiting twenty times farther away from the sun than Neptune.

"Based on my additional calculations, the rogue planet they discovered is not confined to the outer solar system but is on a highly elliptical orbit that will bring it dangerously close to the Earth in the very near future. While the rogue planet, referred to as Planet X, but also known as Nibiru or Wormwood, will not strike the Earth directly, the gravitational and magnetic effects will cause substantial disruption to our planet, including a switch of the magnetic poles. Already, you have heard reports of the Earth's magnetic field lessening in anticipation of this switch, which has taken place several times over the geologic history of our planet whenever Nibiru has come closer to it.

"Moreover, this rogue planet has very likely picked up a train of Kuiper Belt objects—basically asteroids caught in Nibiru's gravitational well, which will be littered along Earth's orbit and fall on our planet as we encounter them. The destruction these will produce cannot be overstated. It will look exactly like the scenes described in the Eighth Chapter of Revelation, with stars and mountains falling to the Earth.

"As further proof that NASA is aware of Nibiru's approach, they have recently launched the Double Asteroid Redirection Test, or DART, mission—which they are explaining away as an operation to redirect two near-Earth asteroids that do not pose a threat to Earth—as a test, in case there should be an asteroid that *does* pose such a threat. But I tell you that the DART mission is not aimed at those asteroids, but at the anticipated trajectory of Nibiru!

"Not only that, but NASA has recently contracted with over forty clergy and lay theologians, ostensibly to discuss the public's reaction to finding life on other planets. In reality, however, they are being consulted as experts on End Time prophecies, and the public's reaction to their eventual announcement of the impending doom.

"This is also the sole reason for the private sector's rapid development of a mission to Mars. The wealthy elite are planning to abandon Earth and start a colony on Mars before disaster strikes. Already they have held demonstration projects of isolated self-sustaining habitations on this very desert, as practice for what they will be endeavoring to accomplish on Mars.

"Look, the dots are all there for anyone willing to connect them. See for yourselves. This concludes my remarks. And I'm sorry, but I really don't have time for questions."

As the dozen or so reporters and TV crew shouted a barrage of jumbled questions at him, Ponomarenko stoically walked into the headquarters building, sat where he couldn't be seen, and waited for everyone to leave.

Then, opening a secure texting app on his phone, he sent a three-word message to a phone number only two other people had.

The text merely read, **Watch the news**.

CHAPTER TWENTY-FIVE

In a secured room adjacent to the small, isolated chapel outside Washington, D.C., the live video webcam feeds of the sealed prophecies had experienced an overwhelming volume of viewers since Boris Ponomarenko's press conference the day before. Had KOTA's IT developers not been instructed to anticipate this level of volume, their servers surely would have crashed, viewership was that heavy. But greater minds than theirs knew how their intended audience would react to such volatile news. In the words of one KOTA Knight, it was akin to a clever shepherd leading a mindless flock of sheep.

Outfitted in his back robe with the gold-embroidered, seven-pointed star on his chest and donning a white mask, Cardinal Damien Challis stepped into the center of the room, the glass cabinet containing the three prophecies behind him. All video cameras were positioned directly on his face as he addressed the world watching the live feed.

"The time has come for hidden things to be revealed. The Catholic Church, my Church, has hidden important knowledge from you, to keep you ignorant and controllable, despite the fact that The End is near and certain things must be done to secure your survival. But according to Matthew 24: *'He that shall endure unto the end, the same shall be saved. And this gospel of the kingdom shall be preached in all the world for a witness unto all nations; and then shall the end come.'*

"Yes, my friends, the time for revelation is at hand, and hidden things shall be made known."

With that, Challis removed his face mask, revealing his true identity. The millions of viewers—the majority of whom knew of this prominent charismatic leader of the Church, anyway—gasped with astonishment. Mindful responses were immediate. *This is a respected cardinal of the Holy Roman Church! The Archbishop of Washington, D.C.! If Challis says this is so, and he obviously has the backing of Rome in that role, it must be true! We are saved at last!*

Challis went on, "The Church has sequestered the true Third Secret of Fátima, but the Knights of the Apocalypse, Guardians of the Truth, Protectors of the Church and Heralds of the End, have been entrusted with this prophecy, and sealed it in its parts, to be revealed in its time, that you may believe and understand."

Before the live cameras, Challis unlocked the glass case with a golden key and removed one of the sealed envelopes. Presenting it to the camera, he opened the envelope and read its contents.

"This is the first part of the Third Secret of Fátima which has been hidden from you:

> *'Behold, in the last days, a heavenly body shall be flung from the heavens. Stars will fall to earth, and a mountain shall fall into the sea, in fulfillment of John's vision. Those whom the Church has appointed to watch the heavens shall see these events before they come to pass and shall be silent, and the kings and rulers of the earth shall hold their tongues. Yet the Voice of Truth shall prevail, and a warning shall be given. And when these things come to pass, repent and be saved, for The End is near.'"*

He placed the paper on the top of the glass case in the camera's view so it could be seen by all.

"Just yesterday," he continued, "an astronomer at the Vatican Observatory sounded the alarm that a rogue planet, a heavenly body called Nibiru, has been flung into the path of the Earth, with a veil of asteroids in its wake, some the size of buildings, and these will rain down like stars falling from the sky, and a mountain falling into the sea, just as predicted in the Eighth Chapter of Revelation. In the words of Luke, *'Today this scripture is fulfilled in your hearing.'*

"Yet neither the Vatican nor the Vatican Observatory, nor NASA, nor any of the world's governments, kings or rulers of the earth, has come forward with a statement, leaving you in darkness.

"But we have brought you into the light. The Knights of the Apocalypse has revealed these things to you, so that you may believe, understand, and be prepared.

"The time is at hand.

"Only the Elect will be saved.

"This is the Second Warning.

"Another prophetic fulfillment is expected soon.

"Be watchful."

FOLLOWING the live revelation of the sealed prophecy, a new page was added to the KOTA website, with a new Web address all its own, announcing a Final Mass event.

> There will be a special High Mass, celebrated at the end of a weekend of prayer, fasting, discernment, confession and reflection.
>
> KOTA has given a special dispensation to those who are able to accept this calling, that those who attend the Mass and drink of the sacred wine, will be spared from the tribulations to come,

and will go to meet Jesus in the clouds prior to his triumphant return to earth. We are calling the Elect to us.

Counselors are standing by to invite you to this special event. Call the number below now to reserve your space.

IN AN UNDISCLOSED LOCATION, Magnus sat at a desk in a small flat with no windows and only moderate furnishings. Not the style of living he was accustomed to, but it would suffice for now.

Picking up a special burner phone from the desk, he dialed a number from memory. When that phone was answered, he began speaking.

"Hello, Lucifer."

"I've told you not to call me that. I did as you instructed. Sooner or later, they're going to figure out that I lied about the calculations. My reputation will be in ruins."

"Yes, that's all probably true. But by that time, it won't matter anymore. You'll be living as a rich man down in the Caribbean. Already the markets are reacting to the announcements, just as we planned. I have just directed the first installment to be deposited into your numbered account in the Grand Caymans, as instructed."

"I hate myself for letting you talk me into this. Some spiritual advisor you are."

"You should have thought of that long before you ran up all those gambling debts in Argentina while I was stationed there. I forgave you then, of course. That is the purpose of confession. But sadly, while confession clears the sinner, absolution does not clear the debts. You owed me."

"Yes, I'm aware of that."

"Stay the course for now, Boris. You want to be around to spend all that money you're making."

With no further words, he terminated the call.

CHAPTER TWENTY-SIX

After the exhausting activities in both Jerusalem and Edinburgh, and all the excitement of obtaining the first key and being chased back to the airport, most of the team settled into their plush seats aboard the Dassault Falcon and curled up for a nap. They didn't know when they might get a chance at a good night's sleep in the days to come, so getting rest was a priority.

As the jet made its approach to Malta, dusk was descending over Valletta, the capital city. The brilliant lights below, with an unusual abundance of neon across the cityscape, met the visitors as everyone looked out the wide oval windows to get a birds-eye view of their new and exotic destination.

Ever the organizer, Hana had arranged rooms for everyone at the Hilton Malta Hotel in St. Julian's. Overlooking the Portomaso Marina, the hotel provided stunning ocean views and the renowned Blue Elephant Thai Restaurant, complementing its seafood restaurant, Oceana, with its unique Maltese Mediterranean cuisine.

As Dominic, Hana, Marco, Sabrina and Rebecca entered the lobby, a large flat-screen TV was broadcasting a CNN special report. The announcement, from the astronomer at Mount

Graham International Observatory in Arizona, concerned a rogue planet on its way to Earth. The announcement itself had created a stir in some sectors, but since Ponomarenko did not have the backing of any official agency, such as NASA or the Vatican Observatory, the initial reaction was largely one of skepticism.

However, when the Archbishop of Washington, D.C. had revealed himself as the head of the Knights of the Apocalypse, and then opened one of the sealed prophecies on live TV confirming the Arizona astronomer's predictions, the reaction had turned more frenzied, especially after the group had made its first prophetic announcement about the current pope being the last pope, according to an ancient prophecy.

Now, KOTA was claiming that the approaching rogue planet named Nibiru was confirming the fulfillment of one part of the Third Secret of Fátima—a prophecy supposedly suppressed by the Vatican for decades. Some Catholic theologians had pointed out that the Third Secret already had been revealed in 2000, and that this must surely be a hoax. However, they had no explanation for how a prophecy from 1917 that was sealed in a glass case for days before could have predicted the astronomer's announcement.

There still had been no official reaction from the Vatican, nor from any world leaders, which coincidently was part of the prophecy's prediction. Churches and spiritual advisors had been inundated with requests for more information, and church officials everywhere were reporting record attendance at even daily Masses. Some Evangelical fundamentalists gloated with self-satisfaction, crowing to their parishioners, "*See? We were right all along,*" while at the same time expounding on the rest of the End Times' prophecies contained in the Bible. Overflowing collection baskets were filling their coffers.

Other self-proclaimed prophets had turned to the works of Nostradamus or other historical precedents for their prognostications, everyone hoping that their predictions would be the next to come true. In larger urban areas many people were inexplicably fleeing the cities, where food and commodities were in short supply from panic buying. Thankfully, owing to its self-sustaining capabilities and sensible populace, Malta had not yet been overtaken by such alarming activity. People generally went about their days as they normally did, and it was business as usual for commercial establishments.

BEFORE TURNING IN, Dominic and his friends decided to try the Oceana Restaurant, each ordering from a succulent menu featuring fusilli with confit of pork belly and mushroom fricassée, slow-cooked leg of lamb with caramelized onions and feta cheese, grilled aubergine and goat cheese pithivier with roasted cauliflower and Moroccan spices, and a cornucopian Mediterranean seafood platter with black mussels, king prawns, vongole, and calamari. Everyone was enraptured, feasting on the best Malta had to offer.

During their sumptuous meal, table discussion turned to the news reports, something they could hardly avoid given their current mission.

"Michael," Lancaster asked, "while reading Jonah's manuscript—and thanks again for allowing me the privilege—I'd like your opinion as to what he wrote compared to what's happening with KOTA now. Are they related to some degree? Are we, in fact, about to experience a cataclysmic end to the world as we know it?"

Dominic put his fork down and dabbed the napkin to his mouth. "Honestly, Rebecca, I don't have a clue. Jonah put a great deal of effort into that book, but I have to believe he couldn't have anticipated KOTA's movements as we're seeing them play out now. And this global panic we're seeing in the news is disturbing, to say the least, but clearly related to their reckless announcements.

"Apocalyptic eschatology—the theological study of the final

events of history—is really not my specialty, though we did cover it to some extent in seminary. The Church has been anticipating the return of Christ for more than two thousand years, but some parts of scripture say that the end will come as a surprise, '*like a thief in the night,*' and that '*no man knows the day or the hour,*' not the angels or even Christ himself. So while there are passages of scripture that show some portents of the end, they are rather vague and have been repeatedly fulfilled throughout history. This kind of End Times fever crops up every few generations. But as is their nature, people have short memories. I am, however, concerned about the effect it is having on society. Look at what's happening, all this panic buying and in certain places people are taking this so seriously they're leaving their homes—but where are they going to go? If the entire Earth is going to be hit, *no place* is safe for the body, and only the examined soul offers safety for what is to come.

"Personally, I think other man-made manipulations are at play here, though that's just an intuitive suspicion. I don't trust the likes of Cardinal Challis, who's nothing more than a two-bit televangelist. I'm surprised he's even achieved a cardinalate. That had to involve a bit of political maneuvering. But I digress."

"So, what are our next steps here?" Hana inquired.

"Well, first," the priest replied, "I'm going to call the Holy Father and brief him on recent events. He has a personal stake in this, of course, since he controls whether the Third Secret is to be revealed at all. I still cannot believe KOTA has the actual prophecy from St. Lúcia, as they claim, but time will tell.

"And second, I need a long run tomorrow morning! All this tension is making me tight, and I can't think properly without a good bit of exercise and soul-cleansing. After that, we'll decide where we go first.

"Meanwhile, as the rest of the world goes mad all around us, we need to be the island of rationality and calm. It's important we maintain our focus if we are to have the ability to turn the tide of this global panic. If you and the others can continue searching for likely places to find that second key, that will be time well spent."

~

In his spare office, Magnus sat watching the news and resulting financial reports, a grim smile crossing his face as he beheld the expected effects of their brilliant maneuvering.

The cell phone on the table next to him vibrated. Picking it up, he opened the secure texting app, Signal, and recognized the phone number messaging him. The text simply read, "**MD2Malta**."

He paused, considering his options, then opened the phone app and pressed a Speed Dial button. When the other party answered, his instructions were brief: "Go to Malta. But do not harm the priest." Nimbus, Knight of the Sword, simply replied, "Understood."

~

Back in his hotel room after dinner, Dominic called the pope's personal line in the Apostolic Palace. The phone was answered promptly.

"This is Michael, Your Holiness. We're in Malta right now," Dominic told Papa Petrini. "We have obtained the first key in Scotland, though not without some complications getting out of there. Clearly, others are on the same path as we are. Tomorrow we're going after the second key, though we have yet to determine where that might be. We have only clues from the Clavis Domini, but I'm confident we'll find it."

"Michael, I am deeply concerned about the reaction to not just the LUCI astronomer's announcement, but to KOTA's dramatic performance. I'm already making plans to reprimand Cardinal Challis for his outrageous behavior, as if he were speaking on behalf of the Vatican, which of course is preposterous.

"I'm also consulting with my advisors about a response from the Vatican Observatory and coordinating the reactions of other governments and religious leaders to see how they're shaping their responses. Hopefully that may help to settle things down. But you say you've had 'complications,' which I take to mean danger, which seems to follow you on these exploits? I won't have you taking any risks, my son. I want your Swiss Guard colleagues with you there in Malta for additional security. We have close ties to the nation of Malta, obviously, and both Sergeants Dengler and Bischoff have diplomatic credentials, which should help move things along there should you encounter trouble with the authorities. And they will be armed. Please, do be careful, Michael."

"I will, Holy Father. I will."

CHAPTER TWENTY-SEVEN

Dressed in his running shorts, Saucony shoes, and his favorite ratty t-shirt from Fordham University, Dominic headed out for his morning run.

While much of Malta has deeply historic roots and fascinating places reflecting its Christian, military, and trading history over the centuries, the Hilton Hotel was situated in a more modernized area. St. Julian's is known for its sandy white beaches and rocky stretches along the coastline, with a seaside promenade featuring restaurants and luxury boutiques for the island's more upscale visitors.

His run took him north to Paceville, an area just south of St. George's Bay Beach known for its boisterous nightlife, upscale bars at Portomaso Marina, and even a few Irish pubs, Lebanese cafés and Chinese dim sum restaurants.

At this early hour nothing but coffee shops and early morning cafés were open, but Dominic relished the peace and quiet as he ran along the boardwalk, the only sounds those of a colony of rare, protected yelkouan shearwater seabirds common to Malta. Curiously, Dominic later discovered, there were no seagulls on the island, due to Maltese hunters having shot them all, so there were none to breed.

Coming out the north end of the hotel near the marina, Dominic had taken the path along the ocean heading northwest, past the huge Westin Dragonara resort and around St. George's Bay. Having looped around the open ground near the desalinization plant, he now headed back toward town. It felt good to be moving. So much of his workdays were spent in the dark, cavernous Secret Archives, where he often felt like a mole living underground. He cherished his ritual morning runs, when the world was fresh and the endorphin rush better prepared him to start each new day. It was during these times he could think things through, or meditate on his life as a priest, and now, erstwhile adventurer.

As he was approaching the Portomaso Marina, his phone rang with an incoming call. Taking it out of his pocket, he noticed it was Sister Teri from the Vatican switchboard. He stopped and answered it, breathing heavily.

"Hey, Teri, how are things going there?"

"Oh, Father Michael, I'm afraid I have some disturbing news," the distraught young nun said. "I happened to be near Sister Mary Oliphant, but around a corner where she couldn't see me, and when I quietly walked behind her as I headed back to my desk I observed her listening in on your call with the pope last night! Our communications displays show which and whose lines are active, and I was shocked to discover her eavesdropping on your private conversation. Of course, I notified the Vatican Gendarmerie immediately and she is now under house arrest. In the several hours that followed, they confiscated her own cell phone and found a number of mysterious text messages to an unknown number—probably a burner phone, they think. But I thought you should hear this from me as early as possible this morning, since I happen to know you're in Malta and it may have some bearing on your business there. Oh, I do hope I've done the right thing. I thought she was my friend, but there's nothing worse than a deceitful, traitorous nun."

"Rest assured you did right, Teri," Dominic comforted her. "It would be helpful to know *who* she was corresponding with, though. Will you let me know if the Gendarmerie figure that out? It could be important."

"Sure, Michael, already on it. I'll let you know whatever we turn up. Meanwhile, take care of yourself there. I understand Karl and Lukas are joining you soon. It makes me feel a lot better, knowing they'll have your back."

"Thanks, Teri, I appreciate you letting me know. You take good care of yourself, and keep me apprised of developments there, okay?"

Disconnecting the call, he leaned on the promenade railing overlooking the marina, pondering how KOTA—if it were indeed KOTA that Sister Mary Oliphant had been communicating with—could have possibly managed to infiltrate the Pious Disciples of the Divine Master, the order to which she belonged.

TURNING TO CONTINUE HIS RUN, Dominic skirted the downtown area, known as Malta's "Sin City," being home to several large casinos, strip clubs and seedy bars, but soon found himself in front of a small, circular Catholic church called Our Lady of Good Counsel. If anyone needed good counsel now, he figured, it was he. Given the abundance of ancient Catholic churches on Malta—a land with one of the largest Catholic populations per capita in the world—he found the chapel surprisingly modern.

Entering, his eye was drawn to a huge oval rainbow in the apse behind the altar, with a magnificent crucifix in front of it. Choosing one of the polished wooden pews, Dominic knelt down and prayed for a bit.

On his reading about Malta on the plane before their arrival, he had been anxious to see St. Paul's Shipwreck Church, up on a northern bay of the island nation. St. Paul, having arrived in Jerusalem in the year 57 after completing his third missionary sojourn, was arrested for allegedly violating certain immutable laws at the time. After a couple years in prison and just before his trial in Jerusalem, Paul claimed he was a Roman citizen, thus exercising his right to be tried by Caesar in Rome. After setting sail for the Eternal City, his ship was ripped apart during a storm off Malta, where he stayed for three months and miraculously cured all manner of illnesses, including those of the father of Publius, Rome's main ruler on the island, who suffered from serious fever and dysentery. Consequently, he became one of the patron saints of Malta.

Finished with his devotions, Dominic walked out of the chapel and continued his run back to the hotel, the shops and restaurants now open and the townsfolk starting their own days under the bright morning Maltese sun.

As he entered the hotel and headed toward the elevator, envisioning a hot shower in his room, Dominic was elated to find Karl and Lukas coming down the stairs, both dressed in running shorts and t-shirts themselves.

"*Father Michael!*" they beamed in unison as they met and exchanged hugs.

"It's so great being here with you," Karl said, his arm resting on the priest's shoulder. "Things were too weird back at the Vatican, with all that's going on." He glanced at Lukas, who was eyeing him for complaining. "Well, they *were!*" he said sheepishly. The other two laughed.

"Well, in any case, it's good to have you both here," Dominic said. "I've a feeling things might get a little precarious. Teri just called to tell me she caught one of the other nuns eavesdropping on my call with the pope, so unknown others are likely aware that we're here on Malta. And KOTA has to realize why."

He went on to tell them about his experiences in Scotland.

The two Swiss Guards' expressions alone comforted Dominic, knowing how much they had fought to protect him in past exploits.

"We're going for a quick run to get the lay of the land, Michael," Lukas said. "Wait for us before you have breakfast, and you can fill us in further."

"Deal," Dominic said. "I have a few things to keep me busy until then. See you back here in the lobby soon, yeah?"

CHAPTER TWENTY-EIGHT

Hana and Marco were the first to arrive in the lobby as they waited for the others to join them for breakfast.

As they stepped onto the polished wooden floors of richly-grained African Shedua, they caught the gentle strums of a Spanish guitar. An old man with short, gnarled fingers and wearing a gray flat cap, accompanied himself in an emotive ballad in Maltese, a Semitic language of Arabic dialect sprinkled with English words.

They took seats in the lobby to enjoy the music, and ordered small cups of the island's unique kafè, a strong, aromatic brew flavored with rosewater and cloves. Inspired, Marco got up and approached the guitarist, nodded his head in appreciation, and dropped a twenty-euro note into his open instrument case.

"That was sweet of you," Hana remarked as he returned to the table.

"I know what it's like. I'd play for a few euros a day when I was a young lad on the streets of Paris. He's not doing it for the money, though. Look at him. He *lives* for telling stories through his music. It's his passion, I can tell." A distant look appeared on Marco's face as he thought back to those carefree days, long before his life took on more brutish dimensions. Hana watched him closely, admiring him anew. *He and Michael are so different, and yet, there are subtle similarities….*

Looking up, she saw the other object of her fascination walking toward them, the priest having chosen light blue jeans and a dark blue, form-fitting polo shirt for their day's outing. Just emerging from the elevator behind him were Karl and Lukas walking together with Sabrina and Rebecca, all chatting amiably. They took seats around the lobby table and ordered kafè, espressos, or cappuccinos.

"Okay, here's my proposal," Dominic began. "There's a nice little spot called Café G, just down the street from a church I passed on my run. From what I hear, the local bread there is amazing, made at a bakery up in St. Paul's Bay, not far from St. Paul's Shipwreck Church. Maybe we'll have time to check that out later. Oh, and they have that traditional Maltese coriander sausage I've been wanting to try. Is it obvious I'm famished?

"Anyway, looking at the map, the Phoenix Restaurant is just outside the walled section of Valletta, so after breakfast we'll go there and see some of the city until the restaurant opens for lunch and find out if the keystone is there. If it's not, we head over to Flames Restaurant. And if that isn't it, then we head back into Paceville to the Fuego Salsa Bar and see if it's there. Ready for a full day?"

"You bet, Michael!" Karl said enthusiastically, turning to Lukas. "We've never been to Malta before and want to see as much as we can."

"Just keep an eye out for any suspicious types," Marco cautioned, "either male or female. Our group of seven might draw attention, and we have to assume they're looking for us—whoever *they* are. So, besides me, who's carrying?"

Three hands raised: Karl, Lukas, and Sabrina. Rebecca looked at her friend with surprise.

"A girl's gotta have protection, doesn't she?" she said, smiling.

"*Très bien*," Marco said with satisfaction. "We're good to go, then."

JUST A FIVE-MINUTE WALK from the Hilton, Café G was indeed small, a narrow slice of tasty wholesomeness tucked between a row of ancient buildings on Church Street.

Once inside, Karl and Lukas pushed two tables together to seat all seven against a canary-yellow leather wall booth. Picking up menus, they variously ordered avocado poached eggs, pancakes with spiced apples, chili scrambled eggs, Maltese coriander sausage, and that uniquely European delight, Nutella pancakes topped with fresh fruits.

Instinctively, Marco sat in the farthest seat on the outside, facing the door. He was slightly on edge, having confided to Karl, Lukas, and the detectives that he was fairly certain they had been followed as they made the trek from the hotel to the café. Knowing Marco wasn't the needlessly paranoid type, the guards took the commando's intuition seriously. Now they, too, were on full alert.

AFTER BREAKFAST, everyone filed out of the narrow doorway and onto the sidewalk, waiting for Hana, who insisted on settling the bill.

Dominic had an idea. "The Phoenix Restaurant doesn't open till noon, so we've got some time. How about a little sightseeing? We can take a couple taxis up to St. Paul's Bay just north of here and see the Shipwreck Church."

With everyone nodding in agreement, Marco hailed one sedan cab, then another, and after everyone split up into the two cars, both headed north.

Twenty minutes later, they arrived at St. Paul's Shipwreck Church, a modest little single-story chapel overlooking St. Paul's Bay, with a small bell hanging inside an arched tower on the roof. Walking up the stone steps, the group looked down, noting an eight-pointed cross made of black-and-white inlaid marble leading to the entrance.

"Look!" Dominic said, startled. "It's the Maltese cross. The same cross is on the Holy Father's papal shield—and the one mentioned in KOTA's press announcement. Wonder if there's a connection…."

"Well, it could just be the standard Maltese cross standing for, you know, Malta?" Hana chided him. "It also represents the eight historic langues, or regions, of the Knights Hospitaller—which I believe included Italy, Germany, France, Auvergne, Provence, Aragon, Castile, and Portugal. And the Knights of Malta are an order of the Hospitallers…."

"*I* knew that," Dominic said, blushing as he smiled at Hana's history lesson.

Entering the simply designed sanctuary, there wasn't too much to see except for the most sacred relic on Malta, that of the wrist bone from St. Paul himself, along with the plinth upon which he was thought to have been beheaded in Rome. There were several paintings on the walls, among them a depiction of St. Paul's shipwreck and the angry seas that caused it, by Giulio Cassarino, a minor painter in the shadow of Caravaggio. The intense mood of doom resonated with Dominic as his mind was jolted once again to the immensity of the havoc being wrought on the world by KOTA.

With Karl and Lukas by his side, Dominic lit a votive candle as they each said a brief prayer, one of urgent supplication for strength and good counsel, then they all headed toward the exit.

Outside now, their arms raised to shield their eyes from the bright sun, Marco noticed a dark gray Mercedes SUV idling in the small parking lot, its two occupants in the front seat staring directly at the group.

As Marco locked eyes with them, their SUV abruptly took off, the driver looking back at Marco with a smug smile, talking on a cell phone held to his left ear as he drove away.

Marco exchanged knowing glances with both Swiss Guards and the two detectives, a silent acknowledgment passing between them that they had indeed been followed. But by whom?

"Okay," Dominic said, checking his watch, "let's head down to the Phoenix Restaurant now. They'll be open by the time we get there. Hana, you ride with me. Your comment about the Maltese cross has me thinking about the new papal crest and what the other symbols might mean to the KOTA plot. Maybe there's a clue for us there."

Not finding any taxis nearby, nor Uber or Lyft postings anywhere on the island, Sabrina asked one of the kids skateboarding near the church if Malta had a ride-sharing service. Replying in English, one of the boys told her to use Bolt, the only service available besides taxis or buses.

Downloading the Bolt app on her iPhone and setting it up with payment details, Sabrina called for a van to pick them up. When it arrived fifteen minutes later, they all piled in for the half-hour trip to the ancient walled city of Valletta.

As the van pulled up to the five-star Phoenicia Hotel, Hana couldn't help but marvel at its classical design.

"We should have stayed *here!* Look at this place. It's magnificent."

"Yes, but *way* out of our league," Rebecca said with a groan. "Remember, Sabrina and I are just civil servants." The two women laughed.

"Well, loving architecture, I can't wait to see the rest of the place," Hana added. "Let's have lunch here. My treat."

Sabrina and Rebecca looked at each other and rolled their eyes. "You do live in a different world, Hana Sinclair."

"Not really. Same world as yours, similar problems, similar

joys. But I love sharing what I can with friends. And I assume we are friends now, right?" She smiled expectantly.

"Of course, we are," Sabrina said after a slight pause, glancing at Rebecca. "If we have nothing in life but a good friend, we're already rich."

On hearing that, Dominic looked over at Hana, and as their eyes met they both realized their relationship went well beyond measurable value. And temptation of a romantic relationship still haunted each of them, particularly now, when they faced the possibility of time running out for them.

Seeing what passed between them or sensing it, Marco reached out and took Hana's hand firmly in his own as they entered the majestic lobby of the Phoenicia, inspiring questioning glances between the two detectives as they followed them in.

SUCCESSFULLY EMBODYING the unique spirit of Maltese architecture, the polished terrazzo floors with inlaid black-patterned marble beneath white, arched, coffered ceilings gave the illusion of spaciousness to an already palatial setting. Towering Areca butterfly palms set against bastion walls dominated the airy room, lending a lush, tropical feel to the more formal Roman Doric columns surrounding intimate seating areas.

Though accustomed to such fineries, even Hana was taken aback by the elegance of the space. "I must keep reminding myself we're here on dire business, or else I'd be exploring the whole place. Now, where's this Phoenix Restaurant? We have a key to find."

Dominic eyed a prominent archway toward the back of the lobby, over which was a sign indicating the restaurant. "There it is," he said, pointing. They crossed the grand room and passed through the door into the sumptuous Phoenix dining room.

The group was seated at a large, round table with alternating Persian blue-and-pale rose chairs, and while the waiter handed each person a menu, Dominic looked around the lavishly appointed room, seeking archways with keystones, but found nothing that might suffice.

"I can't imagine this decor offering anything close to what we're looking for," he said. Then, stopping a passing server, he asked if there was anything resembling a keystone in the building. The priest drew an example of it on a bar napkin.

"No, sir, I'm afraid we have nothing like that," the server replied, "but you might try the bar upstairs." Dominic thanked her, then looked at the menu.

Turning to Karl, he asked, "Will you order me the house club sandwich with smoked chicken? I'm going up to the bar to check it out."

"Sure, Michael," he said. "Good luck."

Dominic crossed the room to the wide arched exit, then ran up the grand staircase two steps at a time. Reaching the bar, he was surprised to find a massive bronzed phoenix rising out of actual flames in a fire pit in the center of the room. He remembered Hana mentioning on the plane how the staff theatrically ignited flaming drinks and *saganaki* for guests in the evening, which seemed a little excessive to him now that he saw it.

Surveying the room, he found no typical keystones anywhere.

"Excuse me," he asked the bartender. "Do you have anything here resembling a keystone?"

The bartender was mystified. "I do not know what you mean by 'keystone,' sir. I'm afraid I cannot help you." Taking one last look around, the priest returned downstairs to the dining room.

"No luck up there," he told the others. "Guess we can cross this one off the list. At least we'll have a fine lunch."

~

SINCE THEY HAD a few more hours before checking out the next candidate on their list—the Flames Restaurant, which didn't open until five—they decided to see some of the sights of Valletta, Malta's capital. A vibrant, bustling city, there were many places to visit, foremost on Dominic's agenda being St. John's Co-Cathedral, home to the Knights of Malta.

Long known as protectors of the Catholic faith from invading Ottoman Turks in the sixteenth century, the Knights of Malta were, by papal charter, deemed a Catholic military order charged with defense of the Holy Land and caring for sick, poor, or injured pilgrims. Originally headquartered in the Kingdom of Jerusalem until 1291, the order moved on to Rhodes, then Malta and numerous other strategic locations in their long and formidable history, setting up hospitals and military fortifications throughout the Holy Land, an area located roughly between the Mediterranean and the Eastern Bank of the Jordan River.

The ruling period of the Knights—from 1535 to 1798, when they surrendered Malta to the invading forces of Napoleon Bonaparte—is often referred to as Malta's Golden Age. It was during this time that architectural and artistic embellishment of the Maltese Islands resulted in improvements to the overall health, education, and prosperity of its citizens, resulting in a near-quintupling of the population from 25,000 to more than 114,000. Music, literature, theater and the visual arts all flourished in Malta during its Golden Age, which also witnessed the foundation and development of many of the Renaissance and Baroque towns and villages, palaces, and gardens of Malta, especially Valletta.

And the centerpiece of Valletta was St. John's Co-Cathedral—with nine chapels featuring opulent gilded walls and stunning ceiling murals by Malta's foremost painter, Mattia Preti—reflecting the significance of the Knights and their core mission of defending the faith and safeguarding the faithful. Built by the Order of St. John between 1572 and 1577 as a symbol of the

Knights' successes, the cathedral featured some of the most beautiful paintings on the island, the most renowned being *The Beheading of Saint John the Baptist* by Michelangelo Caravaggio.

As he strolled through the nearly five-hundred-year-old cathedral, Dominic thought back to the rich history its golden walls had embraced and the many lives lost in its protection by the Knights of Malta, as well as the many souls who had prayed here over the centuries before they moved on to wherever it was souls went to. As with many articles of faith, he was still uncertain about that element of belief himself, something that had gnawed at him throughout his religious career. *What kind of faith is it I have, anyway?* he wondered. It always took the magnificence of such edifices of the faithful to force him to look deeper within, and this was just such a moment.

"You look thoroughly lost in thought, Michael," Hana noticed, matching steps with him as they ambled up the nave toward the altar of the grand cathedral.

"Yes, I was, actually. Experiences like this force me to reevaluate myself: my role in the greater scheme of things, as a priest, as a human being. I go about my life relatively carefree, doing what needs to be done in work and, well, just living. And though by nature each of us thinks the world revolves around us, we're really just inconsequential, when you get down to it. I remember something Carl Sagan, the astrophysicist, once said: 'We live on an insignificant planet of a humdrum star lost in a galaxy tucked away in some forgotten corner of a universe in which there are far more galaxies than people.' And yet I behold grandeur like this"—he waved his arms around, taking in the enormous space"—and yes, even in St. Peter's, and think, *What's it all for?* As grand as these symbols of faith are, they can't come close to depicting the vastness of God's Creation. Or defining our place in it."

"Sounds like the classic existential crisis," she noted. "Maybe it just takes something like this to shake us up, to make us realize that our lives *do* have meaning, that we're not just ants 'in some forgotten corner of a universe.' I look at you and think, *This man is doing the best he can with his life, and it's working out pretty well!* I'm not sure I can say the same thing about Marco, for example. His world is several shades darker than ours, his experiences more hardened. But still, he's a fine man doing the best he can. And if this *is* the end, I'm very glad to be facing it with you.

"Now, are you going to require more therapy, or should we be getting along to find that second key?" She wrapped her arm through his as they continued walking. Dominic looked down at her with clear emotion in his eyes.

"Thanks," he said tenderly. "I don't know how different my life would be without having you in it. You truly are a treasure."

Suddenly feeling a little dizzy, Hana held onto Dominic's arm a bit tighter, but she couldn't bring herself to look up at him. *If you only knew*, she thought.

THE SKY WAS ABLAZE with orange clouds reflecting the setting sun, and a light breeze coming off the Mediterranean brought with it the pungent smells of international foods being prepared in various Vallettan restaurants as Dominic and his friends approached their second destination: the Flames Restaurant, a rustic hideaway located near the rear gate to the University of Malta, not far from St. John's Cathedral.

As they entered the cozy space, they were pleasantly struck by the different sensual aromas. Specializing in a fusion of Turkish- and Asian-inspired dishes, Flames Restaurant represented the different cultures of Malta in the foods their master chefs prepared.

They settled in for dinner at a nice, big table and ordered a mix of duck dumplings, sweet and sour chicken, dolmas, fungi pide, lamb falafel wraps, and kebabs. The room was loud with conversation and laughter, happy people eating sumptuous meals in a casual setting.

Eating family style, on a long table with other local and visiting patrons, food was being passed back and forth while everyone chatted. As Marco passed a plate of sweet and sour chicken to Dominic, his hand didn't quite catch it right and the plate landed in his lap, his polo shirt and jeans now covered with the tasty dish. Red-faced, he got up to go to the restroom to clean what he could of it, then returned to the table.

"Well, now I need to make a stop back at the hotel so I can change." He took his seat and dug into the remainder of his meal.

"Just as well," Hana said. "We've been in these clothes all day. I wouldn't mind freshening up before we head out again."

When he found a moment to hail a busy waiter, Dominic asked him about the keystone, not having seen anything looking like one in the restaurant.

"Keystone?" the young Turk said in flawless English. "You mean like the beer? Keystone beer?"

"You have Keystone beer?! *Here*?" Rebecca asked, astonished. "That's the one I mentioned on the plane!" she said, reminding the others.

"Well, we don't have it here in our restaurant. But I know they serve Keystone at the Speakeasy over the Fuego Salsa Bar, not far from here."

CHAPTER TWENTY-NINE

After dinner, everyone walked the few blocks back to the hotel to freshen up before they headed out to the Fuego Speakeasy. Realizing that he had originally packed for a quick turnaround trip from Rome to Jerusalem, Dominic had only brought one set of street clothes, so until he could get them cleaned, he would have to resort to his priestly attire: black slacks and a black shirt with clerical collar. Though it seemed a bit formal for their night out, no one would mind, least of all himself.

On the walk to Fuego they took in the lively young crowds on the streets, seemingly oblivious to the shattering news rapidly circling the globe. Nightlife in St. Julian's started early, and the team seemed to enjoy the relief from their calamitous mission, especially Karl and Lukas, as the revelers, mostly in their twenties, seemed closer in age to them.

Marco was still uneasy, knowing now that they were being followed. Worse, he kept losing sight of his suspected pursuers, thinking they may in fact be using multiples who traded places using alternating followers. He watched for them as they passed shop windows, where he could catch the reflections of their trackers without looking at them directly.

Finally arriving at the Fuego Salsa Bar on street level, signs led them up a set of stairs to an upper plaza where the Fuego Speakeasy was located, a vibrant outdoor nightspot ablaze with neon lights and a circular orange bar. Comfy padded loveseats embraced intimate, round bistro tables resting on pink neon pillars, and the entire bar lounge area was bathed in blue neon. The ethereal effect bathed both patrons and their theatrical tropical cocktails, the kinds with huge chunks of fresh fruit—pineapples, blood oranges, limes and kiwis—and colorful little paper umbrellas capping each tall glass.

Before they entered, Marco had given Karl a heads-up to watch for anyone suspicious who might be lurking about and observing the others from a distance. Karl had spotted a Häagen-Dazs ice cream parlor across the plaza from the Speakeasy, and he pulled Lukas with him to have a cone while watching the diverse crowd of mostly young people as they did their surveillance.

As the others found a seating area with a wide sofa and accompanying loveseats around a blue-lit rectangular table, Dominic was just about to sit down when he looked up across the plaza toward Hugo's Pub—and was certain he saw Father Lorenzo Marchetti, talking on a cell phone! *That can't be! What's Lorenzo doing on Malta?!* It was some distance, and he squinted through neon haze to make sure it was, in fact, Marchetti.

"I'll be right back," he said to the others, getting up. "Go ahead and order your drinks. I'll get something from the bar."

Moving through the thick rabble of patrons, the priest made his way across the plaza to Hugo's. The man he had seen just moments ago had vanished. Dominic went inside the small pub and looked around, but didn't see him.

Probably just my imagination, fueled by Marco's paranoia....

Breathing a bit easier, he returned to Fuego. He approached the bar and looked up at the selection of liquors against the round backbar. Scanning all the bottles and shelves, he was surprised to find that the backbar itself was a brick arch, at the top center of which was an actual red brick keystone! Then, glancing up above the keystone, his surprise turned to shock, for proudly and inexplicably resting on the keystone of the arch itself was a single blue-and-silver can of Keystone Beer!

Dominic tried to tamp down the excitement overtaking him. *Can it be this simple? However would I have found this had I not simply looked up?! Talk about divine providence….*

Catching a bartender's attention, he asked, "Can I get that Keystone beer up there, please?"

The bartender turned and looked up at the object of the priest's interest. Then he glanced down the backbar to the other bartender. "Billy? This guy asked for the Keystone."

Billy looked down the bar at Dominic, with a look of purpose on his face, then made his way to him while the other bartender passed him in the opposite direction.

"We don't get many priests in here," said Billy, with a clear Australian accent.

"I'm sure," Dominic tossed out. "But I'd like that Keystone beer up there, please."

"You're not from around here, are ya? How 'bout something from Malta instead? Getcha an ice cold Cisk Lager, right up?"

"Maybe I'll try that later, but all I really want now is *that* Keystone." He pointed to the top of the archway, a little irked. "The one at the very top."

"They're all the same, mate," Billy said, a cryptic look on his face. "And that one isn't even cold. You're certain that's the one you want?"

"*Absolutely*!" The priest replied quietly but firmly. "It *has* to be that one…." He looked solemnly at Billy.

Billy motioned for Dominic to join him at the quieter end of the bar. He looked earnestly at the priest, as if he had been expecting someone, someday, to ask for that particular can. It was, after all, his bar, and his duty to protect that particular object.

Glancing up to make sure they could not be overheard,

Billy's face became serious. He had seen something concerning. But there was business to attend to now.

"Before we go any further, you must answer three questions correctly. Are ya game?"

Dominic rolled his eyes, but then thought, *Well, of course, that makes perfect sense.*

"All right. I'm ready." Billy reached into his back pocket, retrieving his wallet. Opening it up, he retrieved a folded piece of paper, scanned it, then began.

Leaning in closer to Dominic, he whispered the first question.

"Who took the last confession of Cardinal Ottoboni?"

Dominic was confused but impressed. *How could this guy or Moshe possibly know of my involvement with Ottoboni?!* He thought back to his previous adventures in Venice, and answered confidently, "Antonio Vivaldi."

"Good on ya, mate. Next question: '*You are my hiding place; you will protect me from trouble.*' If not in Psalms, where is this verse located?"

Thinking back to recent events involving Opus Deus and the secret Masonic lodge Propaganda Due, he responded, a little uncertainly, "In the Vatican Bank?"

"Right-o again. Last question: Tell me, in Latin, what lies hidden behind Raphael's *Transfiguration.*"

Dominic was stunned. Raphael's *Transfiguration* hangs in the Pope's personal office! *This man, or whoever wrote the questions, was clearly given special privileges.*

He leaned in even closer to the bartender, whispering in his ear, "the Petri Crypta."

Billy said nothing more. He took the paper with the questions on it, lit a match to it, then set the burning note in the bar sink. Retrieving a stool from a closet behind the bar and positioning it in front of the archway, he reached up and grabbed the can of Keystone beer. Off the stool now, he handed the can to the priest.

"I wouldn't open that in here, mate. You know anybody else in Malta?"

"No, just the friends I came here with; they're sitting over there." He pointed in their direction. "Why do you ask?"

"A couple o' hoons just came in, and I can tell they're takin' a bit of interest in ya. Looks like they came up the back stairs, so they might have the front ones covered. But you've got a few options going out the front."

"Tell you what," Dominic said, hatching an instant plan. "I'll take two cold Keystone beers to go. I've got some other friends waiting out front too."

"Right you are. Where are you staying?"

"The Hilton."

"Okay, then. Fastest way back is to keep on a straight line when you go down the stairs, between Hugo's and the cab stand. That's Santa Rita, really sleazy street, lots of bars, strip clubs; they probably won't think you'd go that way, bein' a priest and all. That comes out on St. George's Road. Turn right there and take that to the five-way intersection a block away. Then take Triq il-Wilga all the way to the beach. That will lead you to the back door of the Hilton."

"Thanks, Billy, I really appreciate your help."

"No worries, mate. Now, let me see if I can slow these fellas down for ya...."

Returning to the table, Dominic made an obvious gesture of distributing the beers to the others. The 'hoons,' as Billy called them, were watching closely, despite the bartender's trying to distract them.

"I didn't order beer," Sabrina said, surprised.

Hana knew instantly what was happening. *"You found it!"* she exclaimed in a whisper, looking at Dominic.

"Yes, and the key is in one of these cans. But the bartender said there were a couple men in there watching me, so I assume I'll be followed. He's trying to distract them now. Marco, what would you suggest we do?"

The commando considered the situation. "We're going to

play a game of Three Card Monte, try to confuse and split them up.

"Hana, you take the actual can with the key and come with me. Rebecca will take a can, and Sabrina, you just take a Cisk, and Michael can take the other Keystone. I want us all to go down the front stairs and split up into three groups, each going a different direction, and we'll meet up back at the hotel. And be prepared for anything.

"Rest assured, *mon ami,*" Marco said with conviction, "the key will be safe."

Taking out his cell phone, Dominic called Karl, telling him of his success in finding the key and the team's extraction plan. "Wait until I leave, then you and Lukas follow me from a discreet distance. I made a show of taking a can of Keystone with me, so hopefully these guys will think I have the real thing and ignore the others."

Once the group had reached Santa Rita street, they all headed out in their various directions.

FROM THE SHADOWS of Hugo's Bar, Lorenzo Marchetti had his cell phone up to his ear as he watched everyone depart, then split up.

"*Merda!*" he said to the person at the other end. "They're taking different directions. They're probably on to us."

CHAPTER THIRTY

Once on the street, Marco and Hana went up another nearby set of stairs that led to a bridge taking them to the Bay Street Shopping Complex. From their own starting position, Sabrina and Rebecca turned left in front of the 8-Till-Late convenience store, heading toward Casino Malta. Dominic went directly up Santa Rita Street between Hugo's Burgers and a taxi stand.

Marchetti was upset, his expected plans disrupted. Still on the phone, he said, "A-Team is still in the Speakeasy and haven't come out yet. I'm sending B-Team after the girl and the Frenchman. I'll take the priest. Call A-Team and send them after the two women. Tell them they went toward the casino."

Walking up Santa Rita—a lurid section of town awash in flashing neon and scantily-clad courtesans beckoning prospective clientele from the doorways of their bawdy establishments—Dominic passed Angels Strip Club. Not far behind him, wearing a black overcoat and felt fedora, Father Marchetti stayed on the phone, relaying details of his observed activity to someone at the other end. He failed to notice the two Swiss Guards following some distance behind him.

As he passed the clubs, Dominic smiled at the sex workers, sympathetic to the plights that often drive people to such employment. As they in turn noticed his white Roman collar, the catcalls grew louder and more inviting, each of them wanting to tempt and defrock the handsome priest, as if he represented some kind of singular achievement. Drawing more attention than he wanted, he picked up his pace.

After crossing the foot bridge to the shopping complex, Marco pulled Hana aside. "We're going to do an SDR—sorry, a surveillance detection route—to determine if we've picked up a tail. As we pass by the various shop windows, I want you to use them as mirrors. Look behind us as we walk along, trying to see people who stand out for some reason. Remember certain features of them—big nose, high hair, red cap, blue glasses—even those with no outstanding features. Pick anything out and remember it, then keep those in mind in case we see them again. Then we'll know if we're likely being followed."

Then, taking his own advice by pretending to look in shop windows, Marco took Hana's hand and casually strolled down the crowded walkway between the shops. Descending a set of steps back down to street level, they crossed over and went back upstairs, returning to the Speakeasy, then again across the foot bridge. As soon as they reached the top they headed toward the entrance of the Hard Rock Cafe, looked over the menu in the window, then retraced their steps back across the foot bridge to the Speakeasy.

And there they were. Two young men dressed in blue jeans and black t-shirts, their greasy, black, medium-length hair blending in well with most other young men on the streets, had been seen more than once as Marco and Hana made their circular SDR. Marco now had them marked.

~

Entering Casino Malta, Rebecca and Sabrina strolled up the main floor walkway, beer cans in one hand, their bags slung over their shoulders. Changing positions, Sabrina passed behind Rebecca, her hand going into her own bag, then briefly into her companion's. As if by sleight of hand, Rebecca felt the weight change on her shoulder.

"Just a little something in case things get interesting. It's a Makarov I took off a dead Russian mobster in Florence last year. Unregistered and untraceable. So if you have to use it, wipe it down and throw it away. It's loaded eight plus one, safety on. I've got a Beretta Px4 in my bag. We're okay legally, since Italy and Malta have a mutual understanding on the official use of firearms, and I'm deputizing you now as a Carabiniere."

Having made a quick circuit of the casino, they noticed that—likely due to security reasons—there didn't seem to be any other public exits or back doors, only stairs and an elevator to the lobby and upper floors composing the Intercontinental Hotel. They sat down in front of adjoining slot machines where they could watch the front doors. Rebecca set her Keystone beer on the edge of the table in clear view to be seen.

They did not have to wait long before two men appeared looking just a bit too eager and alert. To the seasoned detectives, these guys were clearly looking for something other than gambling.

As the two men stood there surveying the casino, taking in every person, one of them locked eyes with Rebecca. She was accustomed to long looks from men, but this was different. Then she saw him glance at the Keystone beer and a keen look of recognition crossed his face. Smacking his buddy on the arm, he nodded in the direction of the two women.

Just then a young woman, probably in her early thirties, wearing black yoga pants and a gray sweatshirt with a fanny pack strapped around her waist seemed to appear out of nowhere. Stopping between the men and the detectives, she reached into her pack, withdrew a cell phone and a silver tube of lipstick, then activated the phone's selfie camera. As she applied the lipstick, she casually turned, using the phone to look over her shoulder and survey the room behind her. She passed over Sabrina and Rebecca without so much as a pause. Then she lowered her camera and saw the two men walking toward her, focusing on the women.

DOMINIC HAD NEARLY MADE it to St. George's Road when he felt a sudden push on his back just as he was passing by the descending stairwell of the Steam Gentleman's Club. He tumbled uncontrollably down the concrete steps into the dark alcove of the closed club and landed at the base of the stairs. Someone had followed him down, and a hand behind him kept crowding him into the corner, pressing against him to keep him in place. Dominic was in pain, but the surprise attack had his adrenaline up, and he shouted at whoever his attacker was, *"Hey, hey…Stop!"*

"I am told I cannot kill you, Michael, but apart from that, I can make things a lot more painful. Give me the key and that won't be necessary."

Dominic looked up into the twisted face of Father Lorenzo Marchetti.

"It *was* you I saw earlier!" he spat, the deep, aching pain in his ribs making him woozy. "What are you doing in Malta? And what the hell are you talking about?"

"Don't play coy with me, it doesn't suit you. Give me that fucking key. Now!" Marchetti pressed Dominic's head harder into the corner and brought a knee into his low back. The pain was excruciating.

"I don't have any keys!" Dominic shouted. "Search me if you want to!"

Marchetti began feeling around in Dominic's pockets, finding only his wallet, hotel key card, and the Keystone beer. He pulled out the can.

"How clever," he said, admiring the Keystone brand. "I don't know how they got a key inside this thing, but I'll be taking that." Marchetti stood up, holding the can up to inspect it more closely.

Suddenly, as he huddled in the corner of the dark alcove, Dominic heard Marchetti grunt and struggle. Looking up in the dim light, he made out a long arm wrapped around the priest's neck, his back arched toward his attacker. Someone was choking him! Moments later, Marchetti's struggles grew fainter, then stopped altogether.

Dominic was shocked to see Ernesto Vila breathing heavily as he stood over Marchetti's unconscious body.

"The key is safe?" he asked with anxious concern.

"Yes, but… how do *you* know about it?"

"No time for that now, Michael. But your friends are in danger too. We're attending to them as best we can, but right now you must get to Commander Saint-Clair's yacht as quickly as possible. Do not return to your hotel rooms, they are being watched."

Vila turned and ran back up the stairs as Dominic did his best to stand up. As he ran, Vila came upon Karl and Lukas who were looking for Dominic. He stopped them hastily.

"Our friend Father Dominic is in the stairwell there. He needs your attention and will explain what to do. I must go and find the others." With that, Vila ran off.

A few moments later, Karl and Lukas arrived and ran down the stairway.

"Sorry, Michael, we got hung up back there by Michelangelo's—and then you just disappeared! It took us awhile to find you down here. Are you okay? Who's this? And who was that going up the stairs?"

"Too many questions, Karl, give me a minute to catch my

breath." Dominic leaned against the grimy wall of the alcove and realized breathing was painful. Though he couldn't be sure, he thought he might have broken a rib.

"Okay… that was Ernesto Vila, a professor from Portugal; at least that's how I know him. I'm pretty sure he's on our side. And this is—or was—Father Marchetti, an American friend of Jonah Barlow's I met in Rome recently. Turns out he wasn't so friendly, shoving me down these stairs and attacking me, then demanding that I turn over the key. This is all too confusing. Everyone seems to know about these *keys*!

"But Ernesto was adamant that we get to Armand's yacht as soon as we can. The others are in danger as well, but Ernesto said they're being protected. Can't go back to our hotel, though, since bad guys are waiting for us there.

"Let's get to the marina. I know the way. I ran by it just this morning."

PASSING THE HÄAGEN-DAZS SHOP, Hana and Marco headed down St. George's Road toward St. Julian's Bay at a quick pace. Marco was looking for a particular kind of place, a position where they might have a better tactical advantage.

As they came to the end of the block next to a souvenir shop, he quickly assessed his options. They were standing at a five-way intersection, with meandering tourists and locals enjoying the seaside nightlife. A hard right would take them up an alley that didn't look too inviting. A left would take them to the shoreline. A soft right would take them up Dragonara Road back toward town.

Suddenly, the approach of running feet behind them, closing in rapidly, made him aware they were out of time. Grabbing Hana's arm firmly, he headed toward the pedestrian walkway to the right, along Dragonara, past the lively restaurants and shops.

The two men following circled around them, trying to steer them into an alley and away from the crowds.

The closer man tried to grab Marco by the elbow and push him into the alleyway, while the other guy grabbed Hana by both elbows, pushing her in the same direction.

Marco met his opponent's eyes. "So, this is how you want to play it?"

The guy smiled. "You have something our boss wants. Hand it over and you won't get hurt. Too much."

"I like it better when I don't get hurt at all."

The thug was on Marco's left, his right hand holding the Frenchman's left elbow. Seeing Hana being hustled into the alley, he knew he had to act fast. Allowing himself to be moved into the mouth of the alley, Marco reached over with his right hand and trapped the thug's own right hand against his elbow. Swinging his left hand down, he brought it back under the man's right arm at the elbow. Then with a push up and forward, he had the guy in an arm bar, with Marco's right hand controlling the thug's right hand, and with his left forearm now on the man's elbow, forcing him to bend over at the waist. A rapid palm strike with his left hand broke the thug's arm at the elbow. He then stepped forward with his left leg into the guy's armpit and pushed off, sending him head first into a brick wall with as much force as Marco could muster.

One down.

Standing as tall and imposing as he could, Marco slowly turned to the other man, who had by now switched from holding Hana merely by the elbows to holding her from behind with an arm around her throat, his hands clasped together.

"Keep back or I will kill her!"

"That would be a foolish thing to do, *mon ami,* because then there would be no reason for me not to kill you as painfully as I know how. I'll give you one chance. You let go of her and I'll let you run away up that alley. If you don't, well, things will get uglier than you are."

As Marco said that, Hana grabbed the man's arm with both hands and pulled down, holding his arm to her chest and dropping her weight. As she came down to her knees, she rolled her shoulder forward, just as Marco had taught her, and the man sailed over her back and onto the ground in front of her, landing on his back slightly stunned. When Marco's boot hit him between the legs, he was now immobilized and rolled into a fetal position, holding his groin and moaning. One more kick to the back of his head put a temporary halt to his suffering but would add a concussion to his symptoms when he woke up.

Just as Marco was helping Hana to her feet, a man came running down Dragonara. Marco assumed a defensive position, but the man was holding up his arms in surrender.

"I am a friend, senhor," Ernesto Vila said. "You may remember me from Michael's lecture in Portugal. I was just with him; he had been attacked—but he is fine now. Hopefully, his two Swiss Guard friends are now taking him to Commander Saint-Clair's yacht docked in the marina."

"My grandfather is involved in this too?!" Hana exclaimed.

"Yes, senhorita. And you also must go to his boat, the *Sea Chalet*. Do not return to the hotel, for these men are there as well. Your other friends, the two detectives, they are also in danger. Do you know where they were headed?"

"Yes, to the casino, I think they said," Marco replied.

With that, Vila turned and ran back up St. George's Road to Casino Malta.

As THE TWO men started moving toward Rebecca, Sabrina motioned for her to head to the back of the casino. Grabbing the Keystone beer, Rebecca stood and walked between the gaming tables in the direction of the rear of the massive room. She saw Sabrina walking parallel to her along the side wall.

The girl with the lipstick was now standing in the middle

of the casino near a slot machine, appearing to be talking on her phone. As she didn't stand out, neither detective noticed her.

Rebecca's cell phone rang. She fetched it from her bag and answered it.

"Go to the kitchen in the back, just beyond the roulette tables," Sabrina instructed her. "It's a door with a round window; I noticed it earlier when we surveyed the place. There's a service elevator nearby. I'll be right behind you."

Rebecca made her way across the dizzying, garishly-colored carpet common to all casinos and found the kitchen door. Pushing it open, she was blasted by the heat and scents of a large hotel kitchen, smelling of food aromas and an underlying odor of bleach. Long lines of prep tables and cooking stations staffed by several chefs and kitchen workers made for a challenging obstacle course, but she plowed through them anyway while trying to escape her pursuers.

The two men slammed the kitchen door open and pushed through it. Seeing their quarry weave her way through the line staff, one of them picked up a gleaming stainless steel chef's knife as he made for Rebecca.

Various employees shouted at the intruders, *"This is the kitchen…get out of here! You can't be here…get back in the casino!"*

Ignoring the shouts, the other guy moved to the farther aisle to cut Rebecca off before she could make it to the service elevator —or until his colleague could get to her first.

Then Sabrina rushed through the kitchen door. Quickly evaluating the scene, she fished in her bag for the gun, following the man who was running up the farther aisle in Rebecca's direction. Right behind her, Lipstick Girl flung open the kitchen door, coming down the nearer line at a brisk run, heading for the guy with the knife. Instead of the cell phone, her hand now held a black-and-yellow Taser X2. She was quick and lithe and easily dodged between the kitchen staff, making for the guy with the knife. Reaching him in seconds, her hand expertly extended, she let loose 50,000 volts on the back of his neck. He went down instantly.

Rebecca finally made it to the elevator and pressed the call button just as the tased man went down, but the other guy caught up with her as Sabrina was still in pursuit down the line.

"Give me the Keystone!" he demanded, sweat pouring down his face.

"You mean *this* one?" Rebecca asked, as she brought the can up under his chin with every bit of strength she had. The can split, spraying both of them with now lukewarm beer.

Sabrina came up right behind him and slammed the butt of her pistol on the back of his head. Grunting, he turned around and swung a fist at her face. She ducked and stepped back, pointing the Beretta directly at his chest.

"You can't shoot an unarmed man…."

"Don't think so? Watch me." She flipped off the safety and cocked the hammer with her thumb.

Behind him, Rebecca grabbed a meat tenderizer from a prep station, one of those stainless steel models with a smooth side and a knobby side. Choosing the knobby side, she swung it at his head, impacting the man's ear with a sickening crunch. He collapsed to his knees but was still upright—until Sabrina's leg came up and the heel of her shoe caught him under the chin. He went down backward, his head hitting the hard concrete floor.

Just as the elevator door opened, Lipstick Girl got up and ushered both Sabrina and Rebecca into the car, pressing the button for the lobby. Pulling out her cell phone and tapping a speed dial button, she reported, "The team following the two detectives has been neutralized. I'm sending the women to the commander's boat now."

"Who *are* you?" Rebecca asked, confused by the situation.

"That's not important now. Just know that you have friends on the island, Knights and Dames of Malta who work in opposition to those trying to interfere with your work. But you must leave quickly, before they regroup. Go to the *Sea Chalet* in the Portomaso Marina, close to your hotel. It's the biggest yacht on the docks, you can't miss it. But don't go back to your rooms, the threat level there is still too high.

"You may or may not see me again, but do take care of yourselves." With that, the elevator door opened and she ran out through the main entrance.

Sabrina and Rebecca just stood there, looking at each other.

CHAPTER THIRTY-ONE

Marco and Hana hurried past the Westin Dragonara Resort on their way to the marina. Still shaking with the release of adrenaline, Hana was exuberant.

"Did you *see* that?! I can't believe I threw him right over my shoulder, just like you taught me!"

"You were *magnifique, ma chère*. I am so proud of you," Marco said earnestly, pulling her in tightly as they kept walking.

"I can't stop shaking. Do you think I hurt him?" She looked up at Marco, who smiled.

"Maybe a little bit. Hopefully more…We'll work on making that throw more damaging and add a few follow-up maneuvers. You certainly gave me the opportunity to finish him off. We make a good team."

Hana remained silent, thinking of… well, everything. Then she said, "I do hope the others are all right. I should call Grand-père." She fished the phone out of her bag and tapped the speed dial button for Armand's personal phone.

"Hana!" he answered with obvious anxiousness. "How are you, my dear? Is everything all right? I hadn't heard from you in a while."

"Yes, Pépé, I'm fine. Well, Marco and I were attacked by a couple of ruffians, but we fought them off and got away. But someone from Portugal told us to go to the *Sea Chalet*. What's going on? Why aren't we going back on the Falcon?"

"Oh. Well, the pilots discovered a tracking device inside one of the plane's wheel wells. They figure it must have been placed there in Scotland. Obviously, given today's events, someone has been tracking you for some time. I've grounded the plane in the meantime, until it has had a thorough safety inspection and surveillance sweep. Do get here as quickly as you can, my dear. The hotel staff is—secretly, so as not to raise suspicions or tip off followers—collecting everyone's things from your rooms and it will all be delivered to the boat. Will we see you soon?"

"Yes, Pépé, we're just minutes away on Triq Dragonara. See you shortly."

Walking along St. George's Road, Dominic, Karl, and Lukas turned onto Triq il-Wilga heading toward the marina. Reaching the intersection of Church Street and Triq Dragonara, they spotted Hana and Marco across the street, walking at a brisk pace.

"Hey there... hold up!" Dominic shouted as the three of them joined their friends.

"Everyone still intact?" Marco asked.

"Yeah. You guys?"

"No real harm. Hana got first blood, so to speak. And we ran into your friend from Portugal, who told us to get to the baron's yacht *tout de suite*."

"We ran into him, too, and he told us the same thing. I have no idea what he's doing here in Malta, though it seems like he knows a lot more than we do about what's going on."

Then Dominic looked at Hana, his face etched with concern. "'First blood,' Hana? Are you okay?"

"Well, I've had better days. But I did manage to toss one of those goons over my shoulder and take him down. If it weren't for Marco, though, I might not be here to tell the tale." She looked up at the Frenchman with a proud smile that was not lost on Dominic.

"Alright, well, let's get to the *Sea Chalet* before anything else happens," he said. "Has anyone heard from Rebecca and Sabrina?"

Marco looked concerned. "No, come to think of it. I've been so focused on getting out of our own predicaments I had not thought about them. They said they'd be at the casino. I'll give Rebecca a call now. She gave me her number here, somewhere...."

While he was fishing for Rebecca's number, Hana gave Marco a peculiar look he didn't notice. But Dominic saw it. And with just a little shame, he smiled inwardly.

"No answer," said Marco. "It went straight to voicemail. Hopefully it's just on mute in her purse...."

They all kept moving down the last half block of Triq il-Wilga, passing a row of two-story condos painted a cream color with bright blue or teal shutters, seemingly ubiquitous to Maltese housing.

Approaching the Westin Dragonara Resort parking garage on their left, with a row of trailered boats across the street on the right, they heard a couple loud *pops*, and the windows of a car Hana was walking next to shattered in pieces.

Dominic grabbed Hana's arm, driving her onto the ground behind the car. Marco stepped in front of them both, drawing a Glock 19 from his shoulder holster.

"Shooter... behind the boats!" Marco said to Karl and Lukas. "When I engage, you try to outflank him."

The two Swiss Guards crouched low behind the car, waiting for Marco to provide cover so they could move toward cars on the other side of the garage to get an angle on the shooter.

Marco peered up, trying to get a location on the shooter, but another bullet whizzed by his head. He retreated back behind the car.

"*Merde!* He's got a damn good bead on me." While looking for someplace else to gain cover and engage with the shooter, another shot, then two more from different weapons altogether, were heard slightly farther away.

Marco risked another look up and was met with no other shots. Moments later, he saw Rebecca and Sabrina, pistols at a low ready, advancing in crouched positions toward a body on the ground near the boats.

He turned to Karl and Lukas. "Tango down. Let's go, but keep ready, there may be more of them." He reached down to help Hana to her feet, then gave Dominic a hand up as well. The Swiss Guards, both on full alert, kept a rear guard as they all advanced toward the boats.

While Sabrina was frisking the guy on the ground, she found a Beretta 92 FS with a suppressor attached. He had been hit with two rounds from Rebecca's 9mm Makarov. She kept him covered while the others approached.

"Well, this guy is down for the count," Sabrina said as she stood up. "Everyone okay?"

"Yes," Marco replied for them. "Where did you to come from?"

"When we got to the yacht and you weren't there, Armand said you were coming from this direction. So, we decided to come meet you, in case you encountered the same resistance we did at the casino."

Marco nodded. "And we did meet up with some resistance, but everyone was equal to the task. What happened to you two?"

"Nothing we couldn't handle, frankly," Sabrina said. "We'll trade war stories on the boat, but we should get moving now. I might have some shred of jurisdiction here, but even though I deputized her, Rebecca might not pass muster. The Maltese are fickle about such things."

She took the Makarov pistol from Rebecca, wiped it down with a handkerchief and hand sanitizer, then dropped it next to the body. In the distance, two-toned sirens signaled the need to leave the scene.

"Company's coming," Sabrina said. "Time to go."

DWARFING any other craft in the upscale marina, the *Sea Chalet* was no ordinary boat. Built by Benetti, one of Italy's foremost yacht builders, she was a fifty-meter Oasis with an eleven-meter beam. Sleeping up to twelve guests in six staterooms—as well as a ten-person crew with their own shared cabins—the *Sea Chalet* featured three spacious decks above and two more below, with a spiral marble staircase spanning all five decks. The lavish saloon sported some of Armand de Saint-Clair's most prized artworks, including those by Picasso, Miro and Basquiat. The handcrafted walls gave prominence to custom marquetry—a rare craft which uses pieces of veneer in an intricate pattern—portraying the seven wonders of the world: India's Taj Mahal, Rome's Colosseum, Peru's Machu Picchu, Mexico's Chichen Itza, Brazil's Christ the Redeemer, Jordan's Petra, and the Great Wall of China.

Dominic and his six companions finally made it to the marina and were hastily welcomed aboard the *Sea Chalet* by the crew standing by. One of the crew members looked familiar to Dominic—familiar enough to be his own brother.

"Hey, aren't you also the flight attendant on the baron's plane? Carlos, isn't it?"

"Yes, Father Michael. At your service."

"Good to see you doing double-duty here!" Passing him, Dominic joined the others gathering in the main saloon.

Marco had already taken off to run up to join the captain on the bridge, telling him they may still be in danger and that it would be wise to make a hasty retreat. Having been alerted to the situation by the baron, the captain had already instructed the mooring lines to be removed earlier and had been holding the boat to the dock with side thrusters. Once everyone was on board, he instructed the helmsman to head out to the mouth of the marina at max harbor speed.

As they were coming about to port, heading out to St. Julian's Bay, a crewman using night vision binoculars observed three men in a Zodiac rapidly heading toward them, one driving and two on the bow aiming rifles. He informed the captain.

"Marco," the captain said anxiously as he peered through the lenses himself, "that Zodiac has about twenty knots on us. We won't be able to outrun it. There's a marine shotgun in the locker under my bed, with some slugs and flares. That will give you a little more reach than your handgun."

Marco flew out of the bridge, down the steps and onto the lower deck where the captain's quarters were.

"I'll take the helm now," the captain told the helmsman, taking over the wheel. He opened up the boat's turbo diesel engines to maximum power causing the Zodiac to fall back a bit, but when the inflatable's driver gave it more gas the boat leapt back in the chase.

One of the men raised his rifle, aiming it at the *Sea Chalet*. He cranked off a shot that splashed about a meter off the yacht's stern.

He was aiming for a second shot, trying to time it with the bouncing of both craft, when the air was split by the blast of a marine foghorn from behind the Zodiac. A powerful searchlight was directed at the pursuing inflatable, as Maltese Armed Forces Inshore Patrol Boat 21 came past Exiles Beach, previously hidden from view in St. Julian's Bay.

Undeterred, the shooter on the Zodiac took another shot at the yacht, one that hit the stern swim step.

There was a *thud-thud-thud* as the naval crew member manning the Browning M2 heavy machine gun on the bow of the patrol boat stitched three rounds into the water right next to the Zodiac. Suddenly compliant, the driver shut down his engine and let the patrol boat overtake them, the three men now standing up with their hands over their heads. The driver knew his triple Volvo Penta engines could outrun the patrol boat—but he couldn't outrun that .50 caliber.

IN HIS STATEROOM AMIDSHIP, Armand de Saint-Clair's cell phone rang. Checking the caller ID, he smiled and answered it.

"Hello, Eliza. What's the news?"

Lipstick Girl gave the baron the report he had been waiting for. "Lieutenant Borg on P21 tells me you are cleared to depart, Commander. They will attend to those in the Zodiac behind you. Your quasi-diplomatic status here is sparing you a slew of legal entanglements, as you probably know."

"Yes, sometimes rank does have its privileges."

"It was nice seeing you again, Baron," Eliza Spiteri said. "I hope it's not too long before our paths cross again."

"I truly appreciate your help here, my dear. Know that you can call me for anything you need, anything at all. Until then, peace be with you."

"And also with you, Commander." They ended the call.

Saint-Clair picked up the ship's intercom and called the bridge.

"All right, Captain, with all due speed to Porto di Ostia, and keep an eye out for further interference. We might be on our own next time."

Hanging up, he headed out to the main saloon.

Addressing everyone, he said, "Please make yourselves at home. Our next stop is Porto di Ostia at the mouth of the Tiber River just outside Rome, about 380 nautical miles from here. It will probably take us about twenty hours to get there. Your things have been retrieved from the hotel and are being freshened for you. The crew will show you to your quarters when you're ready to retire. Meanwhile, enjoy the amenities aboard the *Sea Chalet*.

"Michael, Hana…I'm calling it a night, but I'll want to speak with you both in the morning. I suppose I have a few things to explain."

CHAPTER THIRTY-TWO

The next morning, everyone having had a feast of food prepared by the stewards last evening before a well-deserved night's sleep, they ambled in one by one and gathered in the main saloon. The galley crew had set out a hot breakfast buffet of scrambled eggs, bacon and sausage, pancakes, French toast, and a number of freshly squeezed juices as well as coffee and an exotic selection of teas.

"I know I've said it before, Hana," Sabrina noted, taking in the sumptuous morning feast, "but you do know how to live well."

"Hey, this isn't *my* boat," she corrected her with a coy smile. "My grandfather is the one who really knows how to live. The banking world has been good to him, sure, but not without the toll it takes on him. I worry about him these days. Though he's still going strong, he is in his nineties now."

"Wow. Coulda fooled me. He seems a much younger man, still vibrant and alert, truly engaged."

"Well, let's hope that's genetic," Hana replied.

Dominic strode up the stairs wearing clean jeans and his blue polo shirt.

"I could smell the bacon all the way down in my stateroom,"

he said, stretching and breathing in the fresh, salty air of the Mediterranean. "What a fantastic morning! It's good not being shot at, isn't it?" he asked of no one in particular, since they had all been shot at. Hana and Sabrina had already loaded up their plates, so he took his turn at the buffet.

"The boys sleeping in?"

"They're young," Hana said, "they need to restore their energy, especially after playing video games in the gaming room most of the night."

"There's even a *gaming room*?! What doesn't this boat have?"

"Grand-père likes to accommodate all tastes. The *Sea Chalet* even has a chapel, Michael, if you ever need to take solace."

Emerging from his master suite, the baron walked down the long, richly appointed hallway and entered the saloon wearing casual slacks, a blue blazer, and traditional Top-Sider boating shoes.

Hana and Dominic were enjoying their breakfast at a large, rectangular table on the aft deck, while Sabrina was now sunning herself on the bow with a mimosa in hand.

"Good morning, my dear. Michael," Armand greeted them as he prepared his own plate. "I hope you both slept well?"

Hana moaned. "I *love* sleeping on the *Sea Chalet*, Grand-père. Something about the rocking...."

"Well, we didn't have too much rocking last night. We kept up a pretty good pace on smooth seas. Still, we won't pull into port until late this afternoon. I trust your activities in Malta were successful, apart from the obvious?"

Dominic responded, "Yes, sir, I think so. We still have some work to do, though."

"Ah, well, so long as that doesn't require going back to Malta right away. I'll leave you two to it, in a moment. But I do need to explain a few things first. Hana, I believe, knows I've been a member of the Knights of Malta for some time now, but she probably does not know of the extent of my involvement.

"As you can imagine, my banking experience has allowed me

to offer significant assistance to the charitable efforts of the order, and now that I'm mostly retired, I spend a fair amount of my time seeing to the distribution of its charitable funds. As such, I am well aware of the activities of the various divisions of the order, since I help make sure they are sufficiently funded to carry out their duties. Also, because the Knights are involved in so many countries—assisting in disaster relief, medical care, and diplomacy regarding humanitarian aid and so forth—as you might imagine, there is a lot of intelligence that can be gained about world affairs arising from those activities. Some of that intelligence makes its way back to the Vatican, sometimes through me by way of the pope's Consulta, and sometimes through other channels."

"I never knew that," Dominic said.

"The current Holy Father knew. As Secretary of State, he was privy to much of the intelligence. When you're running a global organization like that, it helps to know what everybody's up to."

"Yes, I can well imagine. Sometimes I feel too insulated down in the Archives. It's a world unto itself."

"Well, Michael, you seem to do a pretty good job of getting yourself out into the world often enough, and you keep running into trouble when you do, or so I hear."

Both Hana and Dominic blushed. "I can attest to that," she said, laughing.

"Anyway, the Knights of Malta have become aware that these so-called Knights of the Apocalypse, all of whom have split from the Knights of Malta, are up to something. We aren't sure exactly what, but for decades they have been nothing more than a fringe splinter group that could largely be ignored. However, under Archbishop Challis's apparent leadership, the organization has grown exponentially in the last decade, which is why they are able to field new members all over the world, to advance whatever their agenda might be. And by the looks of it, it's a major one.

"The Knights of Malta are not the military order they once

were, but there is still a small contingent that takes on more sensitive or dangerous assignments. You could think of them like a private version of the American CIA. Though you weren't aware of it, several Knights and Dames of the order assisted you in Malta, especially when it became apparent KOTA was mounting a larger and more forceful resistance to your efforts in accomplishing your mission there.

"My being here was no accident. The Knights' leadership called me to an emergency meeting by secure videoconference, and since I was already sailing nearby, off Sicily, I brought the *Sea Chalet* into St. Julian's."

"Excuse me," Rebecca said as she entered the saloon. "I don't mean to intrude, but I need to speak with Michael for a moment."

"That's all right, Rebecca," Dominic said. "You can speak freely with Hana and Baron Saint-Clair here."

"I just spoke with my U.S. partner on the Barlow investigation. We were able to reconstruct some of the documents Father Barlow was working on before he was killed —*if* he was killed; we're still working on that. Anyway, we took the typewriter ribbon from his typewriter and did a forensic analysis. Much of the writing was the same as portions of the manuscript you showed me, but there was also the text of a letter, apparently to one of his sources, expressing concerns about discrepancies between the documents his source provided and copies from other sources. We don't know to whom the letter was addressed. It wasn't on the ribbon and the person was not mentioned by name, but Barlow basically accused this person of creating fraudulent prophecies."

"Well, that would put an interesting twist on things," Saint-Clair noted.

"A copy of Barlow's manuscript was taken from his apartment in Chicago," Dominic said. "If it was KOTA that took it, that might be the playbook they're operating under, thinking those are the actual prophecies that have yet to be revealed."

The baron looked concerned. "Well, we need to figure out what's going on pretty quickly. The global financial markets are in an uproar over these ridiculous prophecy revelations, especially in the U.S. Major swings in commodities futures occur as people react and then adjust to the new announcements. First the Prophecy of St. Malachy, and then that Nibiru thing. It's crazy. Just yesterday, the Dow Jones lost more than ten percent, and the VIX, the volatility index, hit a record high. They stopped trading for several hours until the markets stabilized. If you were betting on a panic, you could have made a killing."

Rebecca stiffened "Say that again…"

"I said, if you were betting on a panic, you could have made a killing?"

"What if you made a killing *because* you were betting on a panic?" she mused.

"I'm not following you."

"Could someone who has read the manuscript be investing in the market, *expecting* these announcements to cause a panic? And could Barlow have been murdered because he might have been on to something, especially if the prophecies were faked?"

"I suppose that's possible," Saint-Clair said, his eyebrows furrowing in thought.

"Baron, would you be able to look at the market data to determine if there was some investor who made a lot of money during this instability?"

"Well, yes, but it could take a while, depending on how sophisticated they were. They could be hiding under a series of shell corporations and automatic trading programs, numbered accounts in places with strict secrecy laws, and so forth. Many Caribbean islands make fortunes sheltering offshore accounts and making it difficult to track such transactions. I'll put some people on it and see what we come up with."

"I honestly think it's worth a shot. Here's my card. Could you let me know if you come up with anything? I'll see if we can put some feelers out on our end. I know a guy at the SEC from an old insider trading case. Started out as a homicide, but turned out the guy committed suicide because he knew the Feds were on to him. Anyway, I'll give him a call. And I have to call Chicago back and let them know what I'm following up on. Maybe we finally have a motive. Now all I need is a suspect."

Rebecca left to join Sabrina on the forward sun deck and began a phone conversation with someone in Chicago.

The captain had taken a run at Naples to get the yacht close to the coast and keep it within range both of cell phone towers on shore and of assistance from the Italian Navy and Coast Guard should they need it. It extended their sailing time a little bit but increased their security. Now they were on the way to the closest port to Rome, Porto di Ostia.

DOMINIC RETURNED to his cabin to fetch something. When he came back, he took a seat next to Hana and set down the fake can of Keystone Beer she had given him after they had boarded.

"I've been toying with how to open this thing since last night, but it had me stumped so I waited to have the gracious assistance of your puzzling skills," he said, smiling at Hana. "Up to the challenge?"

"Always! What have you got so far?"

"Well, it *looks* like a beer can, but it's quite heavy. I tested it with a magnet in my bathroom cabinet last night, and it seems the walls are made of steel, since aluminum isn't magnetic. The top turns, but it doesn't open like a screw cap. I'm afraid it might get damaged if we tried brute force. Which leaves Marco out of the picture."

Hana glanced at him with a rueful grin. "Didn't the Clavis Domini give you any clues, like he did at Rosslyn Chapel?"

"Yeah, he did, but I can't figure them out. He said, '*A dexterous man starts at prime, but a sinister man turns to sext when pushed. The last man returns to none.*' I have no idea what any of that means. Prime numbers, sexting, and nothing. I don't even know where to start."

"Well, we'll leave sexting out of it altogether, *Father* Dominic...."

The priest blushed, not even thinking of the word's trendy meaning until now.

"Don't give up, Michael. The Clavis Domini said you would be uniquely able to figure this out. We just need to determine what you don't know that you know.

"So, let's start with what we do know. We have a safe we have to open, and the top turns." Hana took the can and spun the top around. The top of the can was designed to look like a typical beer can, with a sealed spout and an opening tab. She tried to lift the tab, but it appeared to be welded in place. She felt the resistance as she turned the top, but nothing happened.

"Okay, well, it wasn't going to be that easy, but we had to give it a try. Now, let's start with the first line. *'A dexterous man starts at prime.'*

"A dexterous man is coordinated. Good with his hands, handy. Hmm. Hands. Clocks have hands. A handy clock? Okay, so then *'starts at prime.'* Prime is the first, or most important. Maybe that means one. One is the first prime. So, we should start at one."

She turned the top. "But what do we use as the reference point to know where we are on the clock?" She rolled the can around, looking at the Keystone logo. "Oh, the last three letters of Keystone spells 'one.' It's in italics so only the top point of the 'E' hits the edge of the can. I guess we'll go with that for now."

As if talking to herself, thinking through the process, she muttered, "Now, turn the can so that the 'E' on the side is at one o'clock, then turn the tab to one o'clock. Okay, then the *'sinister man turns to sext when pushed.'* Well, *sext* could be short for *sextus*, or 'six' in Latin, so push and turn to six o'clock." She pushed down on the top, and it depressed maybe a quarter of a centimeter. "*Oh*! That felt like something. Now turn to six o'clock...."

She continued turning the top clockwise until the tab was at six o'clock.

"Now *'the last man turns to none.'* None would be nothing. Or maybe zero, which on a clock is also twelve."

She continued turning it clockwise until the tab was at twelve o'clock. Then she pulled on the top. It didn't budge. Not even a bit.

"Damn. I was hoping this one was going to be easy. Maybe one of these turns is the opposite direction."

Dominic suddenly lit up. "Hey, I think that might be it! *Dexter* and *sinister* are Latin for right and left. So, when the *'dexterous man starts at prime,'* you turn it clockwise, or to the right, and when the *'sinister man turns,'* you go counterclockwise, or left. The last line doesn't say, but most locks go right-left-right, or left-right-left. This one probably goes right-left-right. Try it again."

Hana turned the top a couple times clockwise and stopped

with the tab on one, then pushed in the top and turned it left until the tab was at six, then let go and turned the tab to twelve.

It still didn't budge.

"Well, it was a good try," Dominic said. "We're obviously missing something, although I feel good about the left and right part, and the push part. There must be something else about *prime* and *sext* and *none* that we're missing."

Hana reached for her phone, opened a calculator app, and did a quick computation. "Assuming there are twelve possibilities, there are a little over seventeen hundred potential combinations. We could try them one by one, but that process could take hours, even days."

"*That's it!* Hana, you are brilliant!"

"Well, nice of you to notice, but what did I say?"

"It's the Liturgy of the Hours! Prime, Sext, and None are all times for prayers in the Liturgy of the Hours. In religious life, monks go to prayers seven times a day: Lauds, Prime, Terce, Sext, None, Vespers, and Compline."

"What time is Prime?"

"Six a.m."

Hana turned the top clockwise to six.

"What time is sext?"

"Sext is at noon."

Hana pushed the top in and turned it counterclockwise to twelve.

"What time is None?"

"Three p.m."

Hana let the top pop back up and turned the tab to three. Still nothing. The can wouldn't open.

Hana let out a frustrated sigh. "I thought we had it."

Michael put an arm around her, giving her a side hug. "Oh, come on. You are *not* so easily defeated. Maybe the problem is not with the numbers but with what we are using for the hand of our clock: the tab. Let's try it with the opening as the hand, instead of the tab."

"Hmm. Good point. Okay, here we go. Right to six, push in and left to twelve, out and right to three."

And the moment she finished, lifting the lid easily opened the can, revealing yet another little cardboard tube, just like the one at Rosslyn.

Both Hana's and Dominic's eyes flew open as they sported wide grins.

"It worked! *YES!*" she shouted.

She bounced in her chair like a schoolgirl, then leaned into Michael. She loved these times with him when they used their intellect rather than brute force to solve problems. And she knew Michael valued her for her intellect, not her money or her looks. That meant so much to her. Her eyes started clouding up with emotion.

"You okay?" Realizing he was holding her a little too long, he reluctantly let go.

"Sure. It's just that… well, we've been through so much to get these keys, I'm just happy we got them safely, and we're all okay."

Marco came up the stairs and into the saloon.

"Hey, I heard some shouting. Everything all right?" He surveyed the two of them.

"Yep, all good here," Dominic said as he moved his chair a nudge away from Hana's. "It took a little time, but we managed to get the second keystone open. We were just celebrating."

Getting up from his seat, he twisted the tube open and presented the second key to Marco. "You worked just as hard getting us this far, Marco. Relish the prize. So, mission accomplished. I'm going up top to check with the captain and see how much longer till we get to port."

He left Marco looking at Hana, and as he left, he heard Marco say, "Did I miss something?"

CHAPTER THIRTY-THREE

For days, scientists at the Mount Graham International Observatory had been harassing the media relations office to put a stop to the madness caused by Boris Ponomarenko's press conference.

The more respected among them even threatened to resign unless the observatory issued a clear and thorough statement denying the man's claims. Finally, the director acceded to his team's position and issued the following release:

> The Mount Graham Observatory has investigated the unauthorized press conference given by our former colleague Boris Ponomarenko.
>
> 1. We have reassessed the data relied on by Mr. Ponomarenko and determined that *none* of his calculations were accurate. There is no credible information that verifies even the existence of a rogue planet, much less one that could be heading toward Earth. It is not.
>
> 2. The DART mission is indeed headed to two near-Earth asteroids that do not pose a threat to our planet. This is a demonstration project to test approaches to deter yet-to-be-identified asteroids which might pose a threat to Earth at some

point in the future. The DART mission is not an attempt to deflect Nibiru, which as we have said, does not exist.

3. NASA has contracted with a number of clerics and theologians to explore the public's probable reactions to a discovery of life on other planets, should such a discovery ever be made, which it has not been. They are not being consulted regarding the end of the world due to a collision with a rogue planet that does not exist.

4. In cooperation with NASA, private enterprises are largely funding the mission to explore Mars with plans to eventually start a colony there. However, they are at least a decade away from a manned mission, and longer than that for starting an actual manned colony. This is not an effort by the rich to leave the Earth before an apocalyptic event that is not about to happen.

5. In response to his blatantly false claims and assertions, Mr. Ponomarenko has been terminated from his employment with the observatory.

We reiterate. There is no scientific evidence of the existence of any rogue planet, nor is any rogue planet headed for Earth. We hope this abates unfounded fears and conspiracy theories currently affecting the public.

LUCIFER TURNED off the news on the TV in his apartment after the press release was read on CNN. He glanced over at the stack of cardboard banker's boxes holding the balance of his work of more than ten years at the observatory.

Taking out his cell phone, Ponomarenko sent a text to a number he had committed to memory.

Lucifer: **Terminated**

The response. **Malta. Mdina. Three days.**

CHAPTER THIRTY-FOUR

Making good time cruising at thirteen knots, the *Sea Chalet* was still hours away from Porto di Ostia as the setting sun cast a stunning orange band of light across the broad western horizon of the Tyrrhenian Sea.

"'Red sky at night, sailor's delight,'" Marco quoted to Hana, his arm resting around her blanketed shoulders as they sat on the port side watching nature's dusky spectacle.

"What do you think lies ahead of us when we get to Rome?" she asked.

"Oh, I expect more of the same, frankly. Those guys are not likely to give up so easily, whatever is driving them. But we are prepared for most anything, *ma chère*. Do not be worried."

Just then the captain announced on the yacht's speaker system that Detective Felici would like everyone to join her in the main saloon.

Marco and Hana got up to move inside, while one by one—Dominic, Rebecca, Lukas, Karl and the baron—filed in from different doors to join Sabrina, who was standing at the head of the dining table. Everyone took seats, watching Sabrina expectantly.

"Okay, I think that—given we were attacked each time we

flushed out a key, in both Scotland and Malta—KOTA might try again, knowing we have possession of both keys now. At least we need to be prepared for it, regardless. Marco, Karl, Lukas, Rebecca and I have been kicking around some ideas. We wanted to run some of them by you three"—she nodded toward Dominic, Hana, and the baron—"to see what you think, since Michael is most likely the target of all this. Someone doesn't want you or those keys to reach the Vatican."

"Well, I'm game. What did you have in mind?" Dominic asked.

"We have to assume that the attack could come as soon as we're approaching the port. They could have a sniper anywhere along the shore, in a boat, in a car. Putting ourselves in their position, we've been thinking how *we* might kill you and get the keys, so we have some idea what we'd be defending ourselves against, and then what to do about it. The objective is to get you to the Vatican where the Swiss Guard can keep you safe."

"Gee, thanks. I think."

"Viewing it that way, we now have some idea what we'd be defending ourselves against, and then what to do about it. So, we ran through several different scenarios. One, we could have Shepherd Two fly over and pick you up off the yacht. Not sure the Vatican would permit that, but I'm sure you could have it arranged. But one problem with that could be that they would likely be surveilling the yacht and certainly would notice a helicopter hovering over it. We have no idea how much or the type of ammunition they have, and they just might decide to destroy the helicopter in order to get at you and the keys.

"Second, Fiumicino Airport is right on the other side of the Tiber River from the port, so it would be a quick ride over to the airport to send you back to the Vatican on Shepherd Two. We'd have to worry about getting you to the airport, and we can be fairly certain they are going to have watercraft ready for this type of maneuver.

"Third, Armand has a RIB—a rigid inflatable boat—on the

yacht, a smaller version of the Zodiac that was chasing us off Malta, and it's electric rather than gas-powered, so it's pretty quiet. And doing it farther out and in the dark should keep you out of their sight. One of the crew would take you and either Karl or Lukas off the yacht before we got close, take you ahead up the Tiber, and drop you off at Castel Sant'Angelo, where Swiss Guards can meet you and get you safely inside the Vatican.

"The rest of us will take a van from the Carabinieri and meet you there, kind of as a decoy. We were thinking that Carlos could wear your clerical garb and be seen getting in the van, while you and Karl go up the Tiber on the launch. That's really the plan we like best. Baron, would you mind loaning us one of your crew members?"

"Not at all," replied Armand. "Carlos is the perfect man for the job, and yes, I do see a resemblance now that you mention it. He could certainly pass for Michael."

Dominic thought about the plans. "I'm not all that keen on asking to borrow the pope's helicopter," he said with concern, "nor about asking Carlos to assume risks in my place. But it doesn't sound too risky going from the port to the airport, though I realize there are possible opportunities for an attack taking that route. Maybe the second, stealth option would be best. Being on the yacht is fine, but I'm also not too excited about riding in a little boat in the dark across the ocean."

"If you want, Michael, I could go with you," Marco suggested. "Marine commandos are great swimmers and trained in open water rescue. I couldn't let anything happen to you; Hana would never forgive me." He turned to Hana, who looked at him gratefully.

Karl stood up, gesticulating as he spoke. "No, I'll go. We were thinking that we would put a life jacket on you and cover both of us with a tarp, so it looks like only the driver is on the boat... try to throw them off further even if they do spot the launch. It won't look like anyone they'd be looking for."

"Okay, so it's just one crewman with Karl and me under a tarp in the boat. That works."

THE LAUNCH, a three-meter RIB with an electric water jet engine, was secured to the yacht on a platform behind the bridge. A winch-and-crane arm was used to lift the launch and lower it over the side of the boat. A crew member was lowered with the launch to pilot it back to the aft swim step of the yacht, where Dominic and Karl got in and ducked under the tarp. The crewman let the RIB drift back as the yacht pulled away, and then spun up the water jet, moving parallel to the shore.

It would take about two hours to get to the mouth of the Tiber, and then another thirty minutes to thread their way up the river to the steps of Hadrian's Bridge, which led to Castel Sant'Angelo, virtually next door to Vatican City.

AS THE RIB pulled up to the bridge as silently as possible, Karl pulled the tarp back and surveyed their surroundings. There was one man on the bridge over the river reading a newspaper by lamplight. A homeless person, dressed in rags and surrounded by his belongings, was huddled near the steps. A jogger was coming down the path. Dominic was about to stand up when Karl put a hand on his shoulder, exercising caution.

"Hold up. Before we left, I called a few friends from the yacht. We're just waiting for a signal that we're good to go."

The jogger stopped, looked around, then tied his shoe. The homeless man pulled off his knit cap and brushed the hair back out of his eyes. The man on the bridge folded up his paper and lit a cigarette. All three signals indicated no potential threats from their positions.

"All right, that's an all clear. Let's go."

As Dominic stepped from the boat onto the shore, the jogger

made a turn and preceded them up the stairs, keeping watch in the direction of Castel Sant'Angelo. The man with the newspaper had moved across the bridge about halfway, while checking his rearguard back across the Tiber. As Dominic and Karl walked up the ancient stone steps from the river to the bridge, the homeless man got up and started to follow them up the stairs, looking back down toward the river while carrying a large paper bag, his derelict clothing now enhanced with something much more tactical.

As Dominic reached the top of the stairs and started toward the Castel, a moped turned from a side street and headed toward the bridge at full speed. The jogger yelled *"Contact. Bridge. Far Side. Move the package—go, go, go!"*

The man on the bridge took off at a run to join the jogger, and when he got there, he turned and pulled a pistol from under his jacket aimed toward the moped driver. The jogger had also pulled a pistol from under his shirt with similar purpose.

Karl grabbed Dominic by the arm and started pulling him toward Castel Sant'Angelo. The homeless man had dropped his large paper bag to reveal a short sub-machine gun and was running along beside them. The man with the newspaper was speaking into his sleeve, *"Deploy the SRT, deploy the SRT. Stand by at the gate to receive the package."*

Dominic was almost to the tourist entrance of the Castel when the gate opened and six men dressed in black combat uniforms and carrying tactical gear, the Special Reaction Team, came through it. Four of the men ran past the priest and deployed to his rear. One stayed at the gate, and one covered the area behind them against any possible threats. The guy on the moped tried to make a run past the jogger and the newspaper man, but the jogger dived on him, knocking him to the ground, the moped skidding riderless on its side, a pizza delivery bag on the back flying open and spilling three large pizza pies across the road. The moped driver was quickly handcuffed and searched, but no weapons were found.

The homeless man and the six tactical officers covered Dominic as he was brought inside Castel Sant'Angelo for safety.

"Was all that really necessary, Gardist?" the priest asked them.

"Gardist? You don't recognize me, Father Michael? It's Dieter! Sergeant Dieter Koehl, Karl's friend. And yes, definitely necessary. It's getting crazy out there." Dieter glanced behind them just before the door closed.

Dominic looked back as well to see the jogger and the newspaper man stand the moped driver up and dust him off, apparently apologizing as they removed the handcuffs. Dieter just shrugged, then explained, "A bunch of fanatics has been protesting around the Vatican. Threats against the pope and the bishops. Not to mention the three attacks on you. So we took getting you back here pretty seriously.

"Now, let's get you inside the Vatican where you'll be safe."

THE *SEA CHALET* pulled into Porto di Ostia about eight o'clock that night. The deck crew went about their duties docking and tying off the yacht securely as Lukas, Carlos, Rebecca, and Sabrina gathered on the aft deck to disembark.

Sabrina had called ahead to Carabinieri headquarters and arranged for a passenger van to meet them, which was now idling at the end of the dock.

Before the team left, Dominic had given his clerical garb to Carlos, who everyone agreed resembled him enough to pass as Michael for the purposes of their plan.

Hesitant to be dressed as a priest—as if the pretense were sinful—but keen to please his boss and to be part of the action, Carlos had donned Dominic's black pants and shirt and his white clerical collar. Sabrina stepped off the yacht and gave the area a sharp reconnoiter, seeking anyone who looked out of place, or even the glint of light in a rifle's night scope. Seeing nothing, she signaled to Rebecca, who came down next. Both detectives waited at the dock, keeping watch while Lukas and Carlos stepped down from the yacht, then together they all walked hurriedly toward the waiting black van. Its door now open, they all got safely inside.

"Well, so far, so good," Sabrina said, letting out a breath of relief. "That was the part I was most worried about, where we were the most exposed as a group."

"Right," Rebecca agreed. "Now it's just a leisurely drive to the Vatican."

"Let's hope," her counterpart replied. "It's only about forty minutes to the Vatican on SP8, about the same as on the A91, but there is no such thing as a leisurely drive in Italy, so don't jinx us."

"Yes, I've discovered that in my time here, though I expect it's more dangerous being a pedestrian."

Within a few minutes, the van had made its way through the circuitous streets to Via Tancredi Chiaraluce, a wide boulevard that ran parallel to the Tiber. Looking out the back window several times, Sabrina noticed a motorcycle had been following them from a distance.

The van turned right onto the long access road to SR296 and started to merge into the highway when a black sedan that had pulled out from Ingresso Rimessaggio came at them from the left. The van driver swerved to the right and was forced off the highway, riding on the shoulder of the road as the sedan pulled up right beside them.

The passenger side windows of the sedan rolled down and two submachine guns emerged, aimed at the left side of the van. Both shooters pulled their triggers, raking the left side of the van with bullets. The van driver swerved even farther while applying the brakes in a panic stop. The van turned into the soft earth of a farm field beside the road, the right side tires sinking deep into the turn and bogging down, while the left side tires, still on the harder shoulder, kept going and caused the van to fishtail to the left. When the van was sideways to its direction of travel, the left side tires also entered the soft earth and bogged down, causing the van to start to tilt.

"*Hang on!*" the driver shouted. "We're going over."

Having slowed to thirty kilometers per hour, the van fell onto its left side and started to roll farther, but came back and skidded along the shoulder, the tires now free of the earth but with the van still on its side, gradually sliding to a halt.

The black sedan sped on up the highway, moving away from the incident. The motorcycle turned left at the intersection of SR296 and the port road, then crossed the Ponte della Scafa bridge, disappearing back across the Tiber.

With the van stopped and laying on its side, Sabrina was the first to unbuckle her seatbelt. Preventing herself from falling on Rebecca, she checked everyone's condition. Rebecca, who had been seated on the left side, had hit her head on the window as the van went over and was a little dazed, but otherwise fine. Carlos was also on the left side in the seat behind her, but was in worse shape, as was the driver. Lukas, who had been on the right side behind Sabrina, was hanging in his seat by the seatbelt, trying to unlatch himself without falling on Carlos. Sabrina crawled through to the front of the van, opened the glove compartment, and activated the police radio tucked inside.

"This is Detective Felici in Armored Van 3. We have been attacked; shots fired. I have personnel down. Our 10-20 is on State Route 296 just east of the Tiber. Requesting EMS and backup. I need two ambulances. Suspect vehicle is a black sedan, no plates. Last seen east on SR296."

Massaging her neck, Rebecca was mystified. "They shot at us, but no bullets came through!"

"Yes," Sabrina answered, "I had ordered an armored transport. The sides are lined with Kevlar and the windows are bulletproof. Not much help when they run you off the road, but it could have been a lot worse. I'll have one of the units run you back to your hotel after you're checked out at the hospital."

~

BACK ABOARD THE *SEA CHALET*, Hana and Marco were enjoying glasses of Merlot as they chatted with Baron Saint-Clair. Her grandfather was starting to show his age, and Hana was grateful for every minute she could spend with him before there was no time left.

Not that staying aboard the yacht was much of a hardship, despite the baron's preference that they sleep in separate cabins. Marco was, after all, an employee, and fraternizing with his protectee was frowned upon, especially by her doting grandfather, who otherwise oddly seemed to ignore their obvious closeness.

The launch returned to the yacht about nine p.m., and the crewman reported to everyone that he had seen emergency lights just past the Ponte della Scafa before he departed from the shore, suspecting foul play.

Concerned, Hana tried calling Sabrina, then Rebecca. Neither was answering her phone. But Marco was able to get through to Lukas, who gave him an update on their situation.

"I've already called Karl and told him I'm fine, everybody's okay, though we're going to get checked out at the hospital anyway. Carlos and the driver were pretty shaken up, but they should be good to go. We really owe Sabrina thanks for her foresight in getting an armored van... We were sprayed with machine gun fire, which would have definitely taken us out otherwise.

"We're just entering the Vatican now, Marco. I suppose we'll see you guys soon?"

~

DOMINIC WAS JUST WALKING through St. Anne's Gate, now safely back inside Vatican walls after what seemed like an eternity, when his phone rang. It was Hana.

"Did you make it through all right, Michael? Everything go as planned?"

"Yes, I'm fine. In fact, your cousin Karl had made arrangements with his Swiss Guard buddies to make sure we made it to the Vatican safely. It was all pretty cloak and dagger stuff…those guys are really amazing.

"God, it's good to hear your voice, Hana," he added. "And so good to be back. It seems like ages since I've been gone. I've already asked Father Bannon to have the Vatican locksmith recode the keys to the Petri Crypta tomorrow. Then we'll open the safe and get to the bottom of this mystery. Where are you now?"

"Still on the *Sea Chalet* with Grand-père. But I really wish you were too…."

For a few moments there was silence on the line as Dominic let this thought linger. "Where's Marco?"

"Oh," she said, as if an afterthought, "he's here as well."

Another pause. "Hana, enjoy your time with Armand. And Marco too. I'll be back in my apartment in a few minutes and be hitting the sack. We'll talk tomorrow, okay?"

After saying goodbye, Hana ended the call. She looked wistfully over at Marco sitting on the aft deck, a glass of wine in his hand.

CHAPTER THIRTY-FIVE

Magnus, the spiritual advisor for the Knights of the Apocalypse, was up late, sitting in his palazzo watching Italy's Rai News 24. A reporter live on the scene at State Route 296 was broadcasting video of the Carabinieri's black police van on its side as he spoke energetically about the violent attack and the fact that all occupants survived but were taken to the hospital for treatment.

Angrily punching the TV mute button, he picked up his phone and dialed a number.

"It's me," Magnus said.

"Of course, it's you. Who else would call me from this number?" said Nimbus.

"You need to dial it back. This last action was over the top."

"You wanted him stopped. I tried to stop him. He's a rather determined fellow, your priest, with surprisingly capable associates. What else could we do?"

"Yes, but you were specifically told not to hurt him!"

"Was he hurt?"

"Well, no, but according to the news reports, *he wasn't even in the vehicle!*"

After a brief pause, the response came, "That's impossible! We watched him get in the van!"

"Apparently not. He must have stayed on the yacht and used a double. You *are* still watching it, aren't you?"

"No, once the priest was in the van, I figured there was no need."

"You are an idiot. All right, you're off the case. Recall your BlackCloud goons, I'll take care of him myself."

As Dominic walked through the dark Vatican gardens on his way to Domus Santa Marta and the comfort of his own bed, he caught a whiff of night-blooming jasmine, which was just what he needed to put him in the mood for sleep. He stopped to admire the softly lit paradise that popes for generations had used for prayer and comfort, things he missed. He felt a need to say Mass soon, to get back to his priestly duties and his life working with precious ancient documents in the Secret Archives.

But that would wait until KOTA was stopped.

Two Swiss Guards were placed on either side of the doorway to the Domus, since the building also held the papal apartments. Dominic greeted both men, whom he knew, and entered the building. Making his way up to the second floor, he opened the door to his rooms.

Before even crossing the threshold, he knew something was wrong. Flipping on the light, he found his apartment in utter disarray. It had been thoroughly tossed. Drawers opened, contents dumped onto the floor, clothing from his closets ripped off the hangers, their pockets turned inside out.

But how?! This is the Vatican! How could anyone get past the guards?!

He took out his cell phone and called the Vatican switchboard.

"*Pronto, Vaticano.* How may I direct your call?"

"Teri? Is that you?"

"It is, Father Michael. How can I help you?"

"I need the Gendarmerie here. Now. While I've been gone someone got into my apartment and tore up the whole place. It's a wreck."

"I'll put you through, but I doubt anyone will be there until the morning. You know how they are—"

"Then exercise a little pressure. I want them to find what they can before I get some sleep."

"Of course, Michael. Hold, please."

By the time the Vatican police had left, they had found only one clue as to who was responsible: on Dominic's nightstand they found a black business card with nothing but a seven-pointed star on the front.

The message was clear to the priest. KOTA could get to him. Anytime, anywhere. Even here.

The Gendarmerie had apparently reported the break-in to the Swiss Guard. Before long, there was a knock at Dominic's door. Dieter Koehl stood there, grim-faced.

"Karl is over at the hospital picking up Lukas, so I guess you're stuck with me a little longer tonight. We will have someone outside your door all evening, Father Michael, and will escort you to your office in the morning. Let me give you a hand getting this place back in order."

"Thanks, Dieter. And thank you for being there earlier. I really appreciate it."

When they had gotten the apartment fairly reorganized, Dieter said, "I'll be right outside your door for a couple more hours until I'm relieved. Another guard will be here and will take you wherever you need to go in the morning. If this is an inside job, Father, we can't take any risks."

"Thanks again, Dieter. See you soon."

And with that, Dominic fell onto the bed and into a deep sleep.

THE NEXT MORNING, he showered gingerly, as the events of the night before had left a few bruises, especially from when he was bouncing along on the bottom of the launch for two hours.

Now dressed and ready to face the day, Dominic reached into his bag, withdrawing the two keys they had spent the past few days recovering, put them in the pocket of his cassock, and headed out to meet with the locksmith.

The Swiss Guard outside his door was standing at parade rest, his arms loosely held behind his back, as he stared forward. When Dominic emerged, he snapped to attention.

"Good morning, Father Dominic," he said smartly. "Where to, sir?"

"Good morning. We're going to the Apostolic Palace, the pope's office."

They made their way through the Vatican gardens, around St. Peter's, and into the Palace. Alighting from the elevator to the papal offices, Dominic released the guard and greeted the pope's secretary.

"Hi, Nick. Gosh, it's good to see you again."

"I'll bet," the affable Bannon replied. "I hear you've had quite the week."

"You don't know the half of it. Is the Holy Father in?"

Yes, he's in there with Cardinal Greco and the Vatican locksmith. They're all waiting for you. I'll buzz the doors open."

"That's a quaint phrase. When did this happen?"

"It's a new security feature—given the more violent protests on the streets of late." Bannon was referring to the installation of controlled access to the Holy Father's private office. A button pressed beneath Bannon's desk disengaged the magnetic lock and allowed access to those permitted by Bannon alone. As he heard a soft buzz, Dominic opened the door and entered the office.

The pope and his Secretary of State were standing, talking with a man carrying a small toolkit.

"Good morning, Holy Father, Your Eminence. And you must be the locksmith. I'm Father Dominic."

"I am Luca Balzano, at your service, Father." The two men shook hands.

"His Holiness has just been telling us of your travails in reclaiming the spare keys. I must ask, though: is there any hope of recovering the originals?"

"Well," Dominic said, "while we have our suspicions, Luca, we don't know for sure who took the original keys, so it's an unknown at this point."

Balzano set down his toolkit on a side table.

"Cardinal Greco's key will not open the safe itself," he said. "It can only be used to recode the pope's key. But the pope's key can be used to both open the safe and recode the Secretary of State's key to a new owner. The spare keys have never been coded to anyone, so they can still be set up with the encoder I have brought with me."

Using the key encoder, Balzano paired Cardinal Greco's biometric key to his right thumb, then together with the Secretary of State's key, they encoded the pope's biometric key to Pope Ignatius' thumbprint.

Once that process was complete, the pope pulled back Raphael's *Transfiguration* painting on hidden hinges, revealing a large wall safe, the Petri Crypta. The pope inserted his key, then placed his thumb on the print reader. From inside the safe a single beep was heard. Then the pope turned the key, and the steel locking rods retracted from the lock assembly, releasing the door, which opened just slightly.

"All right," the pope said. "The safe is finally open. Cardinal Greco, I trust you'll keep a very good watch over your key. Signor Balzano, I understand your concerns regarding having no more spares. We may know more soon regarding the originals' whereabouts, I hope. But if not, let us look into replacing the safe with something that has solid security, but is more manageable.

"As for now, I must ask everyone to leave. I do not know what things may be stored under this seal—for the pope's eyes only—and I take that charge quite seriously."

"I understand, Your Holiness," Dominic said. "Would you please let me know as soon as possible if the documents we were looking for are in there? That may help us decide what to do next, and I would like to compare the actual prophecies to the manuscript from Father Barlow."

"Of course, Michael. I will call you as soon as I have inspected what lies within."

SEVERAL HOURS LATER, Nick Bannon called Dominic's office.

"Michael, His Holiness would like to see you immediately. But I must tell you, he's quite upset...."

Dominic dropped everything and ran to the Apostolic Palace, anxious to hear what the pope discovered. Hopefully, he would be able to share everything.

After Bannon buzzed him in, Dominic found the pope sitting behind his desk, his head in his hands. He appeared to be sobbing.

"Holy Father, are you all right?"

Pope Ignatius looked up, his eyes puffy and red.

"I'm afraid I have terrible news, Michael. I have gone through the contents of the safe, and the Third Secret of Fátima is not there! Whoever took the keys must have had full access. He must have encoded the pope's biometric key to someone else who opened the safe. It's the only logical answer. In any event, the Third Secret is not there, and I do not know what else might be missing."

Dominic took a seat, equally distressed over the predicament.

"I would bet my life that Fabrizio Dante is the culprit here,

Holiness. He *was* Secretary of State, remember. And this is just the kind of devious mischief such a depraved scoundrel would take. Don't forget, he has scores to settle with both of us."

"That may well be, my son. But it's not what I *didn't* find that upsets me—it's what I *did* find. You might well imagine the kinds of things that might be secured in a safe intended for the pope's eyes only. But you could never imagine what I've discovered. Reprehensible details of investigations into our clergy, the sheer scope of the problems—they are simply overwhelming. Even as Secretary of State, I never knew how deeply these things had impacted the Church. My heart grieves to now know what has been done by supposed men and women of God.

"Then there were other things. Oh, my dear Michael. Be grateful you do not know. If I had any idea of the scope of such vile information, I would have declined the papacy rather than to learn what I now know. Things I cannot un-see."

Standing up and moving to the window, the pope looked out over St. Peter's Square. Dominic had never seen him so distraught.

"I'm here for you, Father. Whatever I can do, whatever burdens you may need to share, I'm here."

"No man should have to suffer the knowledge I have been given, Michael, and I will not do that to you. I love you too much. Now go. Go back to work. This is my burden alone. This is what Christ has called me to, and I will bear it as my cross, as he bore his."

Dominic went over to his father, pulling him into a warm embrace. Then he quietly turned and left the room, emotion gripping him.

On the way out, Nick Bannon arched his eyebrows with an inquiring look. Michael shrugged disconsolately, then headed back toward his office.

He only got a short way before he, too, began to sob.

CHAPTER THIRTY-SIX

In the offices of his Washington, D.C. archbishopric, Cardinal Damien Challis was sitting at his desk reading and preparing for his next sermon when his program director knocked on the door.

"Come," Challis said bluntly.

The man entered the office. "Your Eminence, a courier just delivered this document from the Vatican. From the pope's personal office, no less! I haven't opened it, of course, since it indicates it must be opened immediately and only by you."

"Well, let's see what the old geezer wants, shall we?"

Challis ripped opened the richly embossed envelope, then read its contents aloud.

> "'Your Eminence, Cardinal Challis'…blah, blah, blah…'You are hereby summoned to appear before the *Congregatio pro Doctrina Fidei* in three days' time. An inquiry is being made into the activities of the organization known as the Knights of the Apocalypse, and its participation in statements regarding prophecies which are not in conformity with established Church doctrine. During the course of this investigation, you are not to celebrate Mass, nor participate in the celebration of Mass, nor

may you hear confessions nor conduct any other ecclesiastic ceremonies or sacraments in the name of Holy Mother Church.'"

"Goodness," Challis said, his voice dripping with sarcasm. "It looks like I'm being suspended. That's not very nice of him. Well, obviously I'm not going to this charade of an inquisition of theirs. We'll tell them I've got a previous engagement. But let's give them a little spectacle in the meantime, shall we?"

"What did you have in mind, Eminence?"

"Issue a press release that I have been requested to come to Rome to lead a seminar for the Curia educating them on the secrets that have been entrusted to us. That we have graciously agreed to come at the request of the pope and have chartered a flight to get us there as quickly as possible, so that we may bring the truth to the whole Church while there is still time. We'll make a big show of getting on the jet, with media at the airport, waving up the airstairs. All that stuff. Can you make that happen?"

"Yes, Your Eminence, absolutely. And the jet… where will it actually be taking you?"

"Why, to Malta, of course. For the Last Mass."

CHAPTER
THIRTY-SEVEN

Early the next morning, Dominic got up, put on his favorite running shorts, a loose-fitting T-shirt with the sleeves cut off, and his well-broken-in Saucony shoes, and headed out the door. Waiting for him in the hallway was Karl Dengler, also dressed for a run, but with a bulky fanny pack around his waist.

"Morning, Karl. I guess you guys were serious about the escort."

"You bet, Michael. Pope's orders. Someone from the Guard will be shadowing you during the day or standing post outside your apartment and office for the foreseeable future. Kind of unusual, I know, but these are unusual times."

"I guess so. Well, I've got a full day ahead, so let's get going. We'll run through the Suburra this morning. It should be pretty quiet this early."

"It's good to know we're not running *from* something, isn't it? Just out for a pleasant morning. I hope."

DESPITE THE LEGION of protestors surrounding the Vatican, with many carrying signs proclaiming "the end of the world is near,"

Dominic and Karl finished up their run without incident, stopping in at Pergamino Caffè on the Piazza del Risorgimento for a quick espresso before starting their workday. The sun had risen a short while earlier, and its warmth flooded the sidewalk outside the café, where each man took a seat at one of the small tables.

"You hold the table; I'll go get our coffees," Dominic said.

Inside he went to the counter, where the delightful Signora Palazzolo was smiling as he approached.

"*Buon giorno,* Padre," she said, her hand coifing her wisps of gray hair for the handsome young priest.

"*Buon giorno,* signora. Just two shots of espresso, *per favore*."

Dominic enjoyed his morning ritual with the pleasant barista, and it felt good being back to his normal routines, especially given the past week's excitement.

Paying for the drinks, he took hold of them and returned to the table outside.

"Michael," Karl began, "I just wanted to apologize again for Lukas and me losing you on Malta in that alley. Michelangelo's caters to… well, a largely male clientele, and the guys outside kept trying to pull us in to dance. While that might have been fun, I knew we had been assigned to your rear guard detail."

"No worries, Karl. The fact is you showed up when I needed you most. It was weird seeing Professor Vila there, too, but I'm glad he was. I'm still mystified by it, though."

"Yeah, there was a lot of crazy stuff going on there. Like that guy who was shooting at us over by the boats. He had some kit on him that I'd seen before, in Africa, when the Swiss military was doing some UN work in the Sudan. These private security contractors work for an outfit called BlackCloud, also known in Latin as *NubesNigrae*. They wore a lot of the same stuff. Kind of strange to see a guy in Malta wearing a specialized outfit like that. I thought these KOTA guys were just a bunch of religious fanatics, but BlackCloud is a huge, multi-national private security company, very much a private army. Many corporations hire them to protect their operations and personnel in areas suffering political unrest. They are always very well equipped, and anyone who kills someone in action is awarded a special dagger called a RainMaker. That guy Rebecca shot? He had one. Then there were the 5.11 tactical pants and the Under Armour boots. Anyone can buy those, they're very popular. But wearing them together was like a uniform for those BlackCloud guys."

"That's actually pretty scary, Karl. A private army? Possibly helping KOTA?"

"I'm in that business, so to speak, and even *I* thought it was scary."

Finishing their espressos, they made their way back to St. Anne's Gate, where a plainclothes Swiss Guard in a black business suit was waiting to take over for Karl, who, after saying goodbye to Dominic, headed back to the barracks to change into his standard uniform.

With his new escort in tow, Dominic returned to his apartment, where he showered and dressed in his clerical suit. Since he had been gone for a few days, work in the Archives had just piled up, and there was much to do.

On arriving, he checked in with Ian Duffy, hard at work in the digitizing lab scanning the contents of the second of fifteen *armadi* in the Archives' Miscellanea section.

"Good morning, Ian. How's it going?"

"Hey, Michael. Just starting in on the second cabinet today. No briefcases in this one; I checked...." He grinned at the memory of finding the briefcase of Italian banker Roberto Calvi in the first cabinet, where it had lain hidden for over forty years since Calvi's murder—Duffy's exciting first week of work many months earlier. Getting the rest of the documents archived in that first cabinet had taken awhile, but he was finally just starting in on the second one. He felt good to have settled into a routine in the lab, one that didn't involve so much danger and intrigue.

Dominic then moved on to the preservation lab, where one of his papyrologists was working on deciphering a mildly deteriorated scroll using their newest piece of equipment, a digital high-energy X-ray machine, one that could reconstruct a rolled-up document by analyzing the layers of ink making up the characters on each page.

Using photographs of scroll fragments with carbon-based writing visible to the naked eye, the X-ray scans were combined with artificial intelligence to pick out and distinguish subtle differences between inked areas and blank areas. Once properly trained, the system could extract data from intact rolled scrolls to reveal the written text within, allowing the technicians to read a whole host of documents that were so old and fragile there could be no attempt made to unroll or separate their pages.

Dominic was enthralled with this new technology, envisioning a new day when, soon, the millions of ancient, previously undecipherable scrolls under the Vatican's care would give up their long-held secrets and add to the world's knowledge of historical people and events.

A SHORT WHILE LATER, Monsignor Diego Ferretti, the papal heraldist, entered the Vatican through St. Anne's Gate, bound for the Apostolic Palace and the pope's office.

While most areas of the Vatican had posted security officers from the Swiss Guard, areas connected to the papal apartments and the Holy Father's office had a higher level of screening, with metal detectors and the requirement of special visitor badges. Obviously, no weapons were permitted, and only authorized personnel were allowed entry.

Since he was still working with Pope Ignatius on the final details of his papal coat of arms and a number of other papal insignia, Ferretti had already been given a badge allowing him unrestricted access.

Ferretti hobbled up to the security station like he had every day for the past two weeks, leaning heavily on his cane. It was beautifully crafted, with a wooden pistol grip T-handle made of highly polished burled walnut, a bronze metal shaft, and a black rubber tip. Simple, but elegant. And more than useful for walking.

As he went through the magnetometer, the buzzer sounded, indicating metal had gone through the archway. He reached out to hand over his cane to the officer manning the accessories bin but started to stumble and caught himself with the cane. The security officer quickly caught Ferretti by the armpit and stabilized him, making sure he stayed on his feet. Nervous, Ferretti began to sweat.

"Oh, my!" said the old man. "That was a close one. Goodness, thank you for your assistance. I'm glad I had my cane. You may take it for inspection now."

"No need, Monsignor," the security officer said helpfully, turning to his colleagues. "I've seen this cane a dozen times the last couple weeks. You can let him through, he's cleared."

The security officer on the other side of the magnetometer stepped aside and let the old man through.

Ferretti hobbled away from the security station, heading for the small office that served as his temporary work area. On the way, he wandered past the pope's outer office, where Nick Bannon was at his desk, just hanging up the phone.

"Good morning, Monsignor," he greeted the old man.

"Good morning, Father Bannon. You look busy this morning."

"Yes, I just got off the phone again with our media relations folks. Ever since His Holiness decided he was going to make a public statement on this whole End of the World nonsense, they've been running in circles getting things ready. Sounds like every reporter and TV crew in Europe is going to be there. The Swiss Guard is clearing St. Peter's Square now, and he will speak from the steps of the Basilica."

"Yes, I was at my main office when that call came in. It got very busy over there in a hurry. I decided to come over here and get away from the craziness. What time is the pope's address?"

"It's set for eleven thirty, so they can make the noon news shows."

"Very good. I'm sure you have a lot to do, Nick. Maybe I'll wander down and watch it from the sidelines."

AROUND ELEVEN FIFTEEN, Dominic was downstairs, deep underground in the Miscellanea section of the Archives, looking for a particular manuscript that Cardinal Greco wanted to review, something he wanted to use for a papal encyclical he was working on.

His mind returned to the previous night, when the Holy Father had opened the Petri Crypta, and how whatever he had found in there had shocked and unsettled him so, despite the mysterious Third Secret of Fátima having gone missing. His heart went out to him, only imagining the burdens that must be weighing on him now.

As Dominic stood in one of the many kilometers of shelving aisles looking for the document, Dieter Koehl came down to relieve the other security guard, who was going off duty.

"Good morning, Father Michael. Everyone else is busy, so you must put up with me again."

The priest groaned. "This whole 'dignitary protection' thing has me rattled, Dieter. I'm not worthy of this kind of valuable resource. I'll have to speak with His Holiness. I hardly need protection inside the Vatican.

"And what's got everybody so busy this morning, anyway?"

"The Holy Father's press conference. Should be happening in a few minutes now."

"*What* press conference?"

"The pope is giving a public statement about this End of the World fanaticism from the steps of St. Peter's. Press from all over

Europe and America are gathered, plus the usual crowd of onlookers."

Dominic thought for a moment, then suddenly panicked.

"Jesus, Mary, and Joseph! No! That was foretold in the manuscript! We've got to stop him, now. They're going to try to kill him!"

"Who? What are you talking about?"

"KOTA! They must have Barlow's manuscript about the prophecies. One of them says the pope will denounce the announcement about Nibiru and will be struck down. And they are going to be the ones who strike him down!"

Dieter jumped into action, the safety of the pope paramount in his duties.

Pulling out a handheld radio from his belt, he spoke anxiously into it, calling his Watch Commander: *"DP3 to WC, DP3 to WC! Emergency Traffic! Over!"*

Nothing but static. They were too far underground.

"DP3 to WC, DP3 to WC! Emergency Traffic! Over!

"Come with me, Michael. We must get up there."

CHAPTER THIRTY-EIGHT

The Swiss Guard and other security personnel had cordoned off the staging area in front of St. Peter's Basilica where the pope would give his address, with hundreds of olive-green wooden barricades keeping the crowds of onlookers and protesters confined to the oval area set back from the ancient church's façade.

The long, concrete ramp and steps leading up to the basilica were packed with the world's media, their tripods and cameras creating an electronic forest filled with snaking cables and crates of equipment scattered on the cobblestoned Square.

The Press Office of the Holy See had erected a small dais between the central pillars at the front of the basilica, as well as a lectern from which the pope would speak to the faithful. The Holy Father's new coat of arms was emblazoned on a massive silk banner hanging from between the colonnades to the entrance of St. Peter's, just behind where the pope would speak, something the papal heraldist had insisted on as its first introduction to the world.

Monsignor Diego Ferretti wanted every reminder possible of just who this pope was, and the coat of arms he had designed was intended to do just that. With the pope standing right in front of it while speaking, the juxtaposition would be dramatic. Soon, the hidden meanings would become clear, and that part of his mission would be accomplished. There was but one thing left to do.

Before leaving his office, Ferretti appraised the two canes in his office. They were practically identical. He had been carrying one into the inner sanctum of the Apostolic Palace, into the papal offices to his temporary office, for some two weeks now. Everyone who mattered was accustomed to seeing him hobble around with a cane. The distinctiveness of its burled walnut handle and bronze shaft was one thing—but nobody forgets a man who walks with a cane.

The cane leaning next to it could have been its double. But it had its own unique build. The bronze shaft in the real cane was hollow. But in the double, about half of its length had been drilled out and rifled, the top end chambered for a single .22 long rifle cartridge. The remainder of the shaft had been drilled out even larger and was filled with a series of baffles that would trap, cool, and disperse the gasses produced by firing the makeshift weapon, ensuring the shot was nearly silent, especially when using sub-sonic ammunition whose velocity did not exceed the speed of sound. With no supersonic crack, and no rapid expansion of gasses at the muzzle, this weapon was as silent as a gunshot could be made to be.

Even the rubber tip of the cane acted as a final seal to the suppressor. It had a notch cut in the side that acted as a front sight. The firing mechanism was cocked by pressing the T-handle down, which pulled the striker back, catching it on the sear, and causing the small spur trigger hidden beneath the handle to protrude below the grip of the cane.

Ferretti took the cane gun with him, leaving the other cane tucked behind his desk to keep it from view should anyone happen to look in his office—not that he expected that in the brief time that was left.

Hobbling down the hallways, greeting the same people he had passed on any other day, Ferretti made his way down to St. Peter's Square.

Since he had already been screened and cleared as a member of the papal entourage, he entered the Square from the door reserved for trusted employees. He presented his Press Office credentials to the guard and was admitted to the restricted area in front of the basilica.

Limping up the wheelchair ramp on the right side of the staging area, he excused himself past others, a couple in wheelchairs and others feeble or elderly. Finally, Ferretti stopped in the right position and looked out over the spectacle. More of the green barricades, covered in white cloth, had been erected at the top of the last flight of steps leading to the stage. Another row of barricades stood at the bottom of the steps, so that the last flight of steps formed a buffer zone between the media and the papal entourage.

The flat open area below the steps was occupied by a mass of press and media personnel, making last-minute adjustments to cameras and microphones. Some of the reporters were doing live introductions of the imminent address by the Holy Father. From where Ferretti stood, against the metal railing of the wheelchair ramp, he had a clear view of the podium at which the pope would speak, about twenty-five meters away from him.

The massive bronze doors of the basilica opened, and the papal entourage emerged into the late morning sunlight. An auxiliary bishop came to the tented podium and made a couple opening remarks, then gave a brief prayer to the assembly.

Then Pope Ignatius stepped up to the podium, his pure white cassock billowing in the light breeze and gleaming in the sun. Even at his advanced age, the pope was a man of surprising vigor, and he climbed the several steps to the top of the dais without using the handrails for support. He paused at the lectern, looking out over the sea of media and beyond to the thousands assembled in the square below. Many carried signs announcing the end of the world, and some denounced the pope or the Church for hiding the truth, while others championed other pet causes. But most were those faithful to the Church and to this beloved pope in particular. He gripped the sides of the lectern and began.

"My brothers and sisters, may the peace of our Lord be with you." He paused for the crowd to render the traditional response, "And also with you."

"We live in tumultuous times," he continued, "with so many entities vying for our attention. We hear so many conflicting things that it is hard to know where to turn for the truth. But I say to you here and now that the Church, this holy Catholic Church, is the repository of truth."

As the crowd vocally responded with their approval, Ferretti took his cane and rested it on the top rail of the ramp, pointing in the general direction of the pope, but not directly at him. A plainclothes Swiss Guard stationed on the right side of the dais noticed the movement and spoke into a radio mike at his wrist, alerting security forces closer to the stairs and the wheelchair ramp to investigate.

Just then, Father Dominic and Dieter Koehl came through the security checkpoint for employees, the same one that Ferretti and others had come through earlier. They scanned the crowd. Dominic had no idea how KOTA intended to attack the pope, only that he was all but sure that this would be the time and the place, based on the wording of Jonah Barlow's manuscript and the pope's specific announcement topic. Michael looked up at the banner of the Papal coat of arms. The motto was still *Faithful to the Last*. Ferretti must be part of KOTA! Dominic could see now how that coat of arms would play into their agenda.

The priest and the Swiss Guard started to move through the crowd toward the dais. The steps were blocked by a crowd of people and two sets of barricades, top and bottom, but the wheelchair ramp was only blocked at the top. Dominic started moving up the ramp, with Dieter following, both trying to gain a better vantage point.

Dieter was about to make another attempt to communicate by radio to the event security coordinator when his radio announced that there was a man at the top of the wheelchair ramp with a cane over the railing. Dominic and Dieter heard the radio chatter and having just made the second U-turn on the wheelchair ramp, the priest broke into a run. Sprinting to the last left turn on the ramp, he saw the man with the cane in front of him—and the cane was now pointed toward the dais.

Swiss Guards stationed on the roof of the Apostolic Palace noticed the running priest on the ramp and alerted security forces, who leapt to intercept Dominic.

Dieter shouted into his radio mike, *"This is Sergeant Koehl! That running priest is Father Dominic! He is* not *a threat!"*

Ferretti looked behind him, gauging his escape route through the thick crowd of onlookers, then lowered himself, crouching down behind the cane, looking down its length, pointing it directly at the pope.

Ignatius was continuing his speech, "... and so I tell you, my brothers and sisters, that there is no truth to the rumors that a rogue planet is on its way to fulfill the apocalyptic visions of John in Revelation, as you have been told by corrupting forces. I have spoken to the astronomers and experts at the Vatican Observatory, and they have assured me of the truth. There *is* no planet Nibiru, and on this I stake my life."

Seeing the man aiming his cane, Dominic raced up the ramp, dodging people on his way. Suddenly, he recognized him—the papal heraldist! With no time to think, Dominic leapt toward the traitor's back.

Too late!

Ferretti had fired off a shot. A sudden muffled spit with a lingering hiss, quieter than a hand clap, escaped the cane gun. A split second later, Dominic landed on the old man, pushing the cane away.

He looked up, saw the pope falling to the ground. Bright red drops of blood splattered the pope's white cassock. Instantly, an army of men in black surrounded the Holy Father, and a platoon of Swiss Guards jumped up onto the stage to form a barrier line as further protection. Several of them pulled out Heckler & Koch MP7 submachine guns from beneath their gala ceremonial uniforms and aimed them into the crowd.

Pandemonium erupted. The press sprung into action—*The pope had just been shot on live television!*—racing to get the best camera position for the action still taking place on the stage.

The pope's personal security detail swooped up his body and whisked him inside to the safety of the basilica. His personal physicians and a paramedic team already were standing by inside.

Quickly assessing his condition, the doctors noted that the bullet had entered his left cheek, grazed the top of his tongue, and exited the other side, barely missing his teeth.

Whoever that priest was that caught the assassin, they considered, had saved the pope's life, for he knocked the shot just slightly off its intended trajectory. Quickly bandaging his cheeks and putting a gauze pad on his tongue, the Commander of the Swiss Guard called for Shepherd Two to be readied for flight immediately to take the pope to the hospital.

Still sitting on Ferretti, Dominic looked up again, desperate to know the condition of his wounded father. Uncontrollable anger welled up inside him. His first instinct was to beat Ferretti senseless, which he was about to do before Dieter interceded, grabbing his shoulder to pull him back.

Swiss Guards suddenly swarmed in around them, weapons ready, looking to neutralize further threats. They quickly separated the crowd away from the top of the wheelchair ramp, and the arrest team converged on Ferretti, Dominic and Dieter. Dieter holstered his weapon and took Dominic by the shoulders as the arrest team grabbed Ferretti, standing him up and cuffing his hands behind his back.

"How could you?!" Dominic screamed at Ferretti.

Turning his head to look at Dominic and seeing the hordes of television cameras trained on him, with a contemptuous smile the old man simply said loudly, "The End is near!"

As the guards led Ferretti away, tears streamed down Dominic's face. Dieter led him toward the Gendarmerie's office, but Dominic could barely walk. The Swiss Guard put his arm around the priest to keep him steady.

Seeing Dominic and Dieter together, Karl and Lukas ran to join them from the other end of the basilica.

"Michael! Here you are!" Karl said, out of breath. "Father Bannon is going with the pope and the doctors in Shepherd Two. He sent me to find you. The pope is asking for you, Michael. We can take my Jeep and meet them at the hospital."

"He's not *dead?!* I saw the blood on his face and cassock, and then he fell. Oh, thank God!"

"No, Michael, he's not dead. It was a very small-caliber bullet, and just hit him in the mouth, through and through. I think he'll have some scars, but he should make it."

Dominic fell to his knees, sobbing in gratitude, for he thought he had lost his father.

As they all got to the parking lot and loaded up in Karl's Wrangler, they heard the chop of helicopter rotor blades, then looked up to see Shepherd Two lifting off and heading toward nearby Santo Spirito Hospital.

CHAPTER THIRTY-NINE

As Dominic, Karl, and Lukas were driving to the hospital, the priest's cell phone rang. He was about to send it to voicemail when he noted it was Hana calling.

"Michael, we were watching the pope's address live! Please tell me he's okay...."

"Yes, thank God. He was just wounded, and apparently not that badly. I'm on my way to see him now."

"Are you okay? From the news video, it looked like you were the one who tackled the shooter!"

"Yes, that was me. I should have known about this sooner, but somehow it escaped me. Jonah Barlow's manuscript said that the pope would be struck down when he denounced the prophet and the prophecy about Nibiru. I hadn't discussed that specific portion of the book with His Holiness, or he would have known not to give that public address—or at least would have been better protected. It's my fault he was up there. I should have warned him."

"Oh, Michael, it's not your fault," she admonished him. "You didn't know he was going to give the address, obviously, or you would have stopped him. And you weren't the one who shot him; in fact, you saved him!"

"I don't know, Hana. There has just been so much going on, I've hardly had time to think. Once we got the Petri Crypta open, he was awfully upset after he read whatever documents it contained. He wouldn't tell me what they were, but it had to have been something terrible. He was in tears after reading it."

"You're right. Whatever it was, to have made him weep, it had to be devastating. Please let him know we are all pulling for him, and that Armand sends his love.

"Oh, and Grand-père has some news for you. It took a lot of work, but his people were able to put certain electronic traps in the market trading systems to spot recent trades that might take advantage of sudden market swings. When the pope was shot, alarms went off everywhere. They're digging through the data now and they think they'll have some names or entities soon, maybe later today. He wanted you to know."

"Yes, I suppose that would make for good reading. Let me know if anyone or anything stands out as regards all this mess. And thanks for calling, dear friend. It means a lot."

They ended the call just as the Jeep was pulling up to Santo Spirito Hospital, where they were met by a media circus. The press was so swift to respond to the pope's shooting that some of them made it to the hospital before the pope's helicopter to stake out positions near the heliport to film the arrival of Shepherd Two and the transference of the pope to the emergency room.

The Carabinieri set about removing all people and equipment in the vicinity before the helicopter landed, just in case there might be another assassin among them. Reporters grumbled in objection, but the Carabinieri brooked no exceptions. In their minds, Papa Petrini was still at risk.

Shepherd Two landed without incident, and the pope, now being swiftly transported on a gurney, was the center of attention for every long-range camera lens, all of them focused on the splotches of red blood in stark contrast to his snow-white garments.

Karl and Lukas used their Swiss Guard credentials to get

themselves and Father Dominic through the massive police cordon around the hospital. The pope was still in the ER, and they were required to stay in the waiting room while he was examined, until he could be moved to the private suite always reserved for the pope.

But the waiting room was already packed with a phalanx of Italian police, Vatican Gendarmerie, and the Commander of the Swiss Guard with a couple aides, all talking over each other. Dominic was accosted by representatives of each agency, who urged him to speak with them regarding his role in the event: how he happened to be on the wheelchair ramp at the time of the shooting, and how he had recognized the shooter in time to at least partly disrupt the shot.

Only when the Commander of the Swiss Guard, along with Father Nick Bannon, stepped in to rescue him was Dominic released to go visit the pope, who had been asking for him.

When he entered the papal suite, the Holy Father, his father, was propped up on the hospital bed, bandages on his cheeks covering the stitches it had taken to close the wounds on each side. At the sight of the wounds, Dominic could not hold back the tears.

With two security guards standing by, His Holiness said, "Please, gentlemen, stand outside. I would speak privately with the man who saved my life."

The guards reluctantly shuffled out to stand just beyond the door.

"I'm so sorry, Fa— Holy Father, this is my fault."

The pope's words were slurred from the swelling of his tongue where the bullet had grazed it, but they were still intelligible.

"No, my son, the fault is Monsignor Ferretti's. He is the one who pulled the trigger, I am told. But I happened to see you running up behind him right before he shot me. You saved me. How did you know?"

"It was in the Barlow manuscript: 'The pope who denounced

the prophet and the prophecy about Nibiru would be struck down.' I should have warned you. I wasn't paying attention and didn't know you were going to give a public address."

"Well, I still would have made the address. I had to, even though it was a last minute decision. But maybe we should have done it in a studio rather than in public. Still, Ferretti was well placed. He probably could have gotten into a studio audience as well, having Press Office credentials."

"Yes, that's true. Maybe it was inevitable. Still, I was so terribly frightened that he might have killed you."

"Michael, I am an old man. I do not have many years left, regardless, and you must be prepared to go on without me at any time. It is the way it has always been. But at least that is not for today. But I sent for you not in order to forgive you, but to thank you. Had you not been there, Ferretti's shot might have had its intended effect. I owe you my life."

"I could not bear the thought of losing you… Father."

Petrini reached out and gathered his son into his arms. They both shed tears of love, and of a loss avoided. After a few moments, the pope released him.

"I assume Ferretti was arrested, but I suspect we will not get much out of him. I doubt that he acted alone, Michael. His attack seems all too closely tied to that manuscript and the prophecies that are panicking the public. So he must be acting in accordance somehow with KOTA. And if so, what are we to do about the people who sent him?"

Wiping his face, Dominic was now determined. "I might have some news about that, soon."

Much of the world had watched in horror as the live events surrounding the shooting of the pope unfolded. The spectacle had, of course, dominated cable news, with the usual talking heads on their various networks commenting on the attempted assassination, and the possible involvement of an obscure order calling themselves Knights of the Apocalypse.

Despite constantly being at odds with Pope Ignatius's more liberal views and actions, the League of Conservative Catholics was perhaps the most vehement voice, denouncing whoever was to blame for defiling Holy Mother Church in such an appalling way—though their concerns were less for the man himself than the office he held.

From the rectory adjacent to his offices at the Archdiocese of Washington, D.C., Cardinal Damien Challis watched in fascination as reports continued to flow in, both on live television and text messages from his associates.

Naturally, he had known of the plot before it happened, and he relished every single moment of it. His exuberance was even heightened when—by sheer luck, thanks to CNN's wide view of the crowds—he actually caught a brief glance of Monsignor Ferretti poised on the barricade, his cane raised just before he took the shot. He clapped his hands together in celebration as it happened, a satisfied grin creasing his face.

Challis had a moment's pity when he watched as Ferretti was taken away, arrested as the prime suspect. But the pity was not for the man but for the other things he'd had planned for Ferretti which now must be altered. But he thought it was a stroke of brilliance that Ferretti had the presence of mind to say, "The End is near," directly to the cameras—thank the Lord they were there!—but the man wouldn't say anything further, Challis was confident. Ferretti was too smart and loyal to the cause to name names.

His phone vibrated with an incoming call. Challis recognized the private number.

"Yes, Your Eminence?" he answered.

"While I appreciate the sentiment, Damien, you should not call me that on the phone," said Magnus.

Challis ignored the reproach. "To what do I owe the pleasure of your call? It seems everything went according to plan today."

"Yes, except that idiot of a heraldist got himself captured. You are sure he can't be traced to us?"

"Yes, quite sure. Ferretti was a very good mole. He has no direct connections to you or to the Knights. The Vatican Gendarmerie will likely consider him a lone assassin and leave it at that."

"When are you going to make the next announcement?"

"I'm thinking of alerting the media about three forty-five. That way, they can tease it on the four o'clock news and carry it live on their five o'clock broadcasts, even if they do a five-minute lead on the shooting of the pope. They won't be able to resist the implied connection of us to the shooting. We will be guaranteed massive exposure."

"Yes, that thought had occurred to me as well. Which is why I am calling. I want you to have our team make a small alteration to our website. Here's what I want you to add...."

AT THE APPOINTED TIME, mere hours after the pope had been shot, Damien Challis strode into the small chapel outside the District of Columbia city limits, again clad in his formal black robe with the gold seven-pointed star on the chest. The live webcams were still set up and running, and they had connected the video feed of the main camera to the wider media's feed.

Owing to the assassination attempt on the pope, the world's major media outlets had all picked up the live feed for Challis's announcements, anxious to not be left in the dark if they could grab any juice to enhance their own reporting and investigative research. Everyone was now watching, waiting, for the next big scoop. Would one of those envelopes accurately predicted this assassination attempt?

Challis looked directly into the camera lens.

"These are perilous times, and it grieves me to have to come to you amid the tragedy that struck the Holy Father earlier today. But I made you a promise when we began this journey together that, when the things which had been foretold—and which the Church has hidden from you—have been fulfilled, then we would reveal them to you so that you might believe.

"Observe closely. I will open the case and take out the next prophecy and read it to you."

Challis lifted open the glass case and extracted the second envelope. As a magician might, he made a show of examining the packet, demonstrating that it was still intact and unopened.

"As you can see, the prophecy is still sealed. And the case has been shown live on camera for all to see, uninterrupted twenty-four hours a day, since the last time it was opened before you.

"Here are the words that were written:

> 'Behold, for it will come to pass that when the prophet has seen the coming fulfilment of the Apocalypse, when the stars will fall and a mountain will descend into the sea, and the waters become Wormwood, and when the prophet has told the people that the Beast will arise and deny the prophet and his prophecy, then he will be struck down at the time of his denial, that the prophecies may be fulfilled.'

"As Luke says in Chapter 24, 'He began by saying to them, "Today this scripture is fulfilled in your hearing."'"

As he finished, Challis held up the letter directly into the camera, confirming to viewers that those were the actual words on the prophecy, removing any doubt that he might be making it up on the fly, after the fact.

"And though he was shot in the head," he continued, "the pope was barely hurt. This is not only amazing; it is a marvel. You might be tempted to think it was a miracle. But it was not. This was just another example of the fulfillment of scripture, for the Book of Revelation, Chapter 13, tells us that the Beast will be grievously wounded in the head, and yet will live, and everyone will marvel that he is alive.

"But marvel not and be warned.

"This pope has told us who he is, though he himself may not realize it. Look at the coat of arms that was on the banner when he spoke. The lion fights the dragon. Christ is the lion, so who does that leave to be the dragon but the pope? And the entire shield tells us of a count-down: an eight-pointed cross; seven-, six-, and five-pointed stars; the four points of the cross; three stars, two beasts, and one cross. He knows that the countdown to the End comes during his reign, and he is warning those of us who know the signs. Even his motto, *Faithful to the Last,* informs us he knows he's the last—but faithful to whom? To the Devil! The dragon!

"The End is near, and nearer with every passing moment. I warned you that the revelations would come faster, as the Lord works to shorten these days for the sake of the Elect, as was foretold in the thirteenth chapter of Mark.

"If you think you are one of the Elect, visit the website on your screen and take advantage of this fleeting opportunity to escape the tribulations that are to come.

"The End is near. The time is at hand. This is the second part of the Third Secret of Fátima.

"Only the Elect will be saved.

"This is the Third Warning.

"You may not get another."

WITH HIS LIVE announcement now finished, Damien Challis was escorted to a waiting limousine, which sped him back to his office a short distance away. Anxious to see how the news was handling the event, he turned on the TV the moment he arrived.

While the shooting of the pope was still the lead story, the revelation of the sealed prophecy had merged with it. There were also recaps of the previous announcement. Challis could not have asked for better publicity. Web traffic to the Last Mass website was through the roof and climbing. People were engaged.

Magnus's changes to the site were also drawing a lot of the attention.

> Can't make it to the Last Mass? For a modest donation we will add your names to the Last Novena. Everyone who participates in the Last Novena will earn an indulgence that will spare you the worst of the tribulations to come.
>
> You will make confession, pray the rosary, and take Communion at your local church, and then certify these acts to the KOTA operators, who will add your name to the list that shall be read and prayed over at the Last Mass, where God's grace will be dispensed upon those who are in attendance, and those who are listed in the roster of the Novena.
>
> Don't miss your opportunity. Operators are standing by.

Genius, Challis thought. The KOTA foundation's coffers would soon be overflowing, just in time to finance the Last Mass.

The burner phone in his pocket vibrated. Fishing it out, the cardinal looked at the number on Caller ID. Not the one he was expecting, but still important.

"Good evening, Sacculus, brother Knight of the Purse. How fare the finances of the order?"

"Good evening, Commander," Sacculus greeted him. "Magnus's suggestion was a brilliant one. We have already begun processing well over a thousand participants for the Novena. That is bringing millions of dollars' worth of assets into the purse. We are faring quite well, as it happens."

"Will I be seeing you at the Last Mass?"

"No, I'm afraid not. There are too many things that I need to monitor and control from here, to make sure that you are not disturbed during the Mass."

"Thank you, Brother. You will be blessed for your sacrifice."

You have no idea, thought Sacculus to himself, replying, "No, thank *you*, Eminence. Oh, and Nimbus, our Knight of the Swords, tells me he won't be able to attend, either. Magnus cut loose Nimbus's private troops for being a little overzealous in deterring the priest from getting back to the Vatican with the keys, though I don't understand why that was necessary."

"All will become clear in time. Please make sure Nimbus is properly compensated for his efforts. We will have enough members at the Last Mass to cover the exits, as it were, so Nimbus's assistance is no longer required anyway."

"It will be done as you say. When will you be leaving?"

"Later tonight. I'm taking a red eye. I'll be there in the morning."

CHAPTER
FORTY

While reporting on the attempt on the pope's life, the Global News Network also provided extensive coverage of the most recent KOTA prophecy revelation, running repeating video segments of the Knight Commander, Cardinal Challis, opening the second prophecy's envelope. Then the news anchor turned to other developments:

> A 6.5 magnitude earthquake shook Jericho and the surrounding areas today, setting off warning sirens across Israel. Initial reports indicate many buildings were damaged or destroyed. Casualty figures are indeterminate at this stage, but so far reports indicate that death tolls are mounting, especially in the poorer Palestinian areas.
>
> With major earthquakes in the area every hundred or so years, this quake should have come as no surprise. Yet many people are upset with the government for not doing more to prepare people for the possibility of seismic activity in the area.
>
> On the other side of the globe, China is rattling sabers in the South China Sea. The Chinese Air Force has moved a squadron of fifteen Chengdu J-20 Mighty Dragon stealth fighters to the airport they built on the disputed Spratly Islands. This gives the

Chinese the ability to strike anywhere in the Philippines or Indonesia without refueling, and with little warning. The Chinese also have moved a number of anti-aircraft missile batteries and radar stations to the islands to defend the planes.

Similarly, North Korea tested a series of medium-range ballistic missiles today, which flew across Japanese airspace and fell into the sea. Japan's Home Defense forces were placed on high alert, but no action was taken once it was determined that the missiles' trajectory would not take them over populated areas. Japan has filed a formal complaint with the United Nations.

We'll be following these developments with more news at the top of the hour.

When the Pope Emeritus heard that Pope Ignatius had been shot, and thinking that it was much worse than it turned out to be, he instructed his personal secretary to draft a memo to the Secretary of State. In it, he indicated that, in this unprecedented circumstance of a living pope being incapacitated while a former pope was still alive, rather than leave the Chair of St. Peter unoccupied, he, the Pope Emeritus, would be willing to return to the papacy on a temporary basis until the current pope was fully capable of reassuming his duties.

To justify the proposal, the memo further stated that the faithful should not be deprived of the spiritual guidance and leadership of the Church during such tumultuous times.

Unfortunately, the Pope Emeritus's secretary misunderstood his boss's intent, and once the memo was drafted and the Pope Emeritus had signed it, a copy was sent not only to the Secretary of State's office, but to the press as well, with the statement appearing on the Pope Emeritus's personal web page.

BEFORE CATCHING HIS PLANE, Cardinal Damien Challis returned for one last visit to the video studio in the small chapel not far from his office. By this time, a permanent media presence had encamped around the chapel to monitor the Web cameras live in anticipation of another prophetic revelation.

Again facing the camera, dressed in his Knight's robe, he began.

"The last twenty-four hours have seen some momentous events of apocalyptic significance. First, I want to draw your attention to the news reports from Israel, where a major earthquake has occurred, and to the reports of Chinese fighter jets deployed to the South China Sea, North Korean missiles flying over Japan, and reports from around the world of food shortages caused by panic buying. All these things have been foretold and must occur, for as Matthew says in scripture, 'And ye shall hear of wars and rumors of wars: see that ye be not troubled, for all these things must come to pass, but the end is not yet. For nation shall rise against nation, and kingdom against kingdom: and there shall be famines, and pestilences, and earthquakes in diverse places. All these are the beginning of sorrows.'

"Yes, my brothers and sisters, these are just the beginnings of such sorrows; sorrows and tribulations that will only grow more wretched as the end draws near.

"Yet more importantly, I want to draw your attention to the Apocalypse of St. John, also known as the Book of Revelation, a book that we, Knights of the Apocalypse, understand uniquely.

"After the unfortunate but prophesied incapacitation of the current pope, the Pope Emeritus has stated that he is willing to come out of retirement to take the current pontiff's place. This was also foretold in the seventeenth chapter of Revelation. It has been an accepted interpretation of this chapter that the prostitute is the Catholic Church, and that the Beast is the last pope. Pope Ignatius is pope, and then not, and is the pope to come.

"How many more warnings do you need to know that we are

truly at the End? So, I invite you once again, to search your souls and see if you are one of the Elect who are called to escape the persecutions and tribulations to come. The Final Mass offers a way to leave these troubles behind and meet Jesus in the clouds. If this is right for you, if the Holy Spirit calls your name, counselors are standing by to take your reservations.

"For the rest: The End is near. The time is at hand. The sorrows have begun, the Beast is here.

"Only the Elect will be saved.

"This is the last warning.

"Peace be with you."

CHAPTER FORTY-ONE

Eliza Spiteri, aka Lipstick Girl, sat in the arrivals area of Malta International Airport's Level 0, just outside the Costa Coffee shop, savoring a hot, foamy caffè latte.

Dressed in ratty jeans and a baggy sweatshirt, her Converse All-Stars propped up on an empty carry-on bag to blend in, her bulky shoulder bag on the chair next to her, she pretended to be reading a paperback romance novel she had picked up at the airport bookshop. From her vantage point, she could see everyone who was arriving in Malta that morning, but she was looking for only one man: Damien Challis.

Since the attacks in Malta had been associated with the Knights of the Apocalypse, she had contacted intelligence agencies for both the E.U. and the U.S., seeking further information on the group, especially its leadership.

Damien Challis was, as far as she could tell, the head of the snake. She had put him and other KOTA members that she knew of on an Interpol Watch List so that she would be notified if they tried to enter the country, especially by air.

Challis's name had appeared on a passenger manifest coming in from Rome this morning, as there were no direct flights from the U.S. to Malta.

Curiously, the Archdiocese of Washington, D.C. had not paid for his flight to Rome, but another entity had: Knight Holdings Group out of the Cayman Islands. In her research, she had discovered that Knight Holdings' leadership, its sources of income, and its stockholders all were carefully shielded by layers of intermediate corporations and entities spread around the Caribbean.

Spiteri had shared these details with Armand de Saint-Clair and Sabrina Felici, who was heading up that part of their investigation. As commander of the Malta Police Force Counterterrorism Unit, her main concern was not Challis's financial dealings, but what he was doing in Malta now.

Two things had put him on her radar: KOTA's probable involvement in the attacks in Malta last week, and Challis's visit corresponding with a sudden surge in religious tourist visits. He was up to something, and it seemed there were a lot of people arriving in Malta to bear witness to it.

EARLIER, Cardinal Challis had boarded the flight to Rome at Reagan International Airport, carrying with him a simple carry-on bag and his clerical garments in a dry-cleaning sleeve, his KOTA regalia carefully pressed within.

On arriving in Rome, Challis kept a low profile. He expected there might be media looking for him, but as his itinerary had not been made public, that shouldn't be an issue.

Luggage in hand, he headed quickly from his arrival gate to his departure gate. The flight to Malta left within minutes. As he boarded that flight, he was relieved that nobody had sought him out.

Ninety minutes later, the plane landed in Malta. Presenting his passport at International Arrivals, Challis watched as the officer scanned the document, asking him the usual questions about the purpose of his visit, then stared for a long while at his screen. Looking back and forth at Challis and his computer, he finally let him pass.

As Challis walked away, the passport control officer reread the message that had appeared on his screen: **Do not detain. Text the Malta Police Force Counterterrorism Unit immediately and relay the following message 'Challis has entered the country**.' The passport control officer did as instructed.

In the arrivals area outside Costa Coffee, Spiteri's cell phone buzzed in her bag. She looked down and read the message from the passport control officer.

Scanning the crowd of arrivals, she spotted her subject coming out of the security area and heading over to the escalator that led to the Level -1 area. As Challis got on the escalator heading down, Spiteri stuffed the book she was reading into her bag, grabbed the carry-on, and followed him at a distance. She stepped on, just as he was about to step off below. As she descended, she watched him make a turn past the food court—past Burger King, KFC, and Fat Harry's—then head down the tunnel to the main car park. She lagged behind, trying to look like just another tourist with no interest in him or anybody else in the area.

Exiting the tunnel to the main car park, Challis got inside a black BMW waiting for him at the green curb, handing his carry-on and garment bag to the driver, who laid them in the back of the vehicle.

Exiting the tunnel, Spiteri noted the license plate of the vehicle and kept walking. As soon as it was out of sight, she pulled a handheld radio from her bag and called the surveillance team standing by outside the airport.

"CT5, CT1, target is in a black BMW 728i, license HQZ626, heading out of the airport's main car park now. Don't lose him."

"CT1, CT5, copy. All units prepare to rotate in as directed. CT5 has target now. Leaving airport on San Tumas northbound."

A short time later, as Spiteri was heading back to the office to monitor surveillance, her phone rang. She pulled it out of her bag and answered.

"Captain Spiteri."

"Subject was dropped off at the Xara Palace Relais and Chateaux in Mdina. We have set up on all exits. Will advise when he moves. One other thing: someone is setting up a huge tent in the fields behind the walled city…."

NOTHING less than the five-star Xara Palace Hotel would suffice for the personal tastes of Cardinal Damien Challis. Even when he was traveling on the Church's budget, his accommodations were rarely less than luxury class.

Having checked into the Xara, Challis was met by two men sitting in the lobby who had been waiting for him: KOTA's spiritual advisor, Magnus, and Father Lorenzo Marchetti. They said little to one another as they made their way up to Challis's reserved suite.

At a predetermined time, Challis sat down at the desk, opened his laptop, and initiated a secure videoconference session. One by one, the seven members of KOTA's Council of Seven appeared in separate windows. As usual, Magnus joined in by telephone—even though he and Marchetti were sitting in the adjoining room of Challis's hotel suite, out of sight and sound of the camera. There was good reason for the evasion.

"Can someone explain to me why we are not in the Mdina Cathedral?"

The Knight of the Lands spoke up. "We would have been, Commander, until Rome called you in and made it clear to Catholic churches everywhere that you had been blacklisted. I would have preferred to have heard that from you. The local bishop called me yesterday and told me that you had been forbidden to celebrate Mass, hold events of any sort, or effect any ecclesiastical celebrations by order of the Congregation for the Doctrine of the Faith. The prefect himself, Bishop Lunesca, made it clear that he wasn't going to go up against the Holy Office for your sake."

"But a big tent just doesn't have the grandeur I had envisioned for the event. I wanted to have people in awe of the classical beauty of the cathedral, not some drab circus tent."

"It won't be so bad, Damien," said Magnus. "Think of all the generations of people gathered in caves and fields. Our Lord himself spoke from hillsides and shorelines, and almost never went into the temples. You have a gift, Knight Commander. You don't need the surroundings to be inspiring. *You* will inspire the people and prepare them for their journey."

"Well, thank you, my friend," Challis replied, his ego having been assuaged. "I accept that. All right, so are there any more issues that need to be decided before the event begins tomorrow?"

"I regret that I am unable to attend," the Knight of Swords said. "Magnus tells me he has everything well in hand. I have pressing engagements elsewhere. Certain things must be in place before… well, before this is all over."

"Yes, I am aware of your situation, Nimbus. That is your choice, of course. I know that the Knight of the Purse is also excusing himself. Anything you wish to add, Sacculus?"

"Yes. Someone is probing at the fringes of the organization, but they have not penetrated our outer defenses. We are secure. I'm not surprised—given the number of people who have committed by this point—that someone is trying to see where their generosity is going. Do not fear: anyone inquiring will see the funds going into the places they were told it was going."

"Very good," Challis concurred. "As for myself, I must prepare my sermon for the Mass. I will see the rest of you in the morning. This is an exciting time, gentlemen. Make the most of it."

Challis ended the call. Magnus hung up the phone then

joined Challis in the main room as he extended his hand to the cardinal.

"Well done, Damien. You will be exalted among the priests and the prophets, the Elect of the Elect. You who have brought all these souls with you as a gift unto the Lord. You will meet him at the head of the multitude, shining like gold."

Challis accepted the praise graciously.

"Come, Father Marchetti, we also have some preparations to make before tomorrow."

Marchetti and Magnus left Challis's room. When they were out in the hallway, the spiritual advisor turned to Marchetti.

"It is time to set the trap. You must report to Ernesto Vila that you *had* to attack Dominic on direction of KOTA, but you would not have hurt him. If you hadn't attacked him, KOTA would have suspected you were a mole. Tell Vila you are still loyal to their efforts. They still do not suspect *me* at this point, but they will soon. That is all according to plan.

"Tell Vila you overheard the planning for the Last Mass, and that the leaders are planning to steal all the money that the people have pledged to participate in the Mass. People have given their entire fortunes to be present at the Last Mass, where they have been told that they will be taken up into the clouds to meet the Lord, and that they will escape the tribulations that are about to begin. Also make sure to tell Vila to inform Dominic that you are sorry, but that you had to maintain your cover."

"It will be done as you say, Magnus," Marchetti said.

"Good. Very good."

As Magnus walked away to his own room in the hotel, the burner phone he carried chimed. He saw it was Nimbus, the Knight of Swords, calling.

"Yes?"

"I was just informed that Lucifer was caught at the airport with enough Botox concentrate to kill half of Malta!"

"Well, that's inconvenient. He should have been clean, with no link to KOTA. But still, the timing could raise questions. I need forty-eight hours. I can't have them making any connections to us."

"If you want him out of jail, you must call the Knight of Laws. He can arrange that. Or are you asking for one of my solutions?"

"I'm still talking to you, aren't I?" Magnus said dryly.

"You know the fee for that?"

"Yes, Sacculus will get it to you."

"This one will be double because it's a rush job."

"Fine, but don't get greedy on us now, Nimbus."

"Remember who you're talking to. You wouldn't want BlackCloud to come rain on your little parade now, would you?"

"I do not appreciate being threatened. We are all in this together. There are fail-safes in place to prevent compromise. You would do well to remember that. Where one falls, all fall."

"Then it will be done as you wish."

The call ended. *Yes*, thought the spiritual advisor, *but I won't be the one to fall.*

SEEKING liquid courage before contacting his handler, Lorenzo Marchetti drove directly to his motel, a dumpy little place outside the walls of Mdina that had maid service once a week and room service when they got around to it. Not being of sufficient stature in the organization to merit a room at Malta's Xara Palace, where the Knights were staying, he settled into the dingy bar of his motel and had a few drinks.

Not a seasoned drinker, when he returned to his room he fell onto the bed, just to close his eyes a bit. Several hours later, he jolted awake. It was now late afternoon. He was anxious that he had kept Ernesto Vila waiting.

Steeling himself for the conversation, he dialed the number. Vila answered.

"This is Lorenzo," Marchetti announced.

"You have some nerve calling me after what you did the other night. Whose side are you on?"

"I realize it looks bad. I think they are on to me. It was a test of my loyalty to them. If I balked, I would have blown my cover. I didn't hurt the priest, though, as instructed."

"It's going to take much more to get me to trust you again, Lorenzo."

"Perhaps this will help," Marchetti pleaded. "I, um… eavesdropped on the KOTA Council meeting earlier this morning. Don't ask me how. But I learned that the Last Mass event starts tomorrow. The participants are being told that on the second day, the Mass will trigger the Rapture, and everyone who has received Communion will, according to scripture, meet Jesus 'in the clouds' and avoid the tribulation that is about to begin.

"To get into the Mass, you have to sign papers that give all your worldly goods—your money and property—to the KOTA Foundation, for use in saving the souls of those left behind. But it's a lie. They are going to steal the money. The KOTA banker, Sacculus, he has made all the arrangements. He and Magnus are going to steal the money and leave Cardinal Challis holding the bag."

"Wait, who are these Sacculus and Magnus characters?"

"I do not know their real identities; those are simply code names. They only communicate by video conference with their Knight Commander, and their faces are obscured. But Magnus knows the priest, Dominic. He said he was glad Dominic had left Malta, so the priest could not identify him."

"All right. I will do what verification I can. If this checks out and you have earned my trust again, fine. If not, you will not appreciate the consequences."

Vila ended the call and considered what had to be done next. Still attending to his duties with the Knights of Malta in Valletta, he decided to call both Armand de Saint-Clair and Eliza Spiteri and inform them of events concurrently.

Setting up the conference call, Vila related to both of them what he had learned.

Spiteri was first to respond. "I have people watching the Xara Palace and the events tent. Everything is shut down for the night there, with security people surrounding the site."

"And we are still digging into the financial records of the trades that occurred before and after the pope was shot," Saint-Clair reported. "As we might have expected, there *has* been suspicious activity, but we should know more tomorrow."

"Which is when," Spiteri continued, "I'm going to try to infiltrate the event, see what I can glean from the attendees and their activities. Meanwhile, I'll contact Father Dominic and see if he might know who their spiritual advisor, this Magnus character, could be, based on what little we know. Shall we plan on reconvening at noon tomorrow?"

"Yes," Saint-Clair and Vila said in unison, then ended the call.

MICHAEL DOMINIC WAS CHATTING with Ian Duffy in the latter's office when his cell phone vibrated. Excusing himself, he walked toward his office while answering.

"Hello, Father Dominic, I am Captain Eliza Spiteri, Commander of the Malta Police Force Counterterrorism Unit. I am investigating Cardinal Damien Challis's financial dealings, and whatever he is orchestrating in Malta. Do you have a few minutes to speak?"

"Yes, Captain, of course," Dominic said, perplexed that such a high-level person in Malta would be contacting him.

Spiteri filled him in on KOTA and Challis's scheme for the Last Mass, and her belief that this was a substantial case of suspected fraud, clearly one on a major scale, given the widespread panic KOTA's announcements were generating.

"It seems there is an individual at the center of all this who has been identified only as KOTA's spiritual advisor. He goes by the code name 'Magnus.' From our intelligence reports, this Magnus is intending to abscond with all the funding the event generates, while leaving Cardinal Challis in the lurch. Magnus also apparently knows *you* quite well, as your name has come up numerous times in our intercepts, and as reported by a mole we have inside the organization. Whoever he is, it's safe to say he doesn't hold you in high regard.

"By any chance, Father, do you know who these 'Magnus' and 'Sacculus' characters might be?"

Dominic's first thought was that a charlatan like Challis deserved whatever fate was in store for him. Then he wracked his brain for who Magnus might be. To his knowledge there were few people who disliked him, apart from those in the Vatican with minor envy due to his close relationship to the pope. But thinking of those, none of them had the standing or wherewithal to take on something of this magnitude.

In Latin, *Sacculus* means 'money bag,' while *Magnus* means 'great,' he considered, so the latter must clearly have a high opinion of himself. And as he pondered that further, one name arose that felt suitable and sickening at the same time.

Dante!

Could it be? Has he finally come back onto the stage? Dominic wouldn't put this kind of scheme past him at all, and the more he thought about it, the more sense it made.

"Captain, does the name Fabrizio Dante mean anything to you?"

Spiteri mulled this over briefly. "No, that name doesn't sound familiar at all. Why?"

"Dante was once a cardinal of the Church. Also Secretary of State at one time, in fact. If anyone has it in for me—and indeed, for the pope personally—it's Dante. And as you describe it, this does seem to be the kind of thing he might align himself with. I wouldn't know where to find him now, though. He spent two years in prison for attempted murder and other charges and was paroled just this past year. You might check into him.

"As for *Sacculus,* that simply means 'money bag' in Latin. I couldn't imagine who that might be."

"Have you got a photograph of this Dante, Father? Our mole might be able to identify him…."

"I'm sure I can find one in his files, yes. I'll email it to you when I find it." They exchanged contact details.

"I am attending tomorrow's event in Malta, the so-called Last Mass, in an undercover capacity," Spiteri said. "I will let you know what I learn."

"Thank you, Captain. And if there's anything more I can help with, you know how to reach me. Good luck."

Pressing the End Call button on his phone, Dominic wondered if this whole debacle was somehow Dante's doing. The more he pondered it, the more likely it seemed.

What is that bastard up to?

CHAPTER FORTY-TWO

KOTA's counselors had done a scrupulous job of carefully screening individuals who would be accepted for participation in tomorrow's Last Mass in Malta. Based on stringent criteria—the primary focus being high net worth and religious fervor—participants were by and large older—at least middle-aged, though most were in their advanced years.

No families had been accepted, only couples and single individuals. In addition to net worth, each also was vetted for an abiding distrust of governments and organizations, a bent toward conspiracy theories, strong susceptibility to suggestion, and a fear of unknown outcomes. They should also be devoutly Catholic, of a conservative nature, and wary or suspicious of the current liberal papacy.

Approximately two thousand of these souls now filled the white folding chairs under the huge white tent.

Captain Eliza Spiteri had been notified that an elderly woman had been brought to the hospital the previous night and had explained that she was in Malta for the Last Mass, before expiring of a heart attack during her intake.

Seizing the opportunity, Spiteri gathered relevant details of the woman, then used her name at registration and received her packet of documents along with a white choir robe with a scarlet, seven-pointed star on the chest. Her hand also was stamped with a similar marking. She was instructed to put the robe on over her clothing and was directed to proceed to the tent. Everyone was told to forfeit their cell phones, wallets, purses, and any other personal possessions. Surreptitiously, Spiteri avoided that instruction.

Flipping through the packet of documents while others were taking their seats for the indoctrination, Spiteri found a number of legal documents that looked to be conveyances of money and property to the KOTA Foundation, matching the intelligence her unit had received.

Above, two huge projection screens begin displaying the agenda for the day. After the opening Mass, attendees would be given an opportunity to have their confessions heard in booths set up around the perimeter of the tent. Ongoing worship was encouraged in the main part of the tent, and prayers of the Novena would be said at particular intervals. In the evening, there would be a candlelit service and Benediction of the Sacrament. If anyone had questions regarding their bequest instruments, counselors were on hand at the back of the tent.

Apart from that, the day was to be spent in strict silent observance of their journey ahead; and talking to other participants was forbidden. Everyone was to focus on being prepared to meet the Lord the following day. Exposition and Adoration would begin again promptly at seven a.m., with Mass beginning at nine. All participants were encouraged to be present and in their seats by seven and spend the last two hours before Mass in quiet prayer and reflection.

Spiteri thought the strict silence guise rather ingenious. No talking to the other participants. No way to compare stories, or misgivings. Keep your mouth shut and follow the program.

A short while later, Damien Challis came out and presided over the Mass—but his homily was not the spectacle of inspiration Spiteri had been expecting based on the cardinal's acclaimed reputation. By all appearances, he looked nervous, as if something was weighing heavily on his mind.

After Mass, she was just exiting the tent when her cell phone loudly rang in her pocket. She had forgotten to mute it. Looking for a secluded place she could take the forbidden call, she ambled over behind one of the smaller tents. But before she could answer it, one of the black-robed KOTA staff came over and intercepted her.

"I'm sorry. We were very explicit that no cellular devices were permitted once you checked in. I need you to hand over that phone. After all, you won't need it anymore."

"I'm very sorry," she said, stuffing the phone back in her pocket, "This is the last call. It has to do with arranging for my, uh…bequeathments. I'll take it out in the parking area. Then I'll turn it in. I promise." With a concerned grimace, the man looked at her skeptically.

Spiteri turned and hurried away, not daring to look behind to see if he was following her. Once she had gone a hundred meters, she pulled her phone back out of her pocket and hit Redial.

"Counterterrorism Unit, Sergeant Grech."

"Spiteri here, calling you back."

"Hey, Commander, you know that guy who was brought in from the airport, the astronomer with enough Botox concentrate to kill half the island?"

"Yes, what about him?"

"He's dead. The jail guard too. Some guy claiming to be a lawyer from the U.S. had an endorsement from the International Criminal Court in the Netherlands. They let him in to see the prisoner, and a few minutes later there was an explosion outside, taking out power in the whole area. The guard came into the visiting area to secure the prisoner, but the alleged attorney took out the guard and the prisoner barehanded. Broke their necks, then used the guard's keys to get out. Everyone was outside dealing with the explosion and fire, so nobody saw him leave."

"Did we get him on CCTV?"

"Yes, but I don't think it will do any good. Doing a sweep of the area, our team found a toupee and professional facial prosthetics—you know, nose, ears, eyebrows—in a trash bin a block away. So, whatever he looked like on video won't help much, since his appearance was changed significantly."

"All right, get forensics in there. I want everything fingerprinted, DNA results, the works."

"You got it, Chief."

"And run that astronomer against everyone we know in KOTA; see if he has any connections to that group. I don't believe in coincidences."

"Already on it," Grech confirmed.

"Keep me informed on this. I'm on my way in now."

Ending the call, Spiteri returned to her car, removed the white robe, then headed back to Valletta from Mdina. She spent the rest of the afternoon visiting the scene of the jail incident, then doing a little digging on Fabrizio Dante.

She was rather alarmed by what she found. The ex-cardinal had been previously implicated in several plots at the Vatican and eventually defrocked and incarcerated at Rome's most notorious prison, Regina Coeli. He had been released from prison on parole this past year, apparently with the help of highly placed connections who helped sway the parole board.

She also discovered that he was involved in some crimes with Opus Deus recently that ended with a cardinal being killed and Father Dominic suffering injuries, after which he and the Prelate of Opus Deus somehow disappeared.

Running Dante's name though the passport database for the days since the affair at the Vatican, she found no record of him ever entering Malta. Then she remembered that Ernesto Vila had told her someone code-named either Magnus or Sacculus was involved in the conspiracy. She ran both of those through the passport control database. No record of Sacculus, even as an alias, was found, but an Albert Magnus entered the country the day after the events at the Vatican, and there was no record that he had ever left.

She picked up her desk phone and called Armand de Saint-Clair. He answered on the first ring.

"Good afternoon, Eliza, what can I do for you?"

"Hello, Baron. How is your investigation going?"

"Well, it seems as if we've encountered a labyrinth of transactions resulting in either dead ends or misdirection."

"I came across something that might help. Remember when Ernesto Vila told us what he learned about the conspiracy to take money from the participants of the Last Mass?"

"Yes, of course."

"Two of the main men involved had code names: Sacculus and Magnus. Father Dominic recognized Magnus as the Latin word for 'great.' So, I ran that name through passport control records and an 'Albert Magnus' came up as having entered Malta the day after ex-cardinal Fabrizio Dante fled the Vatican."

"Are you sure it was Albert, and not Albertus?"

"Yes, I'm certain. I'm still looking at the record on the computer here. Why, Baron?"

"I ask because Albertus Magnus, also known as St. Albert the Great, was a thirteenth-century German bishop. He was very well educated, one of those philosopher-scientist priests. He even taught Thomas Aquinas. That name could be a pseudonym."

"Or Dante just has a rich sense of irony and a sizable opinion of himself."

"Have you looked at the picture on his passport?"

"Unfortunately, we don't capture it when they enter the country, and the surveillance footage from back then would have been deleted by now. The video system only has so much storage space. We really need to upgrade it, but you know how government budgets are."

"So, what are you asking me to do with this information?" the baron inquired.

"Can you pass it on to your financial team to see if Albert Magnus is linked to any accounts we could tie to KOTA?"

"Certainly, yes. Send me all the information you have on this Albert the Great impersonator, and I'll add it to our investigation and see what turns up."

"Thank you, Baron. I'll be here in my office in the meantime. I guess the news media will be carrying the story soon, but to let you know, there was an attack at one of our jails today. Some unknown assailant pretending to be an American attorney got in to see Boris Ponomarenko, the astronomer who made the Nibiru announcement. He showed up here in Malta with enough Botox to exterminate much of the island's population. Then there was an explosion and fire, likely a diversion. But when the guard came in to secure the astronomer, the assailant killed both the guard and Ponomarenko, and used the guard's keys to get out while everyone else was distracted."

"Well, that is alarming news. I wonder what he knew that somebody obviously needed to suppress?"

"Yes, what or *who*…."

"Indeed," Saint-Clair agreed. "All right, I'll call you as soon as I know something, Eliza. Take good care, now."

ABOUT AN HOUR LATER, Spiteri was still at her desk when the phone rang.

"Counterterrorism Unit, Captain Spiteri."

"Hello Eliza, it's Armand again. I have Detective Felici on the line as well. You both need to hear what we've found. It seems that Mr. Albert Magnus is a very wealthy man and becoming richer by the minute. He is the beneficiary of a trust receiving money from the KOTA Foundation in a highly suspicious series of account transfers and apparent money laundering. His scheme will fascinate financial sleuths for years. But my people were better than his.

"We also found someone who could be 'Sacculus.' His name is Edmond Ebanks, a financial manager at a bank in Grand Cayman. He might actually own the bank, but that isn't entirely clear yet. We found his digital fingerprints on a couple of the transfers and can infer the rest. He's a slippery one. But he's for another day, since I verified that he is physically in Grand Cayman. What we need now is to get to Dante, see if he is in possession of any identification that ties him to Albert Magnus. Dante may well be using that name as a cover."

"That's outstanding work, Armand! You and your team may have very well cracked this enigma. I'm going back to the Last Mass. They're doing the Candlelight Benediction of the Sacrament shortly. We'll see if Albert the Great is there."

It was dark when Eliza Spiteri returned to the parking area in the field just outside the walled city of Mdina and as she got out of her car, she donned the white robe. She had left her phone behind so it wouldn't give her away or get confiscated. Walking up to the entrance of the tent, she extended her arm showing the seven-pointed star stamp on her hand from when she had registered, then went inside.

A man in a matte black robe gave her a cream-colored candle with a paper shield to keep the wax from dripping on her hand. She was directed to a larger candle in the middle of the entrance to light her candle; a curious ceremony, she thought. It was dim on the inside, lit only by the flickering of candles dispersed throughout the massive tent. She walked about halfway down on the right side and took a seat. She tried to look around casually, but felt too conspicuous, since everyone else either had their heads down praying or were gazing at the Eucharist, displayed in its monstrance, a receptacle featuring a seven-pointed star in which the consecrated Host was venerated on the altar.

Just before nine o'clock, the congregation seemed to spontaneously break into song as three tall men in black robes came down the center aisle, heads bowed, faces obscured beneath their hoods. They came to the altar, genuflected, then rose again.

The central figure took his flowing sleeves in his hands and grasped the central shaft of the monstrance with the fabric, so his bare hands did not touch it. He raised the receptacle over his head and turned to face the congregation, his features hidden behind it.

Spiteri couldn't see who it was. He began walking back toward the entrance, again bowing his head, the hood covering his face, looking at the floor to guide his steps, symbolically unworthy to look at the body of Christ. She strained to see him as he passed but could not make out his features.

Getting out of her seat, she crouched, trying to keep low as she moved down the side aisle toward the entrance. But as she got close, as if on cue the entire congregation also got up and began moving toward the opening of the tent, crowding the center aisle and both sides. Now she just had to move with the crowd to get out.

Finally, she made it to the exit. But the three hooded men were gone. She waited, looking around. A few moments later, the central figure came out of a small side tent and began walking back toward the main tent. She circled to the side as he came closer. His face was still obscured. But as he was about to enter the tent she called out, "*Magnus!*" The man turned, looked directly at her—and then she knew.

It was the man in the photo Dominic had sent her. It *was* Fabrizio Dante!

Dante turned around swiftly and reentered the main tent. Moments later, several men in black robes came out, clearly on a mission looking for someone.

Spiteri ran to the parking lot under cover of darkness but had not yet started her car. She waited for more of the attendees to begin to leave for the night before returning in the morning for the final day's activities.

Only when others began making their way out did Spiteri start her car and drive toward the exit. Seeing one of the black-robed men near the gate listening on a walkie talkie, she pulled a baseball cap out of the back seat and grabbed her shooting glasses from the glove box. She pulled her hair up under the cap, put on the glasses, and prayed. The ruse worked. Though he was clearly checking out the faces of everyone leaving, the man at the gate let her pass.

As soon as she made it to the main highway, she hit the code lights on her undercover car and rushed back to the office.

BACK AT HER DESK, Spiteri called Baron Saint-Clair, Father Dominic, and Detective Sabrina Felici, merging them into a conference call.

"*He's here!* Dante is here at the Last Mass! He *is* Magnus. Michael, is there any chance you can get here before the morning?"

Dominic thought for a moment. "I doubt it. It's too late to get a flight to be there by tomorrow."

"Honestly, I think we really need you. I'd like to put a wire on you and see if we can urge Dante to make any incriminating statements. If what you say about his irked feelings toward you are any indication, he's likely to boast quite a bit."

"I definitely want to come. I'm certain it was he who stole the keys to the pope's safe and took classified documents from it, not to mention the Third Secret of Fátima. That's theft, and if he faked the copies he gave to Barlow, that's fraud. If we catch him, I need to be there to identify and take possession of the Vatican's property."

"We have enough to nail him for a number of financial

crimes," Saint-Clair said, "but proving them would be fairly complicated, given the banking privacy rules and the different countries involved. It would be cleaner if we could prove them ourselves."

"All right, let me see if I can get a ride to Malta somehow."

"Michael, I insist you take my plane. It will be ready for you."

"Oh, of course, Baron. I forgot who I'm talking to!"

"It's no problem at all. I just had the jet flown to Fiumicino Airport for minor maintenance. Hana and Marco are still here with me on the *Sea Chalet*. But we'll be waiting for you at the FBO terminal in Rome."

"That's great. I'll let His Holiness know. He'll probably send one or two of the Swiss Guards with me. I'm sure we have jurisdiction to arrest Dante and have him extradited for the crimes we believe he committed here, and if we can show he perpetrated crimes in other places we'll just have to fight over the pieces."

"Baron," Spiteri added, "please let me know when you arrive and I'll have transportation waiting for you at the FBO at Malta International."

"Thank you, Eliza, you are a credit to the agency. We'll see you in a few hours."

Dominic hung up and immediately called the pope to inform him of developments, then called Karl and Lukas. "Hey, how'd you two like to go back to Malta and arrest Dante?"

"You mean you want there to be something left of that bastard to arrest?" Karl asked eagerly. "When do we leave?"

"Now."

CHAPTER

FORTY-THREE

Having departed Rome's Leonardo da Vinci–Fiumicino Airport around six a.m., the Dassault Falcon was bound for Malta, a ninety-minute flight. Baron Armand de Saint-Clair had asked the flight attendant to prepare breakfast for everyone after takeoff.

The whole team—Dominic, Hana, Marco, Karl, Lukas, and the baron—enthusiastically tucked into their meals of scrambled eggs, bratwurst, hashed brown potatoes, coffee, and freshly squeezed orange juice as they talked about the day ahead. While they were eager for what was to come, there was some anxiety over potentially uncontrollable elements of their plan.

On arrival at Malta International Airport, they transferred to a Mercedes Sprinter van that Eliza Spiteri had prearranged for them at the Signature FBO terminal. As commander of the Malta Police Force Counterterrorism Unit, she made quick work of clearing the group through Customs, and they all loaded up in the van for the quick trip to Mdina.

Entering the walled city, the van pulled up in front of the

regional police station, a tan, three-story, carved stone building with bright blue double doors, consistent with Malta's passion for color throughout its cities. Ushering them inside, Captain Spiteri took them up to the third-floor conference room, where detectives Sabrina Felici and Rebecca Lancaster were waiting, having flown in the night before. Introductions were made to those who hadn't yet met one another, then Spiteri explained their plan so everyone was up to speed.

"So, to recap, we suspect that ex-cardinal Fabrizio Dante, using the alias Albert Magnus, has masterminded the panic in the financial markets to amass a significant fortune, in addition to stealing assets pledged to the KOTA Foundation from participants and Novena supporters of the Last Mass. But prosecuting him for that fraud will be difficult, given the multitude of accounts and countries that could be involved."

"I'm not sure I see the point of all that," Hana said. "If people do believe the end of the world is coming, why would they bother signing over all their assets to the KOTA Foundation? Logically, there wouldn't *be* a foundation after the Apocalypse! Aren't these people thinking straight?"

"Well, actually," Dominic noted, "they would know, or at least be told, that the world isn't coming to an end immediately. In dispensationalist eschatology, there is a seven-year period after the Rapture during which God pours out his wrath upon the world. If you survive this seven-year period, there is still a chance you could be saved. Jesus returns at the end of the seven years, called the Great Tribulation, along with his army for the final Battle of Armageddon, where evil is defeated, and Christ sets up his heavenly kingdom on Earth for a thousand years."

Everyone in the room was rapt, taking in the vision painted by the priest.

"Yes," Hana acceded, "that would make more sense then. Still, it's all pretty crazy to me."

Spiteri continued. "Moving on, Dante is suspected of stealing more than one set of high-value security keys from the Vatican, and probably removed sensitive materials from the pope's personal safe when he was Vatican Secretary of State. We also suspect he devised the planning of, or was at least complicit in, the murders of Father Jonah Barlow in Chicago, Brother Moshe Hadani in Jerusalem, and probably also the astronomer Boris Ponomarenko here in Malta. There is no question Dante will be arrested. The only question is whether we can get him to confess to any of those crimes, or at least give us information as to where we can gather further evidence.

"Detectives Felici, Lancaster, and I have put together something of a plan. Michael, this is where you come in. We want to put a hidden recording device on you, and have you go in as one of the attendees. We'll be waiting outside the tent, watching for a sign from you—say, running your hand over your hair—so we know when to come in and make the arrest. We need you to engage him in conversation, try to get him to admit he was involved in these crimes—or at least one of them—so we can interrogate him further and break him down on the others."

Dominic was clearly concerned. "Well, I don't want to seem like a coward here, but this man hates me with a passion. What if he has his minions dispose of me on the spot?"

"I agree," said Hana, equally distressed. "Dante is a vile, unpredictable creature. I'm sure I speak for others when I insist that Michael be protected at all times." The others nodded in agreement.

Karl was especially vehement. "What if I go in with him? I want to be there to make sure he comes to no harm. In fact, I insist on it."

"Or *I* could go," Marco added confidently. "Dante wouldn't recognize me."

"That won't be necessary, everyone," Spiteri assured them. "We've got twenty police officers standing by just outside Mdina, as well as soldiers from Malta's Armed Forces 1st

Regiment Battalion and our Quick Reaction Force. These are all Special Operations teams, ready to deploy around the tent from all sides if and when needed. And the arresting team will come in from behind the two large projection screens."

"I'm still concerned that this might be better handled by someone more versed in getting a criminal to implicate himself," Dominic said tersely. "After all, I'm not a police interrogator."

"No, Michael, but you are a priest. And there are other priests on the grounds as well, giving confessions to those seeking to right the wrongs of their lives, so you'll blend in fine. In fact, when approaching Dante, think of it like trying to get a guilty soul to give a full and honest confession."

"Well, now that you put it like that…" he said satirically.

"Great. Stand by while I get the recording equipment."

Spiteri left the room for a few minutes while the others continued expressing their concerns, which Dominic now assuaged with a wave of his hand.

"She's right," he said matter-of-factly. "I'm the only one Dante might engage with. And I do feel better knowing there's an army surrounding me. I'm just concerned the bastard might have a blade on him and gut me where I stand." He shuddered comically, but the others didn't smile.

Spiteri returned, holding a box which she set on the conference table. Reaching inside, she withdrew a device resembling an old-fashioned Walkman, with a lavalier microphone attached on a long wire.

Lancaster and Felici stared at it, then looked at Dominic's trim-fitting clerical garments, then over to Spiteri, shaking their heads.

"I really don't think that's going to work, Eliza," Lancaster said. "You couldn't hide a pack of cigarettes under Michael's shirt, much less something that big." Felici nodded.

Spiteri reexamined everything, then said, "Michael, what are you carrying in your pockets now?"

"Just my wallet and iPhone." Taking both out of his pockets, he set them on the table. Then he stared at the phone for a moment and, picking it up, pressed a speed dial button.

"I have a better idea. Hang on a sec. I have to wake up somebody in Rome."

CHAPTER FORTY-FOUR

With everything set and everyone in place, Dominic was dropped off out of sight by Eliza Spiteri, near the field where KOTA's tent was raised. The priest walked the rest of the way in.

As he entered the large tent, he was impressed at the lengths to which the organizers had gone in creating such a fitting spiritual environment. The logistics alone must have been an enormous feat. A prominent altar took center stage at the front, behind which was a semicircular stained glass apse, replete with burning candles, bouquets of flowers, and saintly statuary. The aromatic scent of frankincense wafted throughout the area, giving it a warm, mystical dimension, its symbolic values being those of purification and sanctification. The gentle strains of Gregorian chant played lightly in the background.

Several throne-like chairs were set side-by-side behind the altar. Rows of white folding chairs, fifty rows deep, with forty chairs on each side of the center aisle, accommodated some two thousand participants. There were also two enormous projection screens displaying in the lower left corners a countdown to the beginning of the Last Mass, with scenes of chaos from around the world above them, apparently live feeds from the internet. Attendees filed in, taking seats. Many were clearly ecstatic; some were weeping, though whether for joy or out of fear was hard to tell.

Fifty men, all dressed in the black KOTA robes, were rolling carts of small, sealed, juice box-like containers up the middle and side aisles, passing out one box to each person in the audience, giving them strict instructions not to open or drink the sacred wine until it was blessed during the Last Mass.

From the rear of the tent, Dominic saw Cardinal Damien Challis, Archbishop of Washington, D.C., standing on the dais, along with several other men wearing a combination of priestly garb and KOTA regalia.

As Dominic started in, he was stopped by a KOTA member in a black robe. The priest was careful to keep his left side away from the person so his phone would not be discovered.

"Can I help you find something, Father?" the person asked.

"Yes, Cardinal Dante requested my assistance."

"Ah, he is up at the front, over on the side there. Go right ahead. Don't want to keep *him* waiting."

Dominic headed farther into the tent.

Then he saw Dante, and his stomach tightened. He was standing just offstage near the altar in his KOTA robe, but also wearing the purple stole and skullcap of a bishop. Sudden feelings of fear and repugnance arose in him as he watched the tall wretch, his hawkish eyes arrogantly scanning the crowd. Dominic knew this man well, and felt only slightly ashamed by the hatred he harbored for him, for the dread the man was causing him to feel in anticipation of what he was about to do.

But he was also eager to see Dante arrested and put away for good, which helped mollify the fear and dread overtaking him. *I can do this,* he thought. *And I'll do it right.*

With his iPhone tucked inside his shirt pocket, the dark camera just peeking out above its black hem, Dominic engaged a preset FaceTime recording button. Fortifying himself with a deep breath, he strode toward the stage.

Walking up behind the man, he said as assertively as he could muster, "Dante, what in God's name do you think you're doing here?"

Dante turned around. Seeing his old nemesis, he didn't even register surprise, much less shock.

"Ah. Father Dominic. So good of you to accept my invitation."

"What invitation? Father Marchetti told us you were here."

Dante looked down haughtily at the priest. "And who do you think Marchetti works for? Ah, there it is. The light of recognition in those blind eyes of yours."

Dominic was momentarily stunned on hearing of Marchetti's involvement—*he was acting as a double agent!* he thought, his agitation mounting.

Forcing himself to stay on point, he asserted, "You *stole* documents from the pope's safe! I want them back. Now."

"Oh, that. Yes, I took the prophecy. If you ever get to read it, you'll see why. But when that incompetent Petrini was elected pope, I had a much better idea. Do you know, after all those years I dedicated to the Church, when I was sent to prison, nobody came to visit me? Well, almost nobody. Father Barlow, my old friend, he came.

"But you know who else came to Regina Coeli? The Evangelicals, looking to steal souls away from the Catholic Church. Some of them are devoutly convinced that the Church is apostate. That the Church is run by the Devil himself. So they see it as their mission to convert the misguided to their 'real' Christianity. They also are wholeheartedly convinced that the end of the world is at hand. They see the fulfillment of scripture in any news out of the Middle East. They are obsessed with the State of Israel. And so they come to the prison, thinking there will be Catholics there who are dissatisfied with the Church, and since they are on a short clock, they must save those poor, deceived souls before it's too late."

"What the hell are you talking about?!" The man was spewing nonsense, as if deranged.

But Dante spoke regally, as if he had everything in control. "I'm talking about *why* you are here. You see, Dominic, people see what they want to see. Those who are conspiracy-minded, they see plots and schemes. The people who think the world is about to end, they see the fulfillment of prophecy. It takes very little suggestion to direct their thinking along those lines. Indeed, Father Barlow was one of those who always believed that the Church was hiding things. Well, and of course it *is!* So it took very little convincing to get Barlow to believe that the prophecies I gave him were the ones the Vatican had been hiding. He saw it as his duty to bring them to light… to expose the corruption and deceit he already believed were so rampant in the Church. He barely questioned their authenticity! At least not until the end. At first, he took my very incarceration as proof that the church was hiding something. However, he was thorough, our Jonah was. He got suspicious toward the end, when what I gave him didn't match some of the information he had gotten from others who knew, or thought they knew, the actual prophecies."

"Are you saying that you gave Jonah *altered* prophecies?"

"Now you're catching on. The actual Third Prophecy did not fit my purposes. I admit that when I took it, I did not know what I was going to do with it. But with everyone blathering on about transparency within the Church, I found my opportunity and then realized it would simply not do to have the actual prophecy released. So I took it and hid it away, and I made a new one that did suit me. I also took the keys, so that nobody would be able to open the safe and see that the prophecy was missing. This gave me time to get everything ready.

"But I digress. I was talking about my time in prison, the prison *you* sent me to, don't forget. You see, those years I spent in

Regina Coeli, I had a lot of time to think about how to take my revenge on you and your *father*. So when Barlow and the Evangelicals visited me in prison, it occurred to me that all this apocalyptic fervor could be turned to my advantage."

"What did you do?" Dominic asked, his distress escalating as moments crept by and he still hadn't said enough specifics on tape to arrest the evil man. A few people filed in to take seats as the black-clad staff prepared various accoutrements for the event about to unfold.

"Be patient. We're getting to that. These KOTA fools, they are some of the people I referred to a moment ago. They *want* to see the world end. Over the past two thousand years, people have been waiting for the End Times; many even yearning for it. So, after I convinced Barlow that the End was at hand—thanks to the altered prophecies—he wrote his manuscript accusing the Church of hiding the true prophecies, certain that the events they predicted would occur.

"I then arranged to have KOTA obtain a copy of Barlow's manuscript. I'm afraid poor Jonah did not survive the acquisition process, but he was making too much noise about going public before I was ready.

"And it was just a stroke of providence that your father's name is Petrini, and that St. Malachy predicted the last pope would be Peter the Roman. It's not too much of a stretch to link Petrini with Peter, although I admit the whole Bishop of Rome thing is a little weak as an explanation for him being Roman, though his ancestors were. But that's the thing about these KOTA fools. They are willing to overlook the weaknesses in things that already fit their worldview. So when I suggested to Jonah that Petrini was the fulfillment of St. Malachy's prophecy, he eagerly ran with it, and so did Damien Challis.

"Oh, and Challis, well, he was ripe for the picking. Cut from the same cloth as Jonah Barlow. Suspicious of the Church, yet thoroughly ensconced within it, convinced the End is near. And oh, so sincere, so charismatic. He could sell atheism to a doorstep Jehovah. And he brilliantly sold everything I suggested to him, following the blueprint for the End that was in Jonah's manuscript —also based on my suggestions—as well as the altered prophecies I gave him. And then all on his own he linked the Pope Emeritus's offer to come back to Revelation 17. Unplanned, but totally helpful to whip up the necessary sentiment among the faithful. He saw what he wanted to see: fulfilment of scripture in present events. It was so easy to convince him that I should be the spiritual advisor to the Knights. He was so busy managing his little empire, after all.

"Then there was that business with the keys. Of course, as Secretary of State, I knew who the Clavis Domini was. I was having him watched the whole time. KOTA has people everywhere. So, when he spoke with the pope, I knew Petrini was going to send someone for the backup keys. What I didn't expect was that Moshe Hadani had become aware that we were watching him. The watchers got a little too close, too overzealous. They spooked him and he sent the keys away. Which, while I didn't expect it, worked out all the better. We were going to take the keys from him anyway, mostly to slow you down and draw you in, but having them spread out across the globe? We just had to add a little pressure to keep you moving, keep you occupied looking in the wrong places while we got everything ready. I'm only a little sorry Moshe died, but we had to know where he had sent the keys. We were playing catch-up there for a while. So yes, you eventually got the keys and found out the prophecy was missing. But I got so much more done in the meantime."

"And what about Nibiru? What about the attack on the pope during his address? Were you responsible for those too?" Dominic tried to keep his excitement from showing, as already Dante had incriminated himself. But he needed more from this greedy and murderous man, enough to send him away for good this time.

Dante looked down at Dominic condescendingly, as if he were slow-witted. Then he sighed theatrically.

"The astronomer, Boris Ponomarenko, came from Ukraine to Argentina to work at one of the large observatories. And while I was there as Archbishop of Buenos Aires, he got himself into a bit of trouble. He had a gambling problem, you see. He came to me for confession, and I absolved him, but I also gave him some help. I got him a job at the Vatican Observatory in Arizona so I could keep track of him. The fool got himself fired, but was able to switch from the Vatican Observatory to the other telescope on the same site, which—in another quirk of irony—was named LUCIFER. And so I pulled in a little favor from Boris, whom I code-named Lucifer, to help me out when the time was right. I had him talk to Barlow to convey to him the details of Nibiru. Boris is another one of those people who had a particular worldview and saw things the way he wanted them to be. There are so many of them… a common human failing, but they can be so useful. Boris had been looking for evidence of Nibiru his whole career. It didn't take a lot to convince him to claim that he'd found it. Then he got into money trouble again. And I helped him out again, as he helped me with that press announcement, and bringing the drugs into Malta which I needed for this Mass. I'm afraid I had to have him silenced so he wouldn't tip off the Maltese authorities before you got here.

"You see, Dominic, it's so easy to make predictions when you know what's going to happen. Predict Nibiru is coming, and then have it announced. Predict the pope will be shot, and then shoot him."

Though Dominic had believed all this to be true, the shock of Dante's exploitable confession stunned him.

"And yes, I'm proud to say I instructed the heraldist to assassinate the pope. Your ever-loving father. It's a pity *you* got in the way."

"You bastard!"

"Oh, calm down now, Dominic. We haven't even gotten to the best part yet."

As Dante spoke these last words, he subtly motioned for three men in black robes to come up behind Dominic.

"Make sure he remains where he is. He is not to leave the premises."

Now surrounded, Dominic felt trapped.

CHAPTER
FORTY-FIVE

Now the white-robed, would-be Elect were filling the chairs, quietly awaiting the Last Mass. But Dante continued, his voice low and menacing, just low enough to be heard only by Dominic. "Let me explain. As you will soon witness, the wine these generous souls are about to drink is infused with carfentanyl and clonazepam, both quite potent individually—but lethal in combination. These people will meet Jesus, all right, but not in the fashion they were hoping for. It will be a mass suicide of epic proportions.

"But you know the best part? This will be all *your* doing! Your name is on the prescriptions for the drugs; you signed for them, in fact…."

"That's ridiculous! Nobody would believe I'd do that! They'd know it was a forgery."

"Yes, perhaps—if that were the only evidence. But, you see, I've been busy since we last saw each other in Rome. Do you remember all those diamonds found in the safe deposit box at the Vatican Bank, the ones stolen from you? Well, it appears that you had separated a few and put them away for yourself, right back where you got them, in a safe deposit box at the Vatican Bank… one registered in your name, by the way, also with your signature on file, which I provided, of course, and to which the key will be found in your apartment.

"And you thought when your rooms got tossed last year, they were looking to take something? No, that was merely to distract you from the one thing they were there to plant: your safe deposit box key, and the access codes to a numbered account at Banque Suisse de Saint-Clair. I thought that was an especially good touch, putting your ill-gotten gains in Armand's bank.

"Yes, Dominic, you earned a tidy sum from the proceeds of this spectacular event here today, as payment for your services in obtaining the drugs, not to mention your shameful indiscretions in selling off documents from the Riserva."

Dante looked into Dominic's eyes. "And there it is again. The light of comprehension. Yes, I had the key to the Riserva, and I took some things from there as well. Things I could sell on the black market whenever I needed money again, which I did after prison and that second Vatican Bank scandal. And I made sure to implicate you in those sales as well. As I see it, you owe me at least the two hundred million you already cost me from my brother's estate, and more for my years in prison, and for stripping me of my priesthood. You and your father owe me a new life.

"I'm leaving after the Mass for a small island with no extradition treaties. I will be rich and untouchable, and you, I'm afraid, will have died in humiliation."

"You're sick, Dante, and totally deranged!"

"*Tut, tut,* my young friend," the old man chided. "There are still finishing touches needed to complete my work here. As Paul wrote in Romans, 'I am Vengeance, saith the Lord.' Well, Dominic—*I am Vengeance!* Here to do the Lord's work.

"How this plays out now is up to you. Get up on this stage and in full view of the cameras and all the media, proclaim the pope to be your father, renounce him for the degenerate fornicator he is, and resign your priesthood in shame. You will also call for your father to abdicate the Throne of St. Peter in disgrace. If you don't do as I say, you will drink the wine as mortification for your sins, and that is how you will be remembered."

Dominic was furious. "You're a *monster*, Dante! You won't get away with this."

"No, you forget—I am *Vengeance!* Now, *make your choice*!"

Dante gestured to one of the men behind him to grab a nearby container of the wine.

"Hold him!" Dante instructed.

Before the men had time to grab him, Dominic, now panicking, suddenly remembered to run his right hand over his head, smoothing back his hair. He had only a moment to decide. Had Ian heard any of their conversation? How long would it take for him to alert the police to sweep in? How quickly would Dante instruct his devotees to drink the poisoned wine? He needed to buy time in any way he could. Time to save these people from a fate they didn't deserve.

Dante took the container from the robed man, opened the pour spout, and held it in front of Dominic.

"What will it be, priest? A sip from the cup, or a speech from the stage? I am weary of waiting. *Choose!*"

Looking directly into Dante's crazed eyes, Dominic simply smiled, then asked, "Did you get all that, Ian?" He hoped his face spoke confidence when, in his heart, he just prayed that his plan would work.

A clear voice emerged from Dominic's breast pocket, saying, "You bet, Michael. Five seconds to replay."

A confused Dante looked down at the young priest. "*What game is this?!*" he asked.

With relief at hearing his assistant's voice, Dominic answered, "Actually, Dante, there's another choice I have. One you hadn't anticipated."

The large screens on either side of the stage flickered, a hazy static replacing the countdown. Two thousand heads turned to look up at the displays as the recorded video of Fabrizio Dante's evil and smiling face filled the screens and the audio came up....

"'Let me explain. As you will soon witness, the wine these generous souls are about to drink is infused with carfentanyl and clonazepam, both quite potent individually—but lethal in combination. These people will meet Jesus, all right, but not in the fashion they were hoping for. It will be a mass suicide of epic proportions....'"

His jaw dropping open, Dante looked up as well, staring at the screens, speechless as the loudspeakers replayed his confession.

CHAPTER FORTY-SIX

There was a sudden hush as people were transfixed, watching the drama play out before their eyes on the big screens, then turning to each other, trying to process what they had just seen and heard. Many wept with tears of disappointment that they wouldn't be going to heaven. A sad few had actually begun drinking the wine, convinced this was some kind of evil propaganda, believing they were indeed facing the End Times. Others shouted at them to stop, trying to convince them that suicide wasn't the answer—that they had been set up!

Then the rumbles of pandemonium began. Angry participants, clearly furious that they had been taken in, rose out of their chairs, looking for retribution.

Suddenly, from all sides of the tent, people watched as two dozen combat blades slit open the sides of the huge tent canvas. Soldiers from all forces and agencies poured through the wide openings as twenty police officers in tactical gear came around from behind the apse of the makeshift chapel. Still on the dais, Cardinal Damien Challis and the other priests were gathered and placed in handcuffs, arrested on the spot.

Outfitted in her tactical uniform, Eliza Spiteri jumped up on stage, approached the podium and flipped on the microphone.

"Ladies and gentlemen, I am Captain Eliza Spiteri of the Malta Police Force. Please remain calm and seated. I will explain what is going on in just a moment."

While she was speaking, Dante had moved quickly from the side altar to the edge of the main stage and up the few steps on the side, still clutching the container of poisoned wine.

Dominic had been joined by Hana, Marco, and detectives Felici and Lancaster near the bottom of the stage steps. Karl and Lukas were maneuvering around to the back of the stage to get behind Dante and come at him from his blind side.

Spiteri spoke again. "Fabrizio Dante, you are under arrest for three counts of murder or conspiracy to commit murder, grand theft, and multiple counts of fraud."

Drawing her firearm, she turned and pointed it at Dante. "Put down the wine and come quietly. There is no way out for you."

Karl and Lukas had gained the main stage and were prepared to jump Dante from the rear. Spiteri saw them in her background and motioned them back out of her line of fire. They stepped to the side and drew their sidearms as well, waiting for Spiteri or Dante to act.

Holding the open container close to his chest, Dante spun around quickly, seeking any avenue of escape. Realizing there was no way out, he had only one option.

Now surrounded by five of them—Lancaster, Felici, and Dominic, with Hana and Marco standing just below him at the base of the steps—Dante stared balefully at Dominic, fire in his eyes.

"Well, aren't you the clever one? Thought of everything, did you? But I don't imagine you thought of this...."

With that, Dante took a swig of the poisoned wine, choking as he swallowed it.

"I'm *never* going back to prison! I'd rather burn in Hell, and I'll take all of you with me."

With a dramatic flourish, Dante flung the remaining toxic liquid from the container in an arc that splashed on all five standing around him.

Rebecca Lancaster, being first in line, reacted almost out of instinct. She shouted *"No!"* as she dove in front of her friend and colleague Sabrina Felici. As she was pushing her out of the way, Lancaster took the first splash of poison across her face, with a deadly portion of the spray falling into her open mouth.

Dominic had slightly more time, but the same instincts. He dove to his right, twisting at the hips to turn his back to the spray of liquid while shielding Hana from the onslaught, pushing her down and away as they fell. He hit the stage floor, landing on top of Hana and holding onto her, afraid to let go. She clung to him, her face buried in his neck.

Marco dove away from the splash, going into a tuck and roll, coming back to his feet as the spray passed him, grasping his pistol from beneath his shirt, looking for a target that didn't exist.

Spiteri had Dante covered, but by the time she realized what he had done, the threat was mitigated. Dante was now on the ground, thrashing in pain from the draught of poison he had ingested, the potent drugs speeding to his vital organs and shutting them down.

Karl and Lukas rushed forward from behind Dante, quickly realizing there was nothing for them to do either—and neither was hardly motivated to try to save Dante.

Now foaming at the mouth, Dante lay there, a guttural groan emerging as he began to convulse violently. One final gasp, and he was gone.

Sabrina was on her knees, holding Rebecca's head in her lap. She shouted for a medic, but Rebecca's eyes quickly clouded over, her pupils constricted to small points by the powerful opiate, and her breaths became raspy and shallow.

"Did we get him?" she whispered feebly, looking into her friend's eyes.

"You bet, Becca. We got him. Shhh, you just hold on. Help is coming. *Medic!* Stay with me, Bec. Don't you leave me! *Medic! Officer down!* Don't you leave me, Becca...."

As she lay in Sabrina's arms, the last thing Rebecca Lancaster saw were the tears rolling down her friend's cheeks.

CHAPTER
FORTY-SEVEN

Seeing the danger had passed, Dominic got up off the ground and helped Hana to her feet. Marco holstered his Glock back under his shirt, then put a protective arm around Hana's shoulders.

Dominic looked at her, then turned away. Hana's gaze followed him.

She watched as he bent over Rebecca, administering Last Rites. Then despite his personal loathing for the man, he knelt over Fabrizio Dante and anointed him as well.

Seeing the priest attend to the one man who had given them all nothing but trouble, Marco pulled back on Dominic's shoulder with menace in his eyes. "Not him," he growled.

Dominic looked up into the face of the commando, and with mercy and forgiveness in his voice said, "Yes. Especially him."

His priestly duties complete, he turned to Eliza Spiteri, who was again addressing the assembly.

"Ladies and gentlemen," she said, "I am sorry for the commotion, but you have been deceived by a deranged man, one who used you as part of a devious plan for vengeance against others, and who was ready to sacrifice you to achieve his goals.

"I'm sure you are upset and confused about what happens now. There will be no Mass. That was all part of the ruse. We are arranging bus transportation for you from here to a facility in Valletta, where investigators will be taking statements from you so that we can begin the process of unraveling the fraud that was committed against you."

His iPhone still engaged on FaceTime, Dominic heard Ian's voice calling to him. "Father Michael, are you there? Can you hear me?"

"Yes, Ian. I'm here."

"I heard it all, Michael, and so did the Holy Father and Father Bannon. They came down to observe everything you were transmitting. In fact, the Holy Father wishes to address the crowd. Now."

"Well, I didn't see that coming. All right, let me get Captain Spiteri."

Dominic went up on stage and, covering the microphone with his hand and pushing it down, he whispered in Spiteri's ear. "The pope wants to address the crowd. Can we do that? Ian, my assistant in Rome, still has a live connection to the projectors."

Stunned at the unusual development, Spiteri said, "Of course! Absolutely. I think that would be a wonderful gesture."

"Okay, Ian, it's a go," he said into his phone.

Moments later, both large projection screens, which had gone dark after playing a portion of Dante's confession, resumed projecting. Suddenly the pope appeared, sitting in the conference room of the Vatican Archives, bandages still covering the stitches on his cheeks, his tongue still a little swollen and thick, giving him a slight slur.

"My brothers and sisters, may the peace of the Lord be upon you. I know you have been through a terrible ordeal, one that was perpetrated against you by a fallen former member of the priesthood, and by the Archbishop of Washington, D.C., who was apparently misled by him, and by the so-called Knights of the Apocalypse, who have no formal standing with the Church. For this you have my sympathy and compassion.

"As I speak to you now, a team of priests and other counselors is being sent to assist you through this difficult time. We, along with the law enforcement and financial authorities in Malta, Italy, the U.S., and elsewhere, will do everything we can to restore you—financially, emotionally, and spiritually. Know that I am taking a personal interest in your recovery and will be kept always informed. In the meantime, I ask that you cooperate with Maltese officials and be patient, for there are many of you needing assistance and Malta is a very small country. They will be doing the best they can, and we will be supporting them in full, but this will take time. You are in good hands."

The pope held up his hand in the familiar gesture of making a sign of the cross. "May the blessings of the Father, the Son, and the Holy Spirit be with you all, now and always. Amen."

The video screens went dark.

"Michael," Spiteri said, "please express my sincere thanks to the Holy Father for his intervention here. His words will help a great deal in the coming days while we figure this thing out. I've activated our civil defense corps. Some people further up the chain will be taking over the investigation from here. I'm sure I will still have some role to play, but my main goal has been achieved. I want to thank you so much for all that you've done. Is there anything that you might need from us? Anything at all?"

"Well," Dominic said thoughtfully, "now that you mention it, yes, there is."

CHAPTER

FORTY-EIGHT

Ernesto Vila was finally heading home to Portugal, his duties to the Knights of Malta completed, at least for now. The new semester was rapidly approaching, and he needed to return to Coimbra to prepare for the upcoming semester, develop his lesson plans, and help to shape the young minds succeeding him.

Sitting in the Departures lounge sipping a cup of coffee, Vila wished he had been able to be there to see the mission to completion at the Last Mass, but he was also glad he had not had to witness the death of Detective Lancaster or, for that matter, of Fabrizio Dante, may the Lord have mercy on him—but not too much.

Still, he could not shake the nagging guilt that if he had been there, perhaps he could have done something to prevent the detective's death. He recognized the pangs of survivor's guilt for what they were and tried to redirect his thoughts. There were already many good warriors there who had not been able to prevent that tragedy. Had he been there, it was likely he would have been as powerless as they were, or worse.

As he looked up and out over the people milling about the international departures area, past the passport control booths, he thought he recognized someone just coming through. He was wearing a hat and glasses, and his hair had been cut nearly to the scalp, but it certainly looked like…

Lorenzo Marchetti!

Their eyes suddenly met, and the man flinched, then started to look away.

Standing up, Vila shouted to the passport control officers and the security officers standing nearby, "Stop that man! Stop him! He is a wanted criminal!"

Suddenly surrounded by men in black uniforms and black berets, pants tucked into the tops of shiny black boots, and carrying Heckler and Koch MP5 submachine guns, Marchetti stopped and raised his hands.

"Don't shoot! I do not know what you are talking about. My name is Timoteo Talpa. Check my passport. That man is crazy. I am not wanted for anything."

Hearing his voice, Vila was more than sure he had the right man.

Addressing the authorities directly now, Vila continued. "This man is a conspirator in the near-mass murder that happened two days ago in Malta. He passed false information from the Knights of the Apocalypse to the Knights of Malta and to the authorities that we were working with. Call Captain Spiteri at Malta's Counterterrorism Unit. She will verify this."

The passport control officers had called for their supervisor, who had hurried over.

"Give me his passport," he demanded. Inspecting it closely, holding up its pages to the lights above, he looked at Marchetti with disgust.

"This is clearly a fake. A very good one, but still a forgery. Officers, take this man into custody downstairs and put him in the holding cell. I will call Captain Spiteri and see what she wants done with him."

Marchetti screamed like a madman as he was marched away.

"Dante was a better man than any of you! I will avenge him. Watch for me, Vila. I'll come for you. I'll come for all of you."

"Get him out of here," the supervisor repeated. "And add terrorist threats to the list of charges. Put me down as a witness."

As the officers led Marchetti away, the passport control supervisor turned to Vila.

Noticing Vila's distinctive lapel pin identifying him as a Knight of Malta, he said respectfully, "Thank you, sir. You have done the order, and the country, a great service. I will send a report of today's actions to the Knights' leadership. You might even get a medal. God knows you probably deserve one."

"Well, not me. But Dame Eliza Spiteri and that Father Dominic from the Vatican. They deserve much more than medals."

The excitement over, Vila returned to his seat, his coffee now cold but his heart was warm, for now he felt like he had completed his mission.

CHAPTER FORTY-NINE

It took a couple days to get the search warrant through the Maltese court system, but since the prime suspect was dead, there was no need to retain the Vatican's documents as evidence.

In accordance with the warrant, Father Michael Dominic was authorized to identify, collect, and repossess any items that Dante had removed from the Vatican. Dominic met with Captain Spiteri, as well as a couple Crime Scene Investigation technicians, at the room where Dante had been staying at Mdina. Immediately prior to the Mass, the ex-cardinal had been staying at the Xara Palace next door to Cardinal Challis, but since coming to Malta he had been renting a small flat in an old stone building just outside the walled city. To Dominic, it reminded him of a monk's cell, comprised of a simple cot, a three-drawer dresser, a desk and chair, and a laptop computer. A simple kitchen and bathroom rounded out the flat.

Starting in the kitchen, the team searched the drawers and cabinets. They looked for items stuck between plates or bowls, pulling out drawers and looking for things taped behind or under them. They searched in the pots and pans, and in containers in the refrigerator. They searched in the toilet tank and took apart the shower head. They found nothing of interest until they got to the medicine cabinet. There, in a bottle labeled as an over-the-counter pain reliever, they found several of the ten-carat octagonal Asscher cut diamonds Michael had found in Roberto Calvi's safe deposit box in the Vatican Bank earlier that year. They then moved to the dresser. In the top drawer, they found the two biometric keys to the Petri Crypta folded into a pair of socks. The keys to the Riserva were rolled up in a pair of briefs.

Dominic moved over to the desk. It was a simple affair, a single column of drawers on the right side and a flat, wide drawer beneath the front of the desk. In the wide drawer, Michael found several pieces of paper with row after row of his own signature. Apparently, Dante had been telling the truth about that. It was a very good reproduction of his handwriting. He set it aside on the desk to be used as evidence later. He also found a passport and Maltese identification card in the name of Albert Magnus, with this flat's address.

He moved to the upper drawer on the right. Inside was a stack of papers, maybe twenty pages in all, and a large manila envelope. On the top was the contrived four-page version of the Third Secret of Fátima, which, at least on the first page, read exactly how he had been told it would read. He briefly scanned the remaining pages and determined that these were other records that had come from the Vatican. He did not explore further. If these documents had come from the Petri Crypta, he had no business reading them. They were meant for the pope's eyes only, and he would honor that.

In the next drawer down, Michael found pages and pages of handwritten notes relating to banking transactions at several institutions spread throughout the Caribbean. These he gave to Spiteri to advance their financial investigation. The bottom drawer contained the missing copy of Barlow's manuscript. Flipping through its pages, Dominic saw that Barlow had handwritten notes in the margins of many of the pages. On one of the pages regarding the prophecies of Nibiru, there was a note reading, 'Boris, the astronomer, does not want this released until he gets approval from his superiors. The public needs to know now.'

Flipping through a few more pages, he found one about the last portion of the Third Secret: 'Dante's copy does not square with Vila's version of the prophecy. Vila is adamant his story is correct, handed down from Cesar. How to resolve? Could Dante's be fake?'

Dominic would have to spend some time going through this page by page once he returned to Rome.

They pulled out all the other drawers and looked under and behind them. There was nothing left to find.

"For someone who allegedly was so rich—at least from what early investigations show he had made by manipulating the financial markets during the panics he created—Dante was living a remarkably simple life. I don't think he was ever a good person, but his time in prison really changed him. He once lived in opulence as a high-ranking cardinal. He also had independent wealth, but this is remarkably spartan."

"Well," Spiteri noted, "he did say he was heading to the Caribbean as soon as the Mass was over. No reason to spend his ill-gotten gains for a place where he wasn't going to stay. But I know what you mean."

"Wait... how did you know he said he was moving to the Caribbean after the Mass? That was something he said to me, before you all came in to arrest him."

"I guess nobody told you. The pope had Ian conference me in on the Facetime call, so we could hear what Dante was confessing to, in case anything happened to the recording, and so we knew when to come in, in case you were unable to give us the signal."

Dominic was aghast. "I'd assumed the bulk of our conversation was heard only by Ian and the pope! So *everybody* heard everything Dante said to me?! *Everything*?!" Panic overtook him, and his voice quavered at the idea that being the pope's illegitimate son had been now revealed to others.

"I'm afraid so, Michael. And by everybody, I mean just Hana, Marco, Rebecca and Sabrina, Karl and Lukas, and me. When we heard what Dante wanted from you, well, afterward we all agreed that we would never speak of it to anyone. I just wanted you to know that your secret is safe with us."

"And does the pope know that you all know?" He was crestfallen.

"He must know that I know, since the call was conferenced into my cell, but I don't think he knows who else was listening in. Don't be alarmed, Michael, we are all very proud of you. There is nothing to be ashamed of. You handled yourself admirably in a tremendously stressful situation. If I'd had any idea what Dante was actually up to, I would never have sent you in there. I'm so sorry for putting you through that."

"It's okay. You didn't know. And I didn't suspect the depth of his depravity, either. Who could have? Still, I have tried to keep my parentage a secret so that it couldn't be used to hurt my father. I'm not ashamed if it. I'm very proud of him, but I would do anything to keep him from being hurt because of me. Dante really knew how to get to me, and that was the most unsettling part of this whole thing. That fear of exposure."

"What would you have done if we hadn't had the option of arresting him?"

"I don't really know. I didn't have the time to think it through, although I've thought about it some in the last couple days. My father and I are both priests, and we are called to lives of sacrifice, to be ready to forfeit whatever it takes for the souls of those we are called to shepherd, just as our Lord gave himself in sacrifice for all. I would have had to give the confession that Dante was asking for to buy as much time as I could to postpone to the ceremony long enough for the police to arrive to put a stop to it and to save the people from dying for nothing."

"You're a good man, Father Dominic. I'm very proud to have known and worked with you."

"Well, I… Oh, look at the time. I have what I came for. Everyone is waiting at the airport with Armand to take his jet back to Rome. Can you give me a lift to the airport, Eliza?"

"Sure thing. The CSI techs here can finish up on their own."

EPILOGUE

Back in Rome, Dominic strode through St. Anne's Gate, exhausted but happy to be back home. With Karl and Lukas by his side, they looked at each other, shaking their heads and laughing.

"We sure do get into some wild adventures with you, Father Michael," Lukas said. "This one was especially exciting. One wonders what's next."

"It's certainly not the quiet life of a priest I'd anticipated in seminary, that's for sure. What are you guys up to tonight?"

"Straight to bed," Karl said. "I could sleep for a week." Waving goodbye, he and Lukas headed for the Swiss Guard barracks on the right, while Dominic decided to drop in on the Holy Father. There was something important on his mind, and it couldn't wait.

Getting off the elevator in the Apostolic Palace, Dominic crossed the foyer and saw Nick Bannon at his desk, smiling.

"Is he in, Nick?"

"Yes. And he's expecting you, Michael. Go on in."

Bannon pressed the button under his desk to unlock the doors to the pope's office. Papa Petrini was sitting at his desk, reading from a stack of papers in front of him. Dominic placed the manila envelope containing the documents retrieved from Dante's room on the pope's desk.

"Here they are, the documents Dante stole from the Petri Crypta. I have not looked at them, other than to briefly check to make sure they are, near as I can tell, those from the Vatican. I have not read them, Holy Father."

"That doesn't worry me at all, Michael. I trust you more than anyone alive."

The pope stood, walked around his desk, and extended his arms to his son, pulling him onto a warm embrace.

"It is so good to have you back, my son. I was most concerned there for a while."

"I suppose you heard all that transpired between Dante and me?"

"Of course. Nick and I stayed in the office with young Ian Duffy to watch the entire event. I couldn't bear to have you going through that alone. I was there with you the whole time in spirit. You performed splendidly, Michael. I am so proud of you. Proud of all of you. I have asked Armand to make a list of the Knights and Dames of Malta who were instrumental in this matter. I have made arrangements to visit Malta soon, and I want to grant them a special audience."

"Yes, I think that's appropriate. So… Nick knows?"

"Nick has known for some time, yes. There are some things you can't keep secret from one of your closest aides. Nick has been by my side for many years. He knows that and much more."

"And Ian Duffy knows, and Eliza Spiteri, and Hana, Marco, Detective Felici, and Karl and Lukas were all listening in too."

"Well. Sounds like our secret isn't so secret anymore." The pope smiled broadly.

"Hana has known for a while now. I trust Ian to keep it a secret. He learned the value of keeping things under wraps when he first started. I think we can trust Marco. Karl and Lukas are good at keeping secrets. I would trust Eliza Spiteri with my life. I guess I did, in fact. My only concern—and it's a remote one—would be Detective Felici."

"Perhaps I could talk to her and ask her to keep this between us."

"I expect she would honor that, yes."

"I must ask, Michael. Had they not been there to arrest Dante, what would you have done?"

"I didn't know at the time. But Captain Spiteri asked me the same thing this morning. I told her I would have made the speech. It was our honor, and the lives of two thousand people, at stake. I know your papacy is not mine to sacrifice, but sacrifice is part of being a priest. Those two thousand souls were being sacrificed for the wrong reason, but I could have made a sacrifice of us for the right one."

"I was hoping you would say something like that, Michael. I know sometimes it is a struggle to be a priest. I know what you have to give up. Believe me, I know that more than most. But you have consistently made decisions that make me proud of you as a son, and as a priest, every day."

Michael looked at his father, tears forming in the corners of his eyes.

"What is it, my son?"

It came out of him in a rush, unplanned. "I don't know if I want to be a priest anymore. I don't know if I ever really did. There are many things that I really respect about it, and I love my work in the Archives. But…"

Petrini waited, a gentle, tender look on his face.

"…but I think I'm in love with Hana, Father."

"Oh, my dear son. You would not be the first priest to fall in love, as you well know. I loved your mother, very much. But I also loved the Church. In the end, we decided to live the way we did. We both made sacrifices to make sure you were raised in a loving home, with as close to a family as we could provide. And from the time you were born to the day Grace died, we lived chastely, in penance for our indiscretion. Together but apart.

"But that was the right decision for us. I cannot tell you what the right decision is for you. The love of a woman is a blessing. Marriage is as much a vocation as the priesthood, but unfortunately, until things change, you can only choose one. I am here for you, in what time I have left, to help you make that discernment. But ultimately, it will be your decision. Yours and God's."

Dominic's tears wouldn't stop flowing. "Thank you, Father. I suppose I need to speak with Hana about this at some point. I don't know how she feels. Well, not for certain."

"Be patient and be gentle. A woman's heart yearns for passion and honesty."

"Yes, Father. I'll keep that in mind."

Petrini returned to his desk, retrieving the documents and the key to the Petri Crypta.

"Could you give me a hand putting these back in the safe, Michael?"

"Of course." He walked over to Raphael's painting of the *Transfiguration* and pulled it away from the wall to reveal the vault. The pope inserted the key and, once his biometric thumbprint was verified and the electronic handshake completed, he turned the key and the metal bars retracted from the safe assembly.

Dominic swung the door open, careful to keep the door between himself and the contents of the safe. As Petrini took the documents and began to place them into the safe, a single sheet of aged paper fell out from between the numerous pages.

Dominic stooped down and picked up the decades-old handwritten letter. He held it up for the pope to read, and, curiously, the pope did not object to his son's reading it over his shoulder. When they had finished, they both stood there, staring at each other in shock at what they had read.

Taking Sister Lúcia's Third Secret of Fátima and putting it in the safe, with his voice trembling, the Holy Father said, "This goes back into the Petri Crypta for good. As Pope John XXIII said, 'This prophecy does not relate to my time.' And I agree.

"We will never speak of this again, Michael."

FACT VS. FICTION

Many readers have asked me to distinguish fact from fiction in my books. Generally, I like to take factual events and historical figures and build on them in creative ways—but much of what I do write is historically accurate. In this book, I'll review some of the chapters where questions may arise, with hopes it may help those wondering where reality meets creative writing.

GENERAL:

As in all my books, vehicles, trains, airports, transportation schedules, restaurants (and their menus), locations, time zones, and travel times are all consistent with reality. As much as possible, events take place in real time, using actual locations and mentioning local buildings and businesses where suitable. Avid readers have often commented that they have come across specific places I describe in their travels, making their experience that much more realistic and enjoyable.

PROLOGUE:

The *Milagre do Sol*, the Miracle of the Sun, was an actual spectacle seen by as many as a hundred thousand people in

Fátima, Portugal, on October 13, 1917, as reported on by newspapers worldwide. According to the legend, Our Lady of the Holy Rosary of Fátima predicted this would occur.

The three shepherd children—Lúcia Santos and her young cousins, Francisco and Jacinta Marto—are on the path to canonization (sainthood) by the Catholic Church as a result of their visions.

And as I describe, the pope is the only person permitted to read the Third Secret of Fátima. It is his decision alone as to whether to reveal it or not. But it must contain something of such terrible magnitude that popes for decades have refused to divulge its true nature. As further described, Pope John Paul XXIII was indeed reported to have fainted upon reading it in 1960, and each succeeding pope has declined to reveal it—except for the allegedly controversial action of Pope John Paul II in announcing what most believe was a different (if not contrived) version of the prophecy. Time will tell as to what the true prophecy holds, if it is ever revealed.

Sister Lúcia's response to questions about the Third Secret were made up for the story, though in real life she was still circumspect as to the full nature of the prophecy up to the day she died.

CHAPTER 2:

Coimbra University in Portugal is one of the oldest continuously operating universities in the world, established in 1290. I chose it for its rich history and geographic relationship to Fátima. Its famed Biblioteca Joanina is well known and highly respected for its superb collection and is considered one of the most beautiful libraries in the world.

FUN FACT: The Joanina Library is noted as being one of two in the world (the Portuguese Mafra Palace Library being the other) whose books are protected from insects by a colony of bats living inside the library. During the night, the bats consume the insects that appear, eliminating the pests. Each night, workers cover the stacks with sheets of leather. In the morning the library is cleaned of bat guano.

The Knights of Malta are, of course, a widely recognized Catholic order founded in Jerusalem in 1099. The order is officially known as the Sovereign Military Hospitaller Order of Saint John of Jerusalem, of Rhodes and of Malta. All facts as described are true as of this writing.

CHAPTER 3:

The Knights of the Apocalypse were once an actual secret society created in Italy in 1693 to defend the Catholic Church against the expected Antichrist. Though long disbanded, I have used the name of this original order (dubbed KOTA) as a fictional entity, but there are apparently many such named groups operating on social media sites as of this writing, which claim to be carrying on the appeal and goals of the original organization. This book has no relationship to any of them.

As used, both the Prophecy of St. Malachy and the Apocalypse of St. Peter are legitimate historical references. I leave it to readers to explore more on those topics as desired.

That Enrico Petrini's surname actually translates as a derivative of "Peter"—as in "*Petrus Romanus*" in St. Malachy's prophecy—was absolute providence. I couldn't believe my good luck, or unwitting prescience, if you can call it that, in originally naming that character years ago.

CHAPTER 5:

Villa Stritch, the housing complex for American priests in Rome, is an actual residential compound, owned by the U.S. Conference of Catholic Bishops. Using photographs and other resources, I have described it as accurately as possible.

CHAPTER 6:

Domus Santa Marta is the Vatican's residential guest house, just southeast of St. Peter's Basilica. The building functions as a guest house for clergy having business with the Vatican, and as the temporary residence of members of the College of Cardinals while participating in a papal conclave to elect a new pope. I have used it as Michael Dominic's permanent apartment—which isn't a stretch, since as of this writing Pope Francis currently uses it as his apartment, forgoing the more opulent suite of rooms in the Apostolic Palace reserved for each pope.

The noted vicious rivalry between Italian football teams Roma and Lazio is real and is among the most anticipated games of the year for Italian football (soccer) fans.

Following is a summary of the three prophecies as used in the book. Two of them—St. Malachy's and St. Peter's—are historically factual. Apart from living popes, no one yet knows what the true Third Secret of Fátima contains, so the third element has been contrived for use in the book and should be considered fictional:

— **The Prophecy of St. Malachy**: stating, among other things, that the last pope would be named *Petrus Romanus*, or Peter the Roman.

— **The Apocalypse of St. Peter**: a vision of heaven and hell, describing the punishments for various types of sins.

— **The Three Secrets of Fátima** (the first two of which have been revealed):

(1) A horrific vision of hell as described by Our Lady of Fátima;

(2) World War I would end, and another Great War would erupt under the reign of Pope Pius XI;

(3) ***Our fictional Third Secret of Fátima:***

(a) The rogue planet of Nibiru (Wormwood) is on approach to Earth and would fulfill the prophecy as described in Chapter 8 of the Book of Revelation;

(b) The pope would publicly denounce the Third Secret and would be struck down;

(c) The pope who revealed the Third Secret would be the last pope, would betray his flock, and the End Times would arrive.

In 1960, the Vatican issued a press release stating that it was "most probable the Secret would remain, forever, under absolute seal."

CHAPTER 8:

The "Petri Crypta" (the Vault of Peter) is an entirely fictional device. I tend to doubt that the pope would have a personal safe in his office—but who knows?

All biblical references throughout the book are legitimate and worked nicely into the plot.

CHAPTER 12:

Papal coats of arms, or armorials, are the personal coats of arms for popes of the Catholic Church, a tradition since the late Middle Ages. Each pope has displayed his own as related to his family history, and in some cases are composed by the pope himself with symbols referring to his past or future aspirations. A pope's personal coat of arms coexists with that of the Holy See, always bearing the Keys of St. Peter and the papal tiara, along with a personal motto. Ron Moore actually devised the coat of arms for Pope Ignatius using symbology fitting the nefarious plot of this book. Don't be surprised if Pope Ignatius chooses a different one soon....

CHAPTER 13:

Obviously, since the Petri Crypta is fictional, there are no backup keys, and the Clavis Domini, or Key Master, is not a real person.

CHAPTER 15:

Each pope does have an actual *Sacra Consulta*—a body of trusted advisors initially set up as a special commission by Pope Paul IV in 1559—upon which popes draw advice on matters related to the Church.

CHAPTERS 18 and 29:

Rosslyn Chapel in Roslin, Scotland is an actual historical edifice with a rich background. It is, in fact (and in another example of unwitting prescience?) owned by the Saint-Clair family of Scotland. It is one of the region's most touristed locations.

Sharp readers of my past books will recognize the questions asked of Father Dominic on his quest to obtain the keys, something only found in consultations with the old scholar Simon Ginzberg, from whom the keepers of the keys obtained the questions.

CHAPTER 19:

Being a puzzle fan myself, I love introducing puzzles into my books, and in concert with Ron, we thought this archaic keystone substitution cipher was a good one to be found at Rosslyn Chapel.

CHAPTERS 20-21:

Forgive our tortured attempts at the Scottish brogue, clearly influenced by Jamie Fraser of Clan MacKenzie in the famed *Outlander* series. (*Ah dinnae ken,* for example, means "I don't know.") Go figure.

Private jets, it turns out, fly much higher than commercial aircraft. Commercial jets fly between 31,000 to 38,000 feet, whereas private aircraft fly at 41,000 to 48,000 feet, allowing for more direct routes away from the most congested areas of the sky.

The Vatican does indeed dabble in astronomy and has for

over two hundred fifty years. Its main telescopes are located at Castel Gandolfo, the pope's summer retreat in the Alban Hills outside Rome. But it also has a prominent observatory, as described in the book, in Arizona at the Mount Graham International Observatory.

The nickname LUCIFER, however, was largely contrived on the internet many years ago such that it became the stuff of legend. At its inception it was called the **L**arge Binocular Telescope Near-infrared Spectroscopic **U**tility with **C**amera and **I**ntegral **F**ield Unit for **E**xtragalactic **R**esearch (hence, L.U.C.I.F.E.R.). But to clarify things—and avoid the obvious unfortunate moniker—the Vatican later named its own unit the Vatican Advanced Technology Telescope (VATT).

Planet X, also referred to as Nibiru and Wormwood, are also real references to the alleged existence of a rogue planet somewhere out there. Two CalTech researchers, Konstantin Batygin and Michael E. Brown, did in fact publish theoretical findings of their discovery of the planet in the *Astronomical Journal* in 2016. Readers interested in further knowledge of this topic are referred here.

CHAPTER 27:

It's true: over the years, Maltese hunters have eviscerated the island's seagull population, the first time I'd ever heard of such a thing. They do have a colony of rare, protected yelkouan shearwater seabirds common to Malta, though; a small seabird widespread in the Atlantic, Pacific, and Indian oceans, mostly in tropical waters.

CHAPTER 28:

If you were to visit Malta, every street, location, building and business establishment is located exactly as and where described. So have fun, those of you lucky enough to visit that beautiful island.

Coors Brewing Company's Keystone beer was another *ah-ha!*

moment for us, as it fit perfectly into the puzzle to find the keys, since everything was related to keystones—those central topmost stones keeping an archway held together at its apex.

CHAPTER 33:

NASA's "DART' Mission (Double Asteroid Redirection Test) is authentic and fascinating. As per NASA's own website:

> The Double Asteroid Redirection Test (DART) mission is directed by NASA to the Johns Hopkins Applied Physics Laboratory (APL) with support from several NASA centers: the Jet Propulsion Laboratory (JPL), Goddard Space Flight Center (GSFC), Johnson Space Center (JSC), Glenn Research Center (GRC), and Langley Research Center (LaRC).
>
> DART is a planetary defense-driven test of technologies for preventing an impact of Earth by a hazardous asteroid. DART will be the first demonstration of the kinetic impactor technique to change the motion of an asteroid in space. The DART mission is led by APL and managed under NASA's Solar System Exploration Program at Marshall Space Flight Center for NASA's Planetary Defense Coordination Office and the Science Mission Directorate's Planetary Science Division at NASA Headquarters in Washington, D.C.
>
> DART is a spacecraft designed to impact an asteroid as a test of technology. DART's target asteroid is NOT a threat to Earth. This asteroid system is a perfect testing ground to see if intentionally crashing a spacecraft into an asteroid is an effective way to change its course, should an Earth-threatening asteroid be discovered in the future.

As for NASA consulting theologians in regard to a planetary impact, in 2015 NASA apparently provided a $1.1 million grant to the Center of Theological Inquiry geared toward a program to study the social impact of finding life beyond Earth. The organization's press release called it funding to "convene an interdisciplinary inquiry into the societal implications of the search for life in the universe."

CHAPTER 37:

The specialized scanning technology that allows the reading and interpretation of an ancient rolled up scroll is actually being used today. It is unknown if the Vatican is using this process now, but it would certainly make sense that they would adopt it at some point. Be watching for this technology in our next book…

CHAPTER 38:

Not restricted to *The Avengers* or James Bond's 007, cane guns are real weapons, though the one devised in this book was developed specifically for fictional use.

CHAPTER 41:

As used here, Botox has no relationship to cosmetic dermatology. Botox is derived from botulinum toxin, a neurotoxic protein that causes botulism, one of the deadliest known toxins. If Botox were to be drunk, as was KOTA's plan, it would cause sufficient paralysis for a quick and painful death.

EPILOGUE:

By sheer coincidence, Pope Francis had just visited Malta in April 2022, when this book was published. We wish him always safe travels and fair winds.

As for Father Dominic and Hana's relationship—one of the most common questions I get from readers—honestly, I have no idea what they will be up to in coming books. Reader feedback has been split in both obvious directions, but my inclination is to have Michael stay true to his vows, as I probably would in his position.

But, as most writers will confess, the characters themselves often choose the direction of their own paths in each story. Will Michael leave the priesthood to explore his relationship with Hana? Would she respect him if he did? Will he stay true to the vows he took in his sacred profession? And where's Marco in all this? Or will there be someone else?

Only time will tell. Keep reading....

AUTHOR'S NOTES

The astute reader will have noted that this is my first book with a collaborator, the brilliant Ron Moore. Like you, he was an avid reader of my work, and some time ago offered to lend a hand when it came to his rich background of skills in law enforcement, crime scene investigations, crime lab analyses, weaponry, and criminal law. He ably assisted me with certain scenes and materiel in *The Opus Dictum*, and at that point I knew he would make a capable collaborator for a few books going forward. *The Petrus Prophecy* is our first work together, but it won't be the last. I feel fortunate to have his assistance.

DEALING WITH ISSUES OF THEOLOGY, religious beliefs, and the fictional treatment of historical biblical events can be a daunting affair.

We would ask all readers to view this story for what it is—a work of pure fiction, adapted from the seeds of many oral traditions and the historical record, at least as we know it today.

Apart from telling an engaging story, we have no agenda

here, and respect those of all beliefs, from Agnosticism to Zoroastrianism and everything in between.

THANK you for reading *The Petrus Prophecy*. We hope you enjoyed it and, if you haven't already, I do suggest you pick up the story in the earlier books of The Magdalene Chronicles series —*The Magdalene Deception, The Magdalene Reliquary,* and *The Magdalene Veil*—and look forward to forthcoming books featuring the same characters and a few new ones in the continuing *Vatican Secret Archive Thrillers* series.

WHEN YOU HAVE A MOMENT, may I ask that you **leave a review on Amazon**, Goodreads, Facebook and perhaps elsewhere you find convenient? Reviews are crucial to a book's success, and I hope for The Magdalene Chronicles and the Vatican Secret Archive Thrillers series to have a long and entertaining life.

You can easily leave your review by going to my Amazon book page. And thank you!

IF YOU WOULD LIKE to reach out for any reason, you can email me at gary@garymcavoy.com. If you'd like to learn more about me and my other books, visit my website at www.garymcavoy.com, where you can also sign up for my private Readers Group mailing list.

WITH KIND REGARDS,

Gary McAvoy

ACKNOWLEDGMENTS

Throughout this series I have had the grateful assistance of many friends and colleagues, without whose help this would have been a more challenging project.

First and foremost, to my exceptional collaborator on this book, Ronald L. Moore. Ron's plotting and scene formulas, his deep research and special contrivances helped make this one of my more action-filled novels, due in large part to his astonishing background in so many areas unique to a book of this nature. He threw himself into the project more than ably, and I look forward to more book projects with him.

Special thanks to reader Ron Petera—whose wife, the Honorable Anne Petera, is a Dame of Malta—for suggesting the island nation of Malta as a prime location for much of this story. We had a great time exploring it on Google Maps and other sources. I expect Ron Moore could actually serve as a Maltese tour guide by now, he knows it so well. Speaking of which, I'm also immensely grateful to Julie Moore for her infinite patience while her husband Ron devoted so much time and effort in helping me build this book. It's not easy being a "writer's widow."

To Gabhán Ó Fachtna of the Facebook Scots Language Forum for his generous assistance getting the Scots diction and phraseology just right in a later revision of this book. Many thanks.

Most authors have a select group of beta readers to review completed books prior to publication, and I'm fortunate to have a great team. You all know who you are, and I count myself lucky to have you. Thanks for your time in helping to put that final polish on the manuscript, with particular notice going to Ben Cheng, Andrea Cooper, Don Reiter and Phil Shallat for their scrupulous read-through and errant discoveries.

To Kathleen Costello and Donna Marie West, my meticulous copyeditors, I owe boundless thanks for cleaning up those pesky rampant punctuation and grammatical issues.

And as always, to my brilliant editor Sandra Haven-Herner, for without her wisdom and remarkable ability to keep everything in mind as she works, my books would suffer terribly, I'm sure.

GM

Printed in Great Britain
by Amazon

46036573R00179